LET
VENGEANCE
BE MINE

DAVID B TWILLEY

LET VENGEANCE BE MINE

A Novel

David B Twilley

Printed in the United States of America

First Printing, 2015

ISBN 0692581782
ISBN 13: 9780692581780

www.DavidBTwilley.com

DEDICATION:

This book is dedicated to the memory of two people
who have greatly influenced me:
Lt. Jeff Tucker with whom I first shared the debates
and discussions of the legal system. As kids, he always
had the dream of becoming a police officer, and he got
to realize that dream.
He was taken far too soon.
William Lockhart, who was simply one of the most
intelligent and witty individuals that I have ever known.
I have done what I can to pattern my life after him.
I miss both of you guys.

PROLOGUE : JILL JUSTICE

"It was a lovely ceremony," Jill Justice thinks as she walks back into her large brownstone townhome on the Upper West Side of Manhattan and tries to keep her mind occupied. A gorgeous, late thirties petite blonde, she looks stunning in her formal black outfit, which perfectly complements her flowing blonde hair and bronze complexion.

Jill walks into her living room, and sits down on the living room sofa and then without warning begins to cry uncontrollably, dropping the paper coffee cup on the floor as she tried and failed to set it on the coffee table.

Jill is consumed with a feeling of loss and complete helplessness.

The large townhome feels so empty as she sits in it all alone, so very quiet now when it had been such a lively place for so many years of happiness. She recalls her earlier phone call and the discussion about loss, and how it affects them both. Both people have lost best friends and it is something that will impact them both forever.

For about fifteen more minutes, Jill just continues to cry, feeling like today would be the turning point in her life that she may never recover from. She thinks how close she was to renewing love and repairing what had become a lost relationship, but now, now it was gone for good.

She knows that love like this does not come around that often, a depth of feeling, a true soul mate, few people ever know love like that even *once* in their lifetimes, much less twice.

Jill realizes that love may have left her forever and she just cannot face this fact.

After sitting on the living room sofa for a few more moments, Jill procrastinates but knows that she needs to go check something. She walks into the powder room in the main hallway of her townhome where she left something sitting on the counter that morning before the ceremony.

Slowly, reluctantly, like a fearful young child, she walks in and fears the worst. She picks up the small white device with the plus and minus signs and looks at it. Sure enough, she sees the plus sign.

Jill Justice is pregnant.

Jill collapses on the powder room floor and cries uncontrollably. What should be a happy occasion is now something that could change her life forever.

"How can I raise a child?" Jill thinks to herself, "If his father is no longer around?"

Things were far simpler a year ago, which is where our story actually begins.

1

CAPTAIN TOM JUSTICE

One Year Earlier:

The phone rings and Tom Justice just shakes his head as he knows what this is, and more importantly, *who*.

"Mayor Lockhart," Tom says as he answers the phone, "good to hear from you, sir."

"Cut the bullshit, Justice!" The Mayor's voice booms over the phone, "Director Maxwell was just telling me how there has been little to no progress over the past several weeks."

"That's not entirely true, sir," Tom replies defensively, "We know that four members of the organization have been operating fairly openly in the lower East side."

"How does that help us?" Mayor Lockhart asks.

"It doesn't immediately, sir," Tom responds, "but we also have word that in the next few weeks there is going to be a meeting either in Manhattan or possibly somewhere in Westchester."

"Give me *something*," Mayor Lockhart responds, "that I can give to Director Maxwell and the Feds to keep them from reclaiming jurisdiction on this case."

"Yes sir," Tom responds, "McWilliams, Parra, and Barnes are currently meeting with some of our confidential informants in the lower East side and I will let you know if they come up with anything."

Mayor Lockhart's tone calms down some as he stresses his point to Tom Justice.

"Seriously, Tom," Lockhart says, "I just don't know how much longer I can keep them at bay. We are probably only looking at a few weeks and it will be out of my hands."

"Tom, I hope I don't have to tell you," Mayor Lockhart continues, his voice calming down significantly, "that you are one of my favorites."

"Thank you, Sir." Tom responds, wondering where this is going.

"I am one of your biggest supporters. My support helped you become one of the youngest captains in the NYPD." Lockhart continues, "but this, I am starting to wonder if this may very well be the end for both of us if you don't make some arrests, and soon!"

"I understand, sir," Tom responds.

Tom hangs up the phone, but only after Mayor Lockhart hangs up his phone first.

Tom walks across his office to his window and looks out onto the streets below.

It is late June in what has started out to be an extremely warm summer for the New York area. It is Monday and the city is alive. Traffic is gridlocked, car horns are blaring and sirens are wailing. Tom looks down on to Midtown Manhattan, which is gorgeous and alive, but he is not in any mood to enjoy any of it.

On East 51st street is the headquarters of the New York Police Department's 17th precinct. Pacing in his office, NYPD Captain Tom Justice wonders what he can do to make good on his promise to Mayor Lockhart.

About ten months prior, Tom and his precinct were assigned to be the leads on a major inter-agency operation to track down a large criminal organization operating in the city. This investigation was originally managed by the FBI, but after a failure on their part, the case was handed over to the Mayor who assigned it to Precinct 17 and Tom Justice personally.

These circumstances are highly unusual because this *case* is highly unusual. Typically a special department such as Major Case would handle it, or it would stay with one of the federal agencies. The Mayor pulled all sorts of strings to get this assignment for Tom Justice, an assignment that could be a career-maker. It *could* be, except that it is not going well at all.

Tom Justice is an impressive individual beyond just his impeccable record. He stands at only 5'10" with a thin, athletic build. His good, if not model handsome, looks along with his exceptionally persuasive manner has led him to all kinds of success.

He excels at commanding a room with his impressive presence. He is the kind of leader that all executives strive to become, one who has the confidence of his superiors and the loyalty of those who work for him.

But right now, he needs help from a trusted ally.

Tom immediately dials the phone to reach out to his friend Lieutenant Shane McWilliams.

Shane McWilliams is Tom's second in command and his closest professional ally. Shane is very similar to Tom in the fact that they both are fast track success stories. Shane came to the NYPD from the FBI and has been in his current position for three years. In this investigation, Shane's connections with the FBI have been very influential in maintaining a good professional relationship across agencies.

This isn't always easy.

"Shane," Tom says, "Lockhart was on me again just now."

"What was it this time?" Shane asks.

"More of the same, really," Tom answers, "The bottom line is that we probably have two weeks. No more than a month and they will pull the case from us."

"That makes no sense, Tom" Shane responds, "The Bureau had their chance already, we just need more time."

"Man, I know," Tom says, "But anyway, have you, Parra or Barnes identified anything useful?"

"Actually, yes," Shane responds, "Based on information provided by two separate confidential informants, we have members of the organization basing at one of three possible condominium complexes over on the Lower East Side."

"That helps, Shane," Tom says, "but we need something more than that."

"Why don't we meet in your office before we wrap up for the day, say 7:30 or so?" Shane asks.

"Yeah, that sounds perfect," Tom replies, "bring some Chipotle if you are coming that way."

"Si, Señor," Shane says as he hangs up the phone.

As he hangs up the phone, Tom thinks more about this current case and realizes that if this case is taken away from him, the political damage for both He and Mayor Lockhart could be insurmountable. The Mayor risks his own re-election and Tom Justice risks any promotion path or political future he may have once had.

He won't likely be fired or suspended, because he has too much clout and too many connections in the department. Also, this case was already bungled by the FBI so he would never receive all of the blame. But it doesn't always matter who messed it up first, often it is the person holding it last that loses out in the court of public opinion.

No, it would just possibly derail any hopes that he had of advancing any further in the department. Any hopes for City Council or the Mayoralty would be at a minimum severely delayed.

He hears the phone ring again and recognizes the number as being that of his real "boss", his wife Jill. He has been avoiding Jill's call all morning and now fears that he can avoid it no longer.

Answering the phone, and expecting the worst, Tom says,

"Hi, Jill."

"Tom," Jill responds sternly, "I was able to get us into Dr. Elsbury on Wednesday."

"Ok, what time?" Tom asks.

"9:30 AM," Jill replies.

Tom hesitates.

"Not sure if I can ma…" Tom says.

Jill interrupts and takes a more aggressive tone, "Don't you *dare* tell me you can't make it. If this is important to you, you *will* make it!"

"Yes, I can make it," Tom says in a conceding tone.

"That's more like it," Jill replies.

"Tom, ever since I have known you, you have had the ability to be charming, to say the right things and persuade people." Jill continues.

"Thank you….I think," Tom replies, expecting the other shoe to drop, and it does.

"But sometimes," Jill says right before she hangs up the phone, "sometimes instead of talking or just waiting for an opportunity to talk… you need to know when to *shut the fuck up!*"

Tom just sits there holding the phone, frustrated to a certain point beyond which most of us would have sent the phone flying across the room.

2

LEMON- FILLED DONUTS

Just before 5 AM the next morning, Lower Manhattan, New York City. Darkness reigns, as two men walk down the street, returning from a cash drop a few blocks away.

The two men are criminals, part of an informal organization or crew that the police have nicknamed "The Reaper Crew". This group is known citywide, and with growing national attention, and is currently pursued by both the New York City Police Department and the FBI.

The first man is Phil Repanelli, younger brother of crew leader Peter Repanelli, also known as "The Reaper". The so-called Reaper is highly regarded for his brilliance but also his ruthlessness. For all of The Reaper's genius and ferocity, his younger brother Phil has none of that.

Standing at over 6 foot 5 and coming in at about 260 pounds, Phil towers over his diminutive friend. Phil is tall and athletic….and impulsive. He is only part of the crew because of nepotism, and his brother is beginning to run out of roles or jobs for him to do.

At the moment, Phil is returning from a basic job with Leonard Gabino, who also has a colorful nickname. This is The Reaper's right-hand man, who is basically here to keep an eye on Phil.

The two men have explicit orders, to make their cash drop to a local group and then return back to the safe house, quickly with a very low profile.

So, despite his orders, and knowing that they must keep a low profile, what does Phil want to do?

Go into a donut shop.

"You don't know what the fuck you are talking about!" an infuriated Gabino says, walking down the street with his colleague.

Leonard Gabino is known to his friends, family and especially to his rivals as "*Mr. Impossible*". This name has stuck with him because no matter how many times he is suspected or investigated, he has never spent a single night in jail.

Slight in stature, only 5'6" and approximately 140 pounds, the brown haired and light skinned man makes up for his small stature with a genius level I.Q.

With his intellect, the man known as "Mr. Impossible" has excelled for years at keeping himself and his superiors out of trouble.

He could very easily have taken the lead of most operations himself, but has always felt that made him too much of a target. He actually prefers to be in the background, providing many of the ideas that ultimately get done, but allowing his superiors the illusion that it was actually their idea.

When he speaks, Mr. Impossible sounds like an authority on any subject he addresses, with a smooth baritone and charming, persuasive voice. He balances this out with a fierce and intimidating voice when he chooses to use it. But the smooth voice has enabled him to diffuse many dangerous situations and manipulate many people to his side.

These powers of persuasion combined with his intellect have enabled him to survive and thrive in a business with far more intimidating physical presences. He manages to convince those around him to not to attempt to bully him for their own benefit.

Where Mr. Impossible struggles is when dealing with stupidity and a complete lack of common sense. He cannot understand impulsiveness, which often puts him at odds with Phil and The Reaper. Whereas The Reaper can be brutal and impulsive, Phil is what Mr. Impossible would describe as, "*Just fucking stupid.*"

Basically, to him, this job is nothing more than babysitting the boss' dumbass brother.

He cannot believe that Phil wants to go into a donut shop, when they are supposed to be keeping a low profile, and should not go anywhere where police might be or if nothing else, the view of the many security cameras in the area.

"This is not the time for donuts, genius!" Mr. Impossible says.

"Just let me get a couple," Phil replies, "I will just be in and out, no big deal."

"No big deal?" Impossible continues, "How about once we get arrested you be the one that tells your brother that it's No *big deal?*"

Shaking off his colleague's objections, Phil continues into the donut store as Mr. Impossible follows him, shaking his head in protest. Despite his verbal objections, Impossible knows full well that there is nothing physically he can do to restrain Phil, who almost outweighs him by over a hundred pounds.

So, Phil enters the Doughnut Factory, the lower east side location of a popular New York citywide chain.

As they enter the small deserted donut shop, there are no customers, but a man working the counter, and two women working in the back. There is a sense of urgency and frenzy as the women bring out trays of donuts and put them on the display racks, trying to be ready in anticipation of the morning rush.

The man at the counter, apparently the owner, still looking as if he has not fully woken up, looks up and greets Phil with a professional, albeit unfriendly "What can I getcha?"

Phil does not reply initially, as he looks at the donuts that are displayed both under the counter and on the racks behind.

Phil puts his hand down on the counter and studies the donut selection.

"I'm not sure that I see them," He mumbles.

"See what, sir?" the owner says curtly. "What can I get you?"

Taken aback by the rudeness, Phil looks up and intensifies his tone. "I don't see any fucking lemon filled,"

"We don't *have* any lemon filled sir" the owner replies, continuing his display of customer service ineptitude. "You will have to pick raspberry or cream filled. That will have to do."

"No lemon?" Phil persists.

"What did I just say?" The owner responds, "Raspberry, cream, no lemon. That will have to do."

Starting to get angry, Phil leans over defiantly, "what do you *mean* that will have to do!?

Looking back even more defiantly, the owner holds his position quite firmly, "I mean, you stupid man, that your choices are three-fold: raspberry, cream or get the hell out of my store."

Mr. Impossible senses rising conflict here, so he decides to intercede.

Stepping up to the counter as a peacemaker, Mr. Impossible leans in and speaks to the clerk with his cool, smooth baritone calming tone.

"Tell you what, how about just a dozen, half raspberry, half cream. No big deal." Impossible says, subtly pushing Phil back a step.

The owner nods in acknowledgment, as he turns around to go to the back donut trays and starts to fill the box with the requested donuts. As he returns back to the counter, he gives Phil a defiant sort of a "fuck you" look

"What are you looking at, old man?" Phil barks.

"I am looking at you 'lemon boy'" the defiant owner snaps back.

"Man, I think I have had just enough of this," Phil raises his voice as he draws a large firearm hidden in his jacket.

Now, the entire tone of the conversation changes.

The owner, now realizing his peril, eyes widening, backs away from the counter with his hands raised.

Mr. Impossible looks the exact same as he realizes this is the last thing they need right now. His eyes are equally widened like saucers and he realizes that he must play the role of peacemaker.

Stepping in yet again, Mr. Impossible says to Phil, "Hey, can we just get our donuts and get out of here? Your brother is going to start to worry and we don't want that, right?"

"Yeah," Phil says, "you are probably right."

Mr. Impossible takes a $100 bill from his pocket and places it on the counter and says: "There, that should make up for the donuts and this little…. *Misunderstanding*. My apologies, you do truly have a nice establishment here."

Mr. Impossible grabs the donuts from the counter and begins to walk out of the donut store, with Phil behind him.

"Come on, Phil, we have most certainly overstayed our welcome."

Phil's eyes appear to calm and his rage appears to dissipate as he follows Mr. Impossible through the door and away from potential conflict.

Before he can exit, however, the owner feels that he must get one last word in.

"This neighborhood," The owner says, as he slowly moves forward towards the counter, "This neighborhood is going to hell because of people like YOU!"

Baited back into the store, Phil turns and re-enters.

"People like me? People like me?" he asks, "What exactly do you mean?"

The enraged owner continues, his voice rises up to a shout.

"I mean useless, thuggish, stupid, criminal….."

He probably shouldn't have said 'stupid'.

Before the owner can finish, Phil raises his weapon and aims it directly at the owner, firing and hitting him square in the forehead.

"I'm not *stupid*!" Phil protests as he shoots.

The force of the blast sends the owner's body back into the rear donut display, sending trays of donuts crashing all around, powdered sugar and pastries flying through the air.

The women working in back hear the commotion and come rushing out front, screaming in abject terror.

As Phil sees the two women come out, he raises his weapon to shoot them also. Mr. Impossible sees this and lunges at Phil, hitting his right arm solidly and knocking the gun out of Phil's hand and on the floor away from him. In the process, a stray bullet fires, but hits harmlessly in the back wall.

The two women continue to scream frantically, one cradling the owner's dead body and the other rushing for the phone and now dialing on it.

Phil sees his gun and wants to move to retrieve it before Mr. Impossible stops him.

"Are you fucking crazy?" Mr. Impossible yells pointing at the woman who is dialing the phone, "She is dialing the cops now, can't you see, so let's get the fuck out of here!"

Finally yielding to common sense, Phil relents and heads along with Mr. Impossible out of the store into the streets for their escape.

Mr. Impossible leads Phil down a side street and through two trash-strewn alleys, and over a barbed-wire fence where the assumption is that they would be safe for now.

Now that he can think more clearly, Mr. Impossible realizes that he made a fatal mistake, one which may have been even a bigger mistake than Phil's dumbass, psycho over-reaction back there.

Mr. Impossible's mind races with conflicting thoughts and most of them bad.

As bad as Phil's move was to shoot the owner, why on earth did he not allow Phil to kill the women? Like it or not, they are witnesses and should be able to provide a description of both men.

And the gun. Damn that fucking gun. The gun, the bullets, the fingerprints.

The goddamned miscalculation.

That was the mistake that they did not need, and the mistake that the boss will likely not be in a mood to forgive.

3

FIRST SHOWDOWN

Three hours later, and the police have finally caught up with Phil and Mr. Impossible.

Mr. Impossible knew the gun was a mistake, but it was too late and it was enough to lead the police right to their lower Manhattan safe house.

A light rain falls on this otherwise perfect summer evening. Five police cars and two SWAT vans move into position at this gorgeous apartment building near the corner of Ludlow and Houston.

This luxury apartment tower is hardly that of a typical stereotypical criminal hideout. The 20 story glass and steel structure shines under the night glow of lower Manhattan, combined with the bright lights of the police vehicles.

All of this for a donut store shooting?

Not quite.

Phil, Mr. Impossible, and their boss Pete Repanelli have been waging a type of war in the tri-state area. The full extent of their crimes is not completely known largely due to the fact that the authorities do not know how wide and/or deep the network goes.

The rumors are that the organization could be multi-national, which adds a great deal of anxiety to the situation. There are rumblings that recent events in Montreal and Vancouver have been tied to the same group, but as of yet there is no proof.

What the authorities *do* know is that Repanelli is either the head of it or is the second in command. Either way, his importance cannot be overstated.

This fact makes his capture alive that much important. The authorities fear that if they do not capture him alive, then the real head of the organization will simply appoint a new lieutenant and it will be business as usual.

Since the crimes were committed in multiple states this case has federal jurisdiction. The Feds (FBI) were brought in to handle the case and they were subsequently butchered. Repanelli found out which hotel they were staying in and had that floor completely bombed.

Just like that, he killed eight FBI agents. Not only that, but also killed over fifteen innocent people who had the misfortune of staying on that floor, just collateral damage.

As a result of this disaster, the Mayor of New York coordinated with the federal government to build a joint federal and local force under the jurisdiction of police Captain Tom Justice and his second in command Shane McWilliams.

Justice and McWilliams work with two detectives in their own department along with two FBI agents. Together they work with the Mayor and Manhattan District Attorney in their pursuit of this criminal organization.

This atypical cooperation is innovative but not without its problems. Questions of jurisdiction and just plain human ego always seem to get in the way.

In most cases such as this, ordinarily the Feds would run the show, but the opinion was that they had their chance so NYPD is getting theirs, along with some federal assistance.

But as Tom Justice discussed with the Mayor earlier, their time is almost running out.

At the moment, Tom Justice can sense the victory, although he is careful not to jinx it in his own mind. He is not exactly sure what to think of it, except to be confident that they are in good shape.

Tom Justice is not dressed in his official police uniform, instead in a white button-down shirt, black blazer, and jeans.

Upstairs in the apartment building, all hell has broken loose.

The leader of the group is the aforementioned Pete Repanelli, also known as "The Reaper". This affectionate nickname is partially a simple play on his surname but also serves to describe both his personality and his method of dealing with both enemies and accidental witnesses.

The Reaper is known for being a cold, calculating killer, all while being charming as a campaigning politician at the same time. It is not exactly known if he is insane so much as he is a true sociopath. He is a clear bully type and loves physically and verbally intimidating his more diminutive ally, Mr. Impossible.

As Mr. Impossible is more into the game for the money and the thrill, The Reaper actually enjoys hurting people and has absolutely no mercy.

Mr. Impossible knows this, and he is sure to protect himself at all times. It is situations like this that he gravely fears because he knows all too well that if pushed into a corner, The Reaper will either let him take the fall or maybe even kill him if it came down to a 'me or you' kind of decision.

As Mr. Impossible is slightly built, The Reaper is strong. He stands 6'1" and over 210 pounds of muscle. While not as big as his brother Phil, The Reaper is a commanding physical presence. In his late 30's with Italian features and dark hair and dark eyes, he is dressed in a simple navy suit and would look completely in place on a Wall Street trading floor.

But now that his lackeys are back and have drawn unwanted police attention to him, The Reaper demands an explanation.

"So why would you shoot the owner of the store Phil?" The Reaper asks,

There was *no* reason boss" Impossible interrupts, "No reason at fucking all. Phil has to know this is the important time so close to the end, he *has* to realize, has to know we are being watched. But still he had to do something so....fucking stupid!"

"Shut up, Impy!" The Reaper commands.

Mr. Impossible walks directly up to The Reaper's face in a defiant and confrontational manner, his anger resonating and starting to become uncontrollable.

"The nickname is 'Impossible', Reaper. 'Mr. Impossible'." **Mr.** Impossible says with escalating rage.

"The name is not 'Impy'. You don't shorten a *nickname*." Mr. Impossible continues, "Besides, 'Impy' sounds like some fucking combination of 'wimpy' and 'impotent'."

"Well," Reaper replies dismissively, "If the shoe fits…."

"Hey," Impossible replies, "I may be wimpy, but I am *not* impotent. Just ask your *sister*." Impossible says half-jokingly with a smile.

"Shut up Impy!" The Reaper shouts, "let's get back into character, this is some serious trouble Phil has gotten us into."

The Reaper walks past Mr. Impossible and then whispers at him dismissively, "Besides, my sister fucks **everybody**."

"Okay, we probably have a few hours before they make their move," The Reaper continues, "until then I have a few ideas…"

"Phil, get on the phone and get Bippus and Mercado over here, we're going to need some more muscle."

"Impy," The Reaper continues, "find some neighbors who are home and with your gun 'invite' them into our apartment."

"Why would they come here now?" Impossible asks.

"I don't really mean to invite them, genius. Don't give them a choice. Somebody will be home. If they don't open their doors, shoot and go in. We need some hostages, some bargaining chips." The Reaper commands.

"Just don't go into either 289 or 290, I have something special in mind for those two." The Reaper continues.

Mr. Impossible is confused, but agrees and moves out to do what he is told. He knows what The Reaper does with hostages, and it's not pretty. He wonders who he should choose, there is that older couple that would be an easy win, Nah. Then he gets it, he thinks that maybe he will get that rich couple that was rude to him earlier this week.

"Little worm." that is what the woman called him, and after all he did was to say "Hi."

"Who's the little worm now?" He thinks to himself as he approaches their apartment door. They might not bother answering it, but that's okay, he will just let himself in.

Back to the ground below, as Tom Justice waits for his second in command Shane McWilliams.

Shane arrives and walks over to greet Tom.

"Tom, I was on the phone coordinating with Frank," McWilliams says, "SWAT is almost in position, and Frank just needs your authorization to go in."

"Good," Tom responds, "Has the building been cordoned off yet?"

"Not yet," Shane replies, "We have the first floor cleared but were not sure if we should go to the second quite yet."

"Yes, before we move let's get the second floor cleared up to about five units away from their apartment. Otherwise, we may risk taking fire."

"Okay, Tom," Shane continues, "let me relay that to the men."

"Before you do that, I have to know," Tom says, "I mean I don't understand how we got this lead. We have been spinning our wheels for ten months on this case."

"Oh you will love this," McWilliams responds, "the only reason we got a lead was because one of them decided to shoot the owner of a donut store."

"Donut store?"

"Fucking donut store." McWilliams continues, "He shoots the owner and then the two women in the back called and reported it."

"And from there, security cameras?" Justice asks.

"Exactly. Parra was able to combine footage from the security cameras which led us back here."

"Nice work," Tom says. "It really helped that your C.I's gave us a target area to start in. There is no way we find them otherwise, donut store or not."

"Right," Shane says, "The timing was almost perfect for the first time in the entire ten month investigation."

As Tom and Shane stand and wait, SWAT Captain Frank Bourn approaches to give them the latest update. Frank Bourn, 49, is a tall, stocky, intense man who heads the SWAT unit coordinating the pending assault.

"Gentlemen," Frank starts, "we have snipers in position in two locations."

"Great," Tom says.

"Yeah," Frank continues, "but none of them have a clear shot."

"Why not?" Shane asks.

"The angle is too difficult and all of the windows are shaded. There is too much motion in there also." Frank responds.

Tom looks up to Frank, "Wait, wait, I want those snipers to stand down, Frank."

"What do you mean?" Frank asks.

"I thought I was clear on this, Frank," Tom says, "We need these two alive, so only shoot to wound if they need to shoot at all."

"I understand, but either way," Frank responds, "I don't like the chances of those hostages."

"Do we know they have hostages?" Shane asks.

"Yes, two hostages that we are aware of," Frank replies, "They have told us that they have two, and will kill them on our approach, but they are not willing to speak to hostage negotiators."

"I think we are on our own," Tom adds.

"Tom, can you share the file on our suspects, so I know who we are dealing with?" Frank requests.

"Oh sure," Tom replies, "Shane has the files right over here. Shane, can you walk Frank through our rogue's gallery?"

Shane brings the file folder over to Frank and starts going over the files and describing the men in question

Shane describes the men as he shows Frank their files with their photos and as much information as they have.

"The identified leader is Pete Repanelli, otherwise and affectionately known as "The Reaper".

"The Reaper?" Frank asks, "Not all that original," He says indignantly.

Shane continues, "His known lieutenant, and second in command is Leonard Gabino, otherwise known as 'Mr. Impossible' because he has never been arrested."

"If he's never been arrested, how do you have this information?" Frank queries.

"Good question, Frank." Shane responds, "The information is not complete, and all that we have on him was provided to us from accomplices so it may not be 100% reliable."

"Rumor has it that he has a genius level IQ and has insight into all legal and procedural operations, keeping him one step ahead of us at all times. This is why he holds such a top spot in the organization."

"Maybe even higher than we think," Tom says.

"What does he mean by that?" Frank asks, somewhat puzzled.

"Tom has this hunch that Mr. Impossible is the actual leader of the group and that Repanelli is really just the muscle, the front man and that Mr. Impossible is the leader sort of hiding in plain sight."

"Either way," Tom says, "we at least need both of these two alive so we can be sure that we have the leader. If not, this reign of terror, this war could go on indefinitely."

"Okay, we are not done with the list yet. Finally, last but probably least is The Reaper's younger brother Phil Repanelli. Phil doesn't have much of a rap sheet, and is really more of a lackey."

"What's his nickname?" Frank asks.

"He doesn't have one yet," Shane replies.

"So, we have 'The Reaper', 'Mr. Impossible', and…" Frank says, looking at Tom.

"..And *Phil*," Tom finishes.

Frank cracks a smile but does not respond.

"If everything is ready, I say that we go in now," Shane adds.

"Shane, let's go ahead and armor up," Tom says.

"Whoa, stop right there," Frank says as the puts both of his hands up in the air in a stopping motion.

"We have got this. My team will take point, you two need to let us handle it and just hang back."

"Frank, we are not hanging back," Tom says emphatically, "we have spent too much time on this case to just 'hang back'."

Shane adds, "I am definitely not hanging back, Frank. These guys are responsible for the deaths of eight FBI agents, two of whom were close friends of mine."

Frank retreats, adding, "Fine, just fine. Don't come complaining to me when you get shot in the ass."

Frank storms off and Tom and Shane look at each other and laugh.

Shane walks over to get the equipment as Tom takes in the entire scene.

Shane returns with the latest state of the art flak jackets and equipment. These are the new Beta Elite models, just recently approved for use by certain select members of the force. In addition to these jackets, the two put on solid Blackhawk Ballistic MICH bullet-resistant helmets and full body suit.

Their equipment is state of the art, the same equipment that the SWAT department uses since Tom and Steve are not meant to be exposed to gunfire. The one difference is that they have even more advanced bullet-resistant helmets.

As they prepare and wait for the "all clear" sign to proceed, back up in the apartment, their adversaries are growing more and more nervous.

The Reaper, Mr. Impossible and Phil all pace nervously in the apartment, anxiously awaiting the next move.

"Ok, I have our neighbor/hostages handcuffed to the front door as per your request," Phil says.

Phil points over to the hostages, a young married couple who are now bound, gagged and handcuffed to the front door. The blonde woman trembles and cries softly, as the man looks very serious as if he were still trying to process the situation.

Mr. Impossible walks over to the front door where the hostages are handcuffed, and pressed his gun against him, giving them a very dirty "you shouldn't have been rude to me" look. They shake and tremble, not knowing what on earth might be in store for them. Whatever it is, it won't be good.

"Good work," The Reaper replies, "what about Bippus and Mercado?"

"No luck there." Impossible says, "By the time they could get over here SWAT had already arrived."

"Fuck!" The Reaper screamed, "That was the help that we needed."

"How are we going to get out of this?" Phil asked.

"They want us alive, so let's make them think we are fine with giving ourselves up."

"Why are you so sure they want us alive?" Mr. Impossible asks.

"They're cops. That's what they do. They cannot just shoot us in cold blood. We have rights."

"I wouldn't be so sure, boss." Mr. Impossible replies, "After the FBI team you took out, I don't know how safe we are from 'accidentally' getting shot while resisting arrest or something else like that."

"He's got a point, Pete." Phil agrees.

"Valid argument I will admit, but they want us alive, I can just tell." The Reaper responds, "The Feds want me in federal court for the hotel bombing, little do they know that I have that already taken care of."

He maintains a stern demeanor, but inside The Reaper is pondering Mr. Impossible's point. On the one hand, the police likely need him for his potential connection to the head of the group, but they could be willing to kill him as payback for the FBI fiasco.

It might not be worth that risk. Either way, there was no easy way out of this.

"Hold on a minute." Impossible adds, "I just got a text from Bippus, he says that the SWAT team appears ready to come in."

"Okay, let's take our positions." The Reaper orders.

"Should I have Bippus and Mercado attempt to engage on the ground?" Impossible asks.

"No, they would be outgunned plus I already have them in place for my contingency plan should we need it."

"Thanks for keeping *me* in the loop boss!" Impossible snaps, "It's no nice to be a part of the team!" Impossible finishes, very sarcastically.

"Need to know basis, you little weasel." The Reaper replies.

The Reaper stares down Mr. Impossible and then adds,

"Be prepared for a full frontal assault!"

"No problem." The Reaper says, "We have our first line of defense in position." as he looks over at the trembling hostages hanging on the front door.

Frank Bourn moves with his team of six men into the building as they go up to the second floor.

Tom Justice and Shane McWilliams follow a little bit behind as the others proceed ahead down the hallway.

Moving cautiously, the team heads towards apartment 291 and waits outside about twenty feet down before the corner.

"Text him now and let him know we are coming," Frank says.

"What do you want me to say?" The SWAT officer says.

"Just give me the damn phone," Frank orders.

Frank types a message to text to the group and it reads: "Ok, come out peacefully and nobody else has to get hurt."

Phil takes his phone over to The Reaper, "Boss you gotta read this."

The Reaper reads the message and says. "Ok, if they want a response let's give them a response."

Phil looks up and wonders what to do. He is becoming as scared as the two hostages who are handcuffed to the front door, bound, gagged and trembling. The young couple, not having any idea what was to become of them when they came home from their date tonight.

"What do you want me to tell them?" Phil implores.

"Tell them that we will be coming out one at a time," The Reaper says.

"What?" Mr. Impossible says, stunned. Inside he sort of expects that he will just so happen to be the first one selected to go.

"You heard me. Tell them that we will be coming out one at a time and that we are unarmed. I just need them to get a little closer and then I have a surprise for them."

Phil texts as per his instructions, and Frank and his team read the message.

"Well good, maybe these guys aren't so stupid after all," Frank says.

Tom and Shane don't agree.

"Maybe it's a *trap*, Frank," Tom and Shane say in unison.

Phil slowly pushes the door open and starts to move outside.

"There," Frank says, "the door is starting to open. Hart, De La Paz, proceed slowly and watch his hands for any possible signs of a weapon. Everyone else, stand down!"

The way that the apartment building is arranged, apartment 291 is at the end of the hallway, and officers Hart and De La Paz are currently standing about ten feet away in front of apartments 290 and 289 which face each other.

Inside apartment 291, The Reaper holds a small electronic remote-looking device and presses the button. The approaching SWAT officers have no idea what The Reaper and his team set up for them only an hour before.

As officers Hart and De La Paz approach, explosions rock outward from both apartments 289 and 290 taking out Hart and De La Paz immediately.

Frank orders the remaining officers to pull back as the smoke and fire persist, creating a wall of fire. Two of the officers run and get the fire extinguishers that are at the end of the hallway and quickly put out the fire as two others remove De La Paz and Hart and take them out of the hallway.

As those officers take care of that, the remaining officers pause and let the smoke clear and assess if there is any additional peril, which they quickly conclude that there is not.

"Everyone else, move in!!" Frank shouts his command.

One by one, the SWAT officers move down the hall, proceeding slowly, and looking around nervously to make sure that there aren't any more surprises waiting for them.

As the other SWAT officers move down the hallway, two of them fire a full round through the front door, the bullets instantly shredding the hostages still handcuffed to the door as they scream out in horrific pain. The SWAT team, of course, has no idea that these innocent people are hanging on the door.

As the gunfire rains down on them, The Reaper, Mr. Impossible, and Phil move back into the rear bathroom behind the front living room.

The SWAT team takes a handheld battering ram and they knock down the door, and two SWAT officers crash through the door, finding none of the key suspects present in the living room.

As they secure the living room, Frank looks back to see the dead bodies of the couple hanging on the back of the front door. By now, only the man is still on the door, the woman's body is down on the floor with about ten bullet holes in her body.

"Where the hell are they?" Frank Bourn yells, "And who are *these* people?"

Frank and the other SWAT officers look at the door, and the now shredded bodies of the hostages, now hanging from the door, the man now on the ground, the young woman still hanging from the door.

"Oh God, these *cannot* be our guys," Frank says.

"No, I am afraid not," Tom Justice says as he enters the room. "This is a standard Reaper tactic. He cuffed the hostages to the door and made **us** shoot them."

"What the hell is the point of that?" Frank asks, "Wait, you expected he would do something like this?"

"No point," Tom says, "he probably first planned to use them as a negotiating point then just felt like doing this. And no, I didn't predict it, but at this point, nothing this bastard does actually surprises me anymore."

Shane McWilliams comes in and helps Frank to align the SWAT team and move them outside of the back bathroom where the three men are hiding.

"No more fucking texts, no more negotiation!" Frank yells, as he marches towards the back bathroom.

"I want you to come out, one at a time, no goddamned weapons or we are firing. We won't make the same mistake twice. I want that door to open up slowly, and I want to see three weapons come out and slowly, very fucking slowly."

Tom Justice leans in towards Frank and whispers to reiterate that they really need to secure The Reaper alive and not dead.

"Alive, Frank" Tom says, "I know emotions are high, I know you are thinking about payback for your two men out there, but we need these two alive. That order comes straight from the Mayor, let's not be hasty. Seriously, Frank, this is our case."

"I am not sure about that." Frank replies, "But I will try."

Back in the bathroom, The Reaper, Mr. Impossible, and Phil cower back there not sure what to do next.

Whether they are aware of it or not, in normal circumstances, the SWAT team would have riddled that door with bullets and not given them another chance. It is only because they were ordered to take them alive that the SWAT team is being so patient.

The Reaper knows that he is really out of options, and feels like they need to surrender. They open the bathroom door, and they roll three pistols across the floor as the two SWAT officers rush forward and retrieve them. The bathroom door then quickly closes.

"I don't like this boss!" Impossible says, "I am not so sure they don't just shoot our asses once we step outside this bathroom."

"I think we have to do what they say. " The Reaper replies, "Impy, you go first and then Phil and I will follow after that."

"Great, I should go out first." Impossible says with impressive sarcasm, "Phil's dumb ass should go first. Answer me this: Shouldn't the moron who got us *into* this situation go first? His ass should be the one to get 'accidentally' shot."

"Impy!" The Reaper repeats firmly, "Get out there *now!*"

Mr. Impossible stands up, and begins to open the door, not knowing what is on the other side of the door, but fearing the worst.

This very well could be it, and Mr. Impossible realizes it. He is not sure they would want to shoot him, but he doesn't really know. He needs to find a way to convince the officers outside that he is not a threat, so decides that humor is his best weapon.

He starts to head out the door, mumbling to himself, "Fine I will go out. First time I have ever been caught and it's because of some fucking idiot. I am caught because some fucking moron has to have his fucking yellow donuts."

"Who eats that shit anyway?"

Mr. Impossible moves outside of the bathroom and keeps talking.

"I am coming out. I am unarmed, please nobody shoot my ass!" Impossible says, with a smooth mixture of sarcasm, bravado, and fear.

He moves slowly outside, where two SWAT officers have their guns pointed directly at him in a menacing fashion.

"Shit, man. I am unarmed; please stop pointing those fucking guns at me, bitch." Impossible says.

The two officers grab Impossible and then pass him back to the officers back in the living room, and finally over to Tom Justice, who looks down at the short little man with an air of confident smugness.

"Mr. Impossible, I presume?" Tom asks.

"Yeah, and who the fuck are you?" Mr. Impossible replies.

"I am the guy that caught you for the first time." Tom says, as he takes and spins Mr. Impossible around, and then he handcuffs him.

"Big fat fucking deal." Impossible replies dismissively.

Back in the bathroom, The Reaper and Phil continue to wait for their signal to come out next.

Frank yells in towards them "Okay, next, come out and like I said, come out extra slowly!"

The Reaper begins talking to Phil, "Phil it's your turn, I will be right behind you."

Before Phil starts to walk out of the bathroom, The Reaper takes a small device out of his back pocket. This device looks sort of like a garage door opener. He clicks it once and unseen by the officers in the room, the plantation shutters on the kitchen window raise, opening the window to the line of sight.

The agent right in front of the window hears something but knows better than to turn away from a suspect who could potentially be armed.

The SWAT snipers have moved from their location looking into that window since agents are now in a position in the apartment itself.

Who has the position then, if anyone?

Phil starts to walk out of the bathroom, but rather than let him go out alone, The Reaper has his semi-automatic weapon in his right hand and starts to walk out also, hiding both himself and his weapon behind his brother's large physique.

As they clear the doorway, before the SWAT officers can see him, The Reaper whispers something to his brother Phil.

The Reaper presses the second button on the remote, and suddenly in the living room, a flash grenade goes off, temporarily blinding the SWAT officers and then The Reaper makes his move.

As Phil continues to walk out into the living room with his brother right behind him, The Reaper suddenly puts his weapon to the center of Phil's back, concealing it as they continue walking out of the bathroom.

The officers are unable to see this due to his hiding it behind Phil's body, and also because they are still disoriented by the flash grenade. As the two men exit the bathroom fully, The Reapers is completely hiding behind his brother Phil.

The Reaper whispers something, this time a little louder to his brother, "Change in plans, Brother."

"I love you, you're my kid brother," The Reaper continues, "but Impy *was* right, you did get us fucking caught!"

Phil appears confused and turns his head slightly to respond, but before he can fully turn around, The Reaper holds his weapon against Phil's back and fires twice, blasting completely through Phil's chest, killing him instantly.

The trajectory of the bullet strikes Officer Gonzalez in the face and knocks him down. Before the other officer can react, The Reaper removes his weapon from Phil's back and fires his weapon at the other officer, Officer Wilson, killing him instantly.

Commotion reigns as if everything is in slow motion as The Reaper fires back and forth and the two remaining, still-disoriented SWAT officers shoot at him but only manage to hit Phil's corpse which The Reaper is using as a human shield.

The surviving SWAT officers take cover and move out of the living room into the hallway, their vision still impacted by the effect of the flash grenade.

The Reaper has managed to kill two of the officers and wounded two others. Frank Bourn is down, and Tom Justice has pulled him out of the apartment. For now, there are no authorities in the apartment at all.

Seeing an opportunity, The Reaper discards his brother's corpse, and sprints across the floor towards the now-exposed kitchen window, diving through it, falling from this second story apartment and landing on the ground below.

This seems like a stupid and rash decision of a madman, but it was actually the planned contingency.

Two of The Reaper's soldiers, Bippus and Mercado, were supposed to be waiting for him on the street below, part of the contingency plan that he discussed earlier. The plan was for them to take out the remaining ground officers and move in and take The Reaper away to safety. He had it timed down to the minute.

But now, there is no Bippus, no Mercado, only a swarm of SWAT officers ready to take him away, but not before they land a few blows for their fallen comrades as they throw him violently into their SWAT van.

Back in the apartment, Justice and McWilliams rush over to the kitchen window to look down at the chaos below.

"What in the hell was that?" McWilliams asks.

"That was absolutely insane," Tom Justice responds.

"What kind of a maniac kills his own brother, then uses him as a human shield, and then takes a dive out of a second story window?"

Tom and Shane just shake their heads.

Shane leaves the apartment to retrieve the handcuffed Mr. Impossible who was in the hallway with another SWAT officer.

"Come over here, I want you to look at this," McWilliams says to Mr. Impossible, as he points to Phil's body on the apartment floor.

"This is what your boss and your organization will do to you too," Shane says, "Tell me, what do you think of that?

Mr. Impossible looks down at Phil's dead body and thinks for a minute.

"What do I think about it?" Impossible says smoothly, as he shrugs his shoulders and shakes his head as he maintains a smug expression,

"I think I am fucking glad that I came out *first*."

Tom and Shane just look at each other and shake their heads as they walk Mr. Impossible outside and down the hallway.

4

LOVE ON THE ROCKS

The following morning, back at the 17th precinct headquarters, Tom Justice sits with Shane McWilliams in his office.

Frank Bourn walks into Tom's office, on crutches as he recovers from his leg wounds.

'Frank," Tom asks as Frank enters his office, "How is the leg?"

"It's fine, I guess." Frank responds, "Quite honestly, I feel lucky compared to what happened to my team."

"I heard that at least Gonzalez was going to pull through," McWilliams adds, "Sorry about Hart, DeLaPaz, and Wilson."

"Yeah I must admit I was stunned about Gonzalez." Frank says "Bullet to the face and he is going to make it. Apparently it just grazed his temple. Lucky bastard."

"Well, at least there is some good news to come out of this," Tom adds.

"I guess. Anyway, I just wanted to come in and let you two know that I am going to take five weeks as a combination vacation and disability. But before I do that, I am going to personally coordinate the funerals of my team"

"Totally understand," Tom replies, "But if you need me for anything just call."

"I am not retiring, I can assure you. I plan to be back in the field in two months or less."

"Thanks, Frank. That's great to hear." Tom continues, "Let us know ASAP about the funerals. I will personally make sure that everyone attends, including the Mayor."

"Thanks, Tom I appreciate that." Frank walks out of Tom's office and shuts the door behind him.

"That's a great man right there," Shane says.

"I know. Well, when do we get to finish the paperwork on The Reaper?" Tom asks.

"I think I am going to have to do that, don't you?" Shane says.

"Why is that?" Tom continues.

"Because you have that appointment with Jill that I think you are already late for."

"Oh shit, the marriage counselor!"

"Yeah, and if you leave *right now* you will only be 15 minutes late, you know based on my initial calculations."

"Damn it, I am a dead man." Tom continues.

"Don't worry, though," Shane says playfully, "I will be happy to complete and submit the report. I can even call the Mayor if it *has* to be done."

Tom mumbles as he hurriedly rushes towards the office door to exit but pausing to look back at Shane with a dirty look, "Biggest arrest of the year, of course you are happy to handle the report, you bastard."

Shane looks up and smiles, "See, I told you they should have made *me* Captain."

***

At that moment, about five blocks away in a midtown Manhattan professional office building, Tom's wife Jill Justice sits alone in the office of Dr. William Elsbury, marriage counselor.

Behind his desk, Dr. Elsbury sits nervously, tapping his pen on the desk, trying to alleviate the obvious tension of the situation.

Across from Dr. Elsbury sits Jill Justice, her gorgeous face not able to hold back an obvious look of frustration and anger. Jill is short, petite, well dressed in a white business suit, her mid-length blonde hair perfectly styled and coiffed.

Jill reaches into her purse and removes her phone. She looks down at it and it reads "9:28".

The appointment was for 9:00.

At that moment, Tom opens the office door and nervously walks inside with that apologetic look like someone walking into class in the middle of a lecture.

"Jill, Doc," Tom starts, "I have no excuse for my tardiness, please forgive me."

Tom sits down on the sofa and attempts to put his hand on Jill's knee, which she coolly deflects as she inches away from his touch.

Tom notices.

"Right," Jill replies smugly, "why would *today* be any different?"

Trying to break up the awkwardness, Dr. Elsbury interjects,

"Seeing as how we only have half a session left, why don't we get down to business?"

"Jill," He continues, "In our last session you said that you wished to pursue a six-month trial separation, are you still thinking that this is the best plan?"

"Yes," Jill replies, as she flashes Tom a dirty look. "Nothing has changed. If anything, I am even *surer of it* now."

"Not so fast Jill," Tom interjects.

Before he can say another word, Jill cuts him off.

"No Tom. We agreed that when we started this that we would be open to all suggestions and at least give it a chance."

Tom hesitates and reluctantly acknowledges, "Yes, I know, but this?"

Dr. Elsbury leans forward and then adds, "It would only be on a trial basis. Six months, you try it out, but there is nothing to say that you cannot get back together sooner than that. After six months, there is an option for continuing an additional six months if more questions remain."

"We could do that," Jill says, nodding.

"Okay Doc, level with me," Tom says suspiciously, "What is the normal success ratio for something like this?"

"A great majority of my clients who try this actually feel quite re-charged and energized by the break. In a way, it's like restarting the relationship with a fresh start."

"And the others?" Tom persists.

"Well, I won't lie to you. Many of these ultimately do go the other way."

Jill sits there, nodding in agreement, as Tom sits with a blank ex-pression on his face, as he is obviously not at all convinced this is the best course of action.

After the appointment ends, Jill rushes ahead and takes the eleva-tor before Tom can get there. Outside of the building, Tom races to catch her, finally catching her about half a block from the office building as she walks quickly.

Tom reaches out and grabs her right arm as she allows him to catch up to her and the couple continues to walk and talk.

"Trial separation?" Tom starts, "Do you really think that things are that bad?"

Jill hesitates for a moment.

"I think we need to try this," Jill replies.

"What is your motivation, Jill?" Tom asks, "Do you, do you really want a divorce?"

"No, Tom, that's not what I want, "Jill replies.

"Well, Jill what *do* you want?"

"Maybe, Tom, I want you to try to figure out what you want in life. Maybe this is the best way for you to do it."

"Jill, I think that deep inside you just want out, but you need to know that I don't plan on letting you go quite so easily."

"Tom," Jill protests, "Let's be adults about this. Sunday we get together at the club with Daniel and Carrie. Not a word about this, promise?"

"So we cannot even tell our best friends about this? That is *un-usual*, to say the least." Tom argues.

"Doctor's recommendations." Jill says, "For the trial separation, we stay under the same roof, we maintain appearances as that of a normal, married couple, but we have the option of seeing other people if we so choose."

"That is not like any trial separation I ever heard of," Tom argues.

"It's not," Jill replies, "but the doctor thinks with your high profile it would be wise to have some degree of secrecy."

Tom stops and thinks for a moment.

"I guess I would rather the guys in the department not know about this," Tom replies.

"The Doctor might actually have a point there." Tom continues, sarcastically, "Then again, the Doc himself might actually have a thing for you. No *wonder* he endorsed the trial separation idea."

"Tom, be serious," Jill responds, "This is pretty important, not like one of your and Daniel's jokes."

"I know, I know." Tom concedes, "I just think this is the wrong move. You know how hard it is to not tell Daniel."

"Well, you *have* to." Jill says, "I know you are going to see him in court tomorrow, so please, seriously, do not say anything."

Tom looks straight ahead, not sure if he can keep his promise.

5

THE DEFENSE RESTS

The next day, Tom and Shane begin to walk up to the New York Supreme Court building from the street, after parking about five blocks away. It is an absolutely fantastic summer morning, perfect for a morning walk.

What a day, with clear skies, about 70 degrees, no humidity and a perfect beach or baseball day if you are so fortunate, but alas Tom and Shane have work to do.

Less than twenty-four hours have passed since Tom made his promise to Jill not to reveal the trial separation and now he is talking to Shane, who just asked Tom how the counselor visit went.

"Not so good," Tom replies, "Jill has requested a trial separation….which I *never told you about*, right?"

"And the marriage counselor agreed with that?" Shane asks.

"Yeah, I suspect that he sort of planted the idea in her mind."

"Damn, sorry Man" Shane says, trying to console his friend.

"Jill says she feels that it will benefit the marriage, but I really have my doubts," Tom adds.

"I don't see how any separation can help a marriage, Tom."

"My point exactly and that's what I said to Jill," Tom says.

The two continue walking and talking as they walk up the courthouse steps and reach the front door of the courthouse.

"Not meaning to abruptly change the subject," Tom says, "but we may have some bad news in regards to The Reaper case."

"What are you talking about?" Shane replies, pausing slightly to look around, "Also, I didn't want to bring it up before but what are we doing over here at the courthouse, anyway?"

Tom looks straight ahead and shakes his head.

"I can't believe that after all these months of tracking them, all of this time..." Tom begins, "that now we get to deal with *this*."

Shane's expression goes from one of confusion or bewilderment, to complete shock as he looks up as if he has had a "Eureka" moment.

"Oh don't tell me..." Shane says.

"Yes, sir, The Reaper has hired *Daniel* as his defense attorney."

Daniel Aronson has been Tom Justice's best friend since the fourth grade. Many times they have ended up on opposite sides of the courtroom, but none of those other cases were this personal.

Daniel even has changed his mind on a few occasions and elected not to defend certain clients at Tom's request. This violation of legal ethics bothered Daniel, who vowed never to do that again regardless of how much Tom persisted.

Tom and Daniel followed the same path for quite some time until they deviated.

Whereas Tom's path went to criminal justice, Daniel was able to get his law school financed and became a lawyer.

On several occasions, men that Tom Justice and his precinct have put behind bars have been subsequently freed due to Daniel's tactics, some of which border on unethical.

There were two cases in the past that Tom was able to successful persuade his friend not to take, and he is strongly hoping that this is one of them.

Tom and Shane proceed into one of the courtrooms, opening the door and moving inside and taking a seat.

A trial is currently in progress, and at the front of the courtroom, Daniel Aronson is questioning a witness. Daniel looks like a male model or Hollywood lawyer stereotype as he stands confidently and almost poses there in the courtroom directly in front of the jury box.

Approaching the witness stand in his impeccable custom tailored bespoke Navy pinstriped suit, he approaches a man who is almost the exact opposite of himself. Daniel Aronson is a confident, borderline cocky attorney, one who enjoys the game as much as the law.

Daniel is what would be described as 'sharp' with his perfect chestnut brown hair, his custom suit, and his neatly-trimmed, hip beard. He just has that look and manner of a sharp, successful lawyer and that is exactly what his clients get when they hire him.

On the witness stand is one Will Harrison, early 30's, African American, slight build with thick glasses and a wrinkled, double-breasted suit that was in style....back in *1998*.

"Mr. Harrison," Daniel begins his line of questioning, "You are not a bad guy, right?"

"No sir," Harrison responds.

"I mean," Daniel continues, "you are practically a genius-level inventor. You have your engineering degree from Georgia Tech and a P.H.D from M.I.T"

Daniel turns towards the jury as if to play to them as he shrugs and says, "That's *kind of* smart, right?"

The jurors, especially the female ones, smile and chuckle at Daniel's last comment. Right then, the confident Daniel knows he's got it.

"Well yes and no." Will Harrison replies, "No I am not a bad guy, and yes, yes I have those degrees that you mentioned."

Will is obviously uncomfortable being on the stand, as would we all be, but Will especially does not like the attention.

"So, you're not a bad guy, have advanced degrees, so what is your crime exactly?" Daniel continues, "Do they say that your inventions are too good?"

"Essentially yes," Harrison responds, "they say that my inventions could be used to hurt people. Basically, my former partner was jealous and reported me; it's nothing more than a vendetta, really."

"But," Daniel continues, "Have any of these devices been used to hurt anyone?"

"No sir. Not to my knowledge, they have not." Harrison replies.

"That's what I thought," Daniel says.

Daniel walks over to the defense table and retrieves and opens his briefcase, retrieving a small round device he approaches the bench.

Daniel absolutely loves this part of what he calls "the game". He knows all too well that his client was arrested for far more than what he is about to show the jury. Some of the inventions and technical items were quite deadly, but Daniel successfully managed to have them excluded from evidence.

He arrogantly, but accurately, believes that if he can show one harmless technical item then he can remove the perception of a threat.

"Your Honor, please allow me to introduce into evidence Defense Exhibit 12?" Daniel continues, as he approaches the bench.

"It is so noted." The judge responds.

"Now Mr. Harrison," Daniel begins, "could you please tell the court what these devices are for?"

"Yes, sir, these are my 'Professor Light' devices."

Several members in the courtroom laugh.

"'Professor Light' devices?" Daniel repeats, with a sardonic grin on his face, somewhat mocking the name, and playing into the courtroom laughter to belittle and trivialize these devices.

"Perhaps," Daniel continues, "you should demonstrate and explain."

"Objection!" The prosecutor stands and barks, "Relevance your honor?"

"Your honor," Daniel responds, "This man is on trial for supposedly making dangerous weapons that can hurt people, this demonstration is absolutely relevant to show the *true* nature of his inventions."

The judge hesitates and then finally adds, "I will allow it."

"I assure everyone that these devices are perfectly harmless" Daniel continues as he hands the device over to Will.

"Mr. Harrison," Daniel says, "Can you please tell the court what these devices are and then show how they work?"

'Yes, sir. Well, these devices are designed to defend against a frontal assault."

"Okay, how so?" Daniel replies.

"If an attacker comes at you," Harrison continues, "and you fear for your life. You can....oh I suppose some of you should cover your eyes."

"Way ahead of you pal," Daniel says as he dons a pair of black tinted, extra thick sunglasses.

"So, right," Harrison continues, "say that you see an attacker and need to disable them, you can do this."

Will Harrison clicks a button on the device and it releases an intense burst of light in all directions such as police or military floodlights but to the power of ten.

The courtroom emits a communal *"Ahhh"* as they all cover their eyes and are stunned by what has occurred, including Judge Hartwell.

As the courtroom recovers and order is restored, Daniel approaches the witness stand again.

"Thank you for providing me these special glasses earlier, I really appreciate it."

Turning his attention to the jury, Daniel walks towards the jury box and begins addressing the jury directly,

"Ladies and Gentlemen of the jury, my client here may be guilty...." Daniel starts,

"Sure. He may be guilty of....developing something of little practical value."

Daniel continues, speaking rhythmically and confidently, "He may be guilty of...*being a poor dresser.*"

A few of the jurors laugh softly.

"But" Daniel continues, "He is not guilty of *these charges.*"

"These devices, may, may be something out of the ordinary, but they are not harmful, in fact, they are wildly creative and could actually be beneficial if modified in certain ways."

Daniel again makes eye contact with two of the female jurors, whose nods and looks of agreement lets him know without word one being spoken that he has got this.

"If anything," Daniel says, "we might want to be nice to Mr. Harrison and who knows; maybe he will let us in on his IPO when his company finally goes public and we all become rich."

Daniel finishes this sentence and then walks over to the jury box, stands, and almost poses as if secure in his victory.

"The Defense Rests," Daniel concludes firmly and almost arrogantly, walking with a confident stride bordering on a strut as he sits down at the defense table.

About an hour later, Tom and Shane wait outside the courtroom when Daniel finally comes out. Tom walks over towards him looking confrontational.

"You know Daniel," Tom starts, "we arrested that guy because he had more than just *blinding light* devices."

"Yes he did," Daniel admits, "but none of those were admissible in court now were they?"

"Bastard," Tom says, knowing he can't win the argument.

"I have been ever since the fourth grade, jackass."

Shane looks at Daniel and adds, "That was quite the performance out there."

"Daniel," Tom intercedes, "I don't think you have ever met my Lieutenant. Shane McWilliams, this is the infamous Daniel Aronson."

"Pleased to meet you, Shane," Daniel says, "I hope that you are the level-headed one in this partnership and that you keep my pal here on his toes."

"I try, but it's not all that easy," Shane says, "I must say I was impressed today. I mean I had heard the legend but I have never actually seen you in court."

"Oh, well this was a relatively easy case." Daniel says arrogantly, as he somewhat dismisses Shane and turns his attention back to Tom, "Tom, are we still on for tennis on Sunday?"

"Yes, Sir. The wives will be drinking wine by the pool while we kill ourselves on the court." Tom quips.

"Sounds great. See you guys there at 12:30, Court 4 is already booked." Daniel replies.

"Work on your serve man," Tom says, jokingly. "Don't let me take you in straight sets like last time."

Daniel walks away smiling at the dog-out from his best friend, continuing to talk as he walks away.

"That was just a lucky match. It's my turn now." Daniel says confidently.

Unknown to Tom, Daniel really did let him win.

Sort of like letting your boss win when you play golf with him, Daniel likes to let Tom win a few when Daniel could easily beat him whenever he wanted. Yeah, Daniel is that kind of a guy, that rival that is always a little better than you in every single way.

Irritating.

"Oh, and one more thing," Tom says as Daniel walks away, "I loved the wrinkled suit bit, did you pick that one out yourself?"

Daniel continues walking without speaking, but then turns around and winks.

"I've seen him do that twice before, totally makes the defendant look incompetent and sympathetic," Tom says.

As Daniel continues to walk away, Shane turns to Tom and looks a little surprised.

"I thought you were going to ask him not to take The Reaper case?" Shane asks.

"I *was*," Tom responds, "but I think I will wait until at the club and approach it then."

"This is a sensitive issue," Tom continues, "it has conflict of interest written all over it, so I need to tread lightly. Daniel has told me that he will no longer be persuaded not to take cases."

"Do you think even Daniel could prevent The Reaper from being convicted?" Shane asks.

"I don't know Shane, but I don't want to take that chance."

6

AT THE CLUB

Sunday Morning, Trump National Golf Club Westchester, Briar Cliff, New York. It is yet another gorgeous midsummer morning, and perfect tennis weather on the grounds of the Trump National Westchester.

This stylish playground of the rich features unbelievable golf, a lovely swimming pool area, and four tennis courts. The initiation fee is not for most of us, over $200,000, and that does not include monthly dues.

For Daniel Aronson, as a well-paid defense attorney, this is no financial problem but for Tom Justice, it should be another matter. A police Captain should not be able to afford to be a full member of the club, not an honest one maybe.

It helps to have a rich wife.

Yes, Jill Justice is the money in the family. Her late parents were both senior executives with the old Texaco Corporation (now ChevronTexaco) and had a fortune derived from vested stock options. By fortune, I mean over 30 million dollars. Jill did not inherit all of it but got the majority as she was the favorite child.

With Jill's inherited wealth, she and Tom are able to live the life of luxury and leisure. A constant source of conflict between Jill and Tom is the fact that he continues his work as a police captain when the financial reality is that he simply does not have to.

This is part of the reason they are having marital issues right now. The current case, The Reaper and his crew, has meant long hours, travel, and significant shifting of priorities for Tom.

What Jill simply cannot understand is the fact that Tom does not do the work for the money; it is truly an honor thing with him. In a way, since he did not earn his wealth, he is that much more determined to work as he cannot otherwise enjoy his money without the guilt that accompanies it.

By staying in his job and performing well, he sleeps better at night knowing that he is contributing in some way, and is not just some entitled and privileged member of the elite class.

Back on point, quite literally actually, Tom and Daniel finish up a point over on Court 4 of the lovely tennis courts. Court 4 is in the corner adjacent to some small woods.

Daniel fires a serve from the Ad side, hitting the corner of the service box and going untouched for an ace. This is his best serve and Tom was not ready for it at all.

"Oh man, ACE for me" Daniel exclaims, "That wraps up the first set at 6-3 me."

"Hey, 'Nadal', not sure if you know it, but this is not Wimbledon," Tom responds half playfully and half irritated, "We're not on center court, you are not Raffa or Roger."

"And since when do you call out the score when you win? Who does that?" Tom continues, "Nice tennis etiquette."

Daniel and Tom walk over to the area between the courts, which feature a nice wooden table with four chairs. Since there is no other match going on, the two sit at the table for a little set break. They reach into their respective Babolat tennis bags and retrieve an alcoholic beverage.

"Sorry about the smack talk." Daniel concedes.

"I actually expect it man from a cocky bastard like you" Tom responds playfully, "I just hope you wouldn't do that to someone you did not know well like in your City Finals match or something."

Daniel looks surprised at the implication, "Man, I wouldn't do that."

"I don't know," Tom replies curtly.

"We have known each other *forever*. I can say that sort of shit to you that I would never say otherwise."

"You do have a point, though," Daniel replies, "I have been known to get a little too familiar too soon, which can rub some people the wrong way."

"Especially in *these* circles." Daniel continues, as he gestures putting his arms up, alluding to the country club that they are in.

"No doubt," Tom replies, "I am not completely sure if I will ever feel comfortable here, but I am trying."

"I have no problem with it" Daniel responds, "I did a little bit at first, but after a few rounds with people like the Donald, and Presidents Clinton and Bush, the awkwardness has worn off."

"Yeah, but you *earned* this position, this wealth" Tom contends, "I am only here because of my in-laws, because of my wife."

"You can't think that Tom." Daniel says, "Do you remember why I went to law school and you didn't?"

"Your in-laws paid for your law school."

"Exactly. If Dave and Marie had not been there to pay for my law school, then no way am I here today."

"You make a great point."

Tom continues, "And speaking of law school...."

This is the segue and break in the conversation that Tom was waiting for and enduring small talk and tennis to get to. He strongly feels like he must persuade Daniel to drop The Reaper case. Now is this a conflict of interest? Oh absolutely.

Does that mean he will not do it? No, it does not.

"I may have made it through law school, but I don't know that I ever could have defended some of the people you have. I mean some of them are just evil, plain and simple."

'I don't think you can just dismiss them as evil, Tom." Daniel replies.

"Not evil?" Tom continues, "What about that energy trader, Ballenger, who killed his wife and buried her on Staten Island?"

"They never found the body," Daniel replies dryly.

"Come on, Daniel" Tom protests, "Be real. Stop talking like a damn lawyer for a minute and use some common sense."

"Honestly, Tom, I asked him several times point blank if he did it, and he denied it every single time. I told him the information was privileged and he still would not confess to any of it."

"He was *guilty*." Tom presses.

"Even so, Tom, guilty or not, he deserved a fair defense" Daniel responds.

"That's our system, so I suppose so," Tom says, reluctantly.

"Morality is a tricky thing," Daniel says, "The world is not some sort of black and white, good and evil place."

"How do you mean, Daniel?" Tom asks.

"I mean sure there are people I defended that were guilty, but I did my job, I defended them and that is the law." Daniel says, "But I understand and even feel guilty sometimes that what I may be doing might not be moral."

"But you still do it?" Tom asks.

"I do it, first of all because I love it," Daniel responds, "I enjoy the challenge of winning a case that I have no business winning. I guess that's the competitive asshole in me." Daniel finishes with a half-smile.

"What about *this* case Daniel?" Now Tom goes in for the kill.

"I am seriously asking you to reconsider. I understand our system, I understand your point about a fair defense, but this one, this one is different, Daniel. You talk about morality, but in my view, it would be immoral to take this case."

"How exactly is it different?" Daniel asks.

Tom ponders for a moment, his eyes looking around as if he is thinking of the best way to phrase it.

"Well, you didn't see this man like I did. I watched as he shot through his brother's body then used him as a human shield and dove out the window!"

Daniel replies smoothly, "and you mean to tell me that is not a case of *mental defect?*"

"Goddamn, I knew it!" Tom exclaims, "I think he even knew he was going to try this type of defense."

"What, you think he *planned* on running through the apartment, just hoping that the entire SWAT team would not fill him with bullets, just to give him the opportunity to try out a mental defect defense???"

Tom stammers, "No..well... yes, well I don't know."

"The defense *rests*," Daniel says as he chuckles smugly.

This is a running joke between the two of them whenever they have an argument. Since Daniel argues for a living, he wins easily about 90% of their arguments. And so, once Daniel feels that he has won, he ends his argument with that line.

Tom just hates that shit.

"I understand your position, Tom," Daniel continues as he gets up from the table, "but, for now, let's get back to tennis. We only have another hour and we need to meet the ladies for lunch."

Tom gets up as well, grabbing his tennis racket.

"Just an hour?" Tom asks.

"Yeah," Daniel continues, "that should be plenty since we only have one more set to play." Daniel says, his subtle implication being that he will win in straight sets.

Slightly over an hour later, after Daniel has backed up his boast, the two enjoy a post-tennis drink across the property. Daniel and Tom sit at a nice outdoor table on the lovely patio at the club. They sit, sipping their alcoholic beverages as they await their spouses who had been swimming, or more accurately, lounging by the pool for the past few hours.

About fifteen minutes later, Jill Justice and Daniel's wife, Carrie Aronson, approach from behind and greet their husbands.

Jill is dressed fairly conservatively in tennis attire, as she has a doubles match after lunch, but Carrie who is about seven years younger than Jill is dressed more revealingly.

Carrie has a black bikini top on with a cold shoulder beige lace cover up on top. Carrie is a tall, strikingly gorgeous dark brunette with olive skin and green eyes. She stands in stark contrast to the petite blonde, Jill.

"Well, look who finally decided to grace us with their presence" Tom quips, as he is the wiseass who prefers playful banter to being sweet.

"Ladies, please have a seat," Daniel adds, as he stands up acting like a gentleman and plays the role of charming attorney all of the time even when he is not in the courtroom.

"We have your mimosas waiting here for you." Daniel continues, as he pulls Carrie's seat back for her and gets her situated.

"Well thank you, Daniel," Jill replies as she gives Tom a playful dirty look, "It's good to see that *someone* is thinking about us."

Jill and Carrie sit down and begin to sip their mimosas as the gentlemen retake their seats as well.

"I am sorry, Jill," Tom says, "I was just a little too busy giving old Daniel here grief about yet another tennis beat down."

"Oh no, not again," Carrie says, "Now I will be hearing about this until you guys finally play again."

"You know how serious he is about his tennis, Tom" Carrie continues, "He is…"

Tom interrupts, "…the most competitive person in the world. Trust me, Carrie I know."

Tom continues, "Besides, I was just kidding. He took me in straight sets yet again."

"Yes I did," Daniel says with a smug grin on his face, leaning back in his chair. "And thank you for setting the record straight."

"Speaking of competitive," Jill interjects, "Tom, did you ask Daniel about that case you were so concerned about?"

"I am still working on him, Jill, but I don't think he is buying my argument."

"Not one bit." Daniel replies, expressionless.

Jill turns to Carrie, "If you think Daniel is competitive, just wait and see how Tom reacts if Daniel is able to secure an acquittal for this man."

"This isn't personal, Tom," Daniel says, "I just think it's what I have to do."

"Daniel, it's just that we *know* he is protecting someone" Tom continues, "To be honest with you, now I regret telling SWAT to take him alive."

"Tom, we will just have to agree to disagree and move on."

Carrie looks as if she needs to change the topic, and speaks.

"Not so subtly changing the subject, Jill and Tom, I just want to say how glad I am that you could both make it to the club today. I realize how busy both of you have been."

"I am glad too," Jill adds. "If we can only get these two to stop talking work stuff then we should be fine."

"I see your point, ladies." Tom concedes, "No more 'shop talk'. So tell me, what have you ladies been talking about today, anything good?"

"Actually," Jill replies, "we have been talking about Carrie and her recent...er...procedure."

Jill motions towards Carrie's chest and everyone understands the implication that she is referring to some recent breast enhancement surgery.

"Ah yes," Daniel says, kicking back and taking a smoke on his now-legal Cuban cigar, "money well spent indeed."

There is a bit of an awkward laugh, and then a pause and then Tom speaks up.

"Well yeah," Tom says, "now that you ladies brought it up I must admit I did notice earlier, and must say they did an *outstanding* job."

Daniel, Tom, and Carrie laugh awkwardly, Jill not as much.

"Tom!!" Jill says, not laughing, and slapping him playfully on the wrist.

"Well, wait, wait just a minute now." Tom starts to defend himself.

"I was wondering about the social protocol here," Tom continues, "and after thinking about it for a while, I concluded that we are all at the level of friendship that I can say something like that and not sound like a total perv."

"Doesn't offend me," Daniel replies, "I think that they did a great job too."

"I understand that it is an awkward topic," Tom continues, "but the entire reason Carrie did it was to feel better about her appearance, right?"

"True," Carrie replies.

"And I am merely acknowledging that improvement, right?"

Daniel adds, "Like noticing someone has lost weight or something."

"Exactly, or a new hairstyle" Tom continues.

"Well, Tom," Carrie adds, "I take it as a compliment, thank you very much. An *awkward* compliment, maybe, but still. Thank you." Carrie adds with a smile.

Tom nods towards Jill, feeling as if he has won the mini-debate.

"The Defense Rests," Tom says, as He and Daniel both laugh at the reference to Daniel's own catch phrase.

Daniel has to get the last word in, though.

"Now, while we are all great friends here at this table," Daniel says, as he continues to puff on his cigar, "Tom, I do hope that you have the common sense and good taste not to walk up to a woman at the precinct or at church and blurt out:

'Wow, that **new rack** looks great!'"

Everyone at the table laughs, as Tom reaches across the table to give Daniel that cliché of clichés, the fist bump.

For the next hour, the two couples enjoy a very pleasant meal and great and lively conversation that only longtime friends can share.

Daniel cannot stay much longer, as he has a meeting of a different kind scheduled.

***

Later that day, in a small café in the Upper West side, Daniel sits waiting for someone to join him.

About fifteen minutes later, a young late teen African-American man comes in and joins Daniel at his table.

"Richard, thanks for meeting me down here," Daniel says as he stands to greet the young man.

Richard says thank you and then sits down for a discussion.

Richard Murphy is a very sharp, successful student who happened to be in the wrong place at the wrong time and was arrested on suspicion in a gang-related murder. This is ironic because he is not a member, nor has he ever been affiliated with this gang. Richard is not a member of any gang but was arrested anyway.

"I just can't thank you enough for handling my case, Mr. Aronson," Richard says, his eyes beaming with true appreciation and gratitude.

Daniel smiles and replies, "I was happy to do it, Richard. Once I heard about your case I knew that I had to take it."

"Well, I really do appreciate it." Richard replies.

"It also helped," Daniel says, "that the prosecution didn't have a shred of real evidence, and it was relatively easy to have this case dismissed."

"That's what I never understood Mr. Aronson," Richard says, "I mean, I don't want to make that big a deal about the race thing, but I really think that it did play a big part in this."

"No doubt that it played a big part in this," Daniel responds, "These cases are examples of what I am working to correct in this city. I am taking cases such as this to try to help any way that I can."

"Well, I am forever in your debt, sir," Richard says.

"You said that you had a favor to ask of me, Richard?" Daniel says.

"Yes, yes of course," Richard replies, "It's about my brother Charlie."

"What's going on with your brother?" Daniel asks.

"It seems that he has developed a bit of a shoplifting problem, and he has been hanging around some bad influences," Richard says.

"Not gang types are they?" Daniel asks.

"Not even close," Richard replies, "In fact, they are these two white kids from Charlie's advanced classes."

"Oh, I see," Daniel says.

"Right, so I was wondering if you could maybe just talk with him and explain to him the risks and stuff, you know things that he doesn't want to hear from his 'stupid' older brother."

"No problem, Richard." Daniel replies, "Give me his cell number and I will call him up."

"Thanks, Mr. Aronson," Richard replies as he hands Daniel a piece of paper with his brother's phone number on it.

"I will call him, and then let you know what we talked about," Daniel says.

"Thanks, Mr. Aronson." Richard says, "Well I better be going, I still have to finish my English report for tomorrow."

"Ok, well I will let you know as soon as I have spoken to Charlie," Daniel replies.

"And one more thing Richard."

"What's that, Mr. Aronson?"

"Call me Daniel, Richard. Call me Daniel."

"Okay, well thanks, *Daniel*, I really do appreciate all of this," Richard says as he walks away with a smile.

***

Before Daniel can make good on his promise to Richard, merely a day later at an Upper West Side bodega, young Charles Murphy and two of his friends walk into the store and talk.

"Just get two packs of gum," Drew says to Charlie, pointing to the racks of bubble gum in front of them.

"No, man, I don't want any part of this," Charlie replies.

"What are you afraid of, you pussy?" Drew replies, "Take two packs of gum put them in your socks, and then cover them up with your jeans. It's so easy my five-year-old brother can do it."

"Well if it's so damn easy, why don't **you** do it?" Charlie asks.

Drew rolls up his jeans leg to show four packs of gum stuffed in his sock.

"Already did," Drew says.

"In fact, to hell with gum, if you are going to be a part of our group that you desperately want to be a part of, you need to get us something good," Drew continues.

"What do you mean something 'good'?" Charlie asks.

"Wait here a minute and I will be right back," Drew says as he goes out the front of the store.

As Drew exits, Charlie just stands there a little bit lost as to what is going on. As Charlie stands towards the back of the store, the owner moves closer to the register where he can apparently keep an eye on the young African-American kid.

Drew returns to the store along with another friend Jonah. Drew is a cocky, blonde-headed kid with Jonah, the brown, curly headed kid from Israel. The owner recognizes Drew because Drew comes into the store very frequently and talks to everyone in the store. For a 14-year-old kid, he has the persuasive ability of a young man five years older.

The owner does not, however, recognize Charlie and definitely does not remember Jonah, even though he has seen him several times and really should recognize him by now.

As Drew walks into the store, he makes his way up to the counter and as he does so, motions with his eyes for Charlie to stay in position.

Drew addresses the owner behind the counter as if they were old friends.

"Mr. Irving, how are you today sir?" Drew asks.

"Can't complain, young Drew, what can I do for you, young man?"

"Well, I just came into some birthday money, spoiling grandparents you know, and would like to look at the new iPhones that you have under the counter here."

"Before I take them out can I see the cash? I know you, but I don't need you wasting my time now." The owner says.

Drew takes out his wallet and puts six one hundred dollar bills on the counter.

The owner's eyes widen.

"Spoiling grandparents indeed. Man, you kids got it good." The owner mumbles as he walks back to get the keys to the electronic display case underneath the main counter.

The owner places two devices on the counter and begins explaining them to Drew.

"We have a 64GB device here, which is perfect for all of your gaming, music, and all those app things you guys use." The owner says.

Drew holds both of them and starts to examine the boxes, and then sets them down on the counter. "I am not sure which one I want."

At that same time, Jonah flashes some sort of "Go" signal to Charlie, to which Charlie responds.

Suddenly, Charlie dashes towards the front counter, grabbing the two devices that are on the counter, conveniently shielded between Drew and the side counter so the owner cannot reach over to grab them.

Charlie has the devices in his hands and there is no way that the owner can catch him. He darts towards the front door and envisions a clean getaway and being a hero to his friends.

And he trips.

Yeah, he trips. His leg hits against a pastry and donuts end cap display, and he falls right to the ground on his face.

The owner now has time to come out from behind the counter and nab the would-be shoplifter and starts to take him into the back of the store as he will then call the police.

"He did it," Charlie screams, "This was all *his* idea!" Charlie says, pointing at Drew.

The owner stops for a moment, and asks Drew, "Drew, is this true, were you working with this kid? You did have me take the devices out in the first place, and I saw you talking to him just a few minutes ago."

Drew looks up with a cold and confident look, makes eye contact with Charlie, whose eyes have an unspoken "come on man, please tell them," look to them and Drew replies.

"Sir, I have never *seen* this kid before today in my life," Drew says, "Actually he was asking me for money earlier."

Charlie protests as the owner takes him into the back office.

"*He* did it, it's not true, he made me do it!" Charlie's cries fall on deaf ears, as Drew and Jonah take advantage of the distraction to leave and take a few additional items with them on their way out the door.

About an hour later, Officers Martinez and Kinzer arrive and put Charlie in handcuffs and put him in their squad car to take him down to the station. The charge will be felony shoplifting since the values of the goods were in excess of one thousand dollars.

Charlie worries what his mother will think, and God only knows what his father will do once he finds out about this. These are thoughts which a 14-year-old boy should not have to deal.

Two hours later, young Charles Murphy is on a hospital stretcher, being wheeled into St. Joseph's hospital as the E.R. doctors desperately try to stabilize him from his gunshot wounds.

As they rush him on the stretcher towards surgery, a frightened young boy looks around, looks for a familiar face, a friend, a family member, anyone who could bring him some comfort.

He is scared. He is in pain.

A single tear falls from his left eye as he takes his final breath and dies.

***

Four hours after that, Daniel Aronson's phone rings.

Daniel can barely say "Hello" before a frantic voice calls out to him on the other end of the line. It is Richard Murphy and he is in a panic.

"They killed my brother, Mr. Aronson!" Richard screams.

"What….what are you talking about Richard? I need you to slow down a little." Daniel replies.

"My brother, he was picked up for shoplifting," Richard says.

"And? You are telling me he was killed because of shoplifting?" Daniel asks.

"Yes, they said he was resisting arrest and tried to take the officer's gun, so they shot him," Richard says.

"Oh, my God!" Daniel says.

"I told you that that crew he was running with were bad news, why didn't you even talk to Charlie, Mr. Aronson, I was afraid something like this was going to happen!" Richard says.

"I…I am so sorry Richard," Daniel says.

"Sorry means nothing, Mr. Aronson. Would a 'sorry' bring my brother back?" Richard asks.

"No, no it won't, Richard," Daniel says.

Richard disconnects his phone without saying another word. Daniel disconnects his phone and walks away.

Daniel Aronson throws his phone across the room as he shouts in frustration and anger.

7

READY FOR COURT

Tom Justice sits back at his office desk in the busy precinct headquarters. The office is somewhere between functional and Spartan, with his desktop computer with triple monitors, some plaques on the wall and other indicators of a successful career. What his desk lacks is the typical photo of the spouse, for reasons we have already discussed.

District Attorney Garcia knocks at his office door. Tom nods to him, and motions for him to enter his office.

Garcia walks in and sits down in one of the leather chairs in front of Tom's desk. Garcia is an average looking Latin man in a basic gray suit. He has dark, slightly graying hair; dark eyes and is in his mid 50's. Originally from Cuba, Garcia's family immigrated to Miami in the early 1980's and he dedicated his life to the law at an early age.

He has decided to prosecute this case himself, which is fairly unusual, but is certainly warranted considering the magnitude and importance of this case. He, like Tom Justice, is greatly concerned about the possible outcome and potential backlash as a result of this case.

"Mr. Garcia," Tom starts, "What brings the district attorney to my humble office?"

"The Mayor wanted me to come see you" Garcia replies curtly, "to inform you of the timeline for the Repanelli trial."

"No problem, what else can I do for him?" Tom asks.

"First, the good news," Garcia says, "Thanks to the high-profile nature of this case, we have been able to reject any postponement requests by the defense."

"That's great!" Tom exclaims, "What about the bad news?"

"Yes, the Mayor and FBI Director Maxwell met with me last week and told me to make a deal with Gabino."

"Mr. Impossible?" Tom looks up, surprised.

"Yes, we have provided him immunity for his testimony."

Tom is enraged and slams his fist on his desk.

"Whose brilliant idea was this?" Tom says loudly, so loud that several officers on the precinct floor stop what they are doing to see what is occurring.

"Not mine I can tell you that," Garcia replies, "This came down from Washington, not from the Mayor. I could tell that Lockhart was equally taken aback by the idea."

"They don't understand what's at stake here." Tom continues.

Garcia replies, "Yes, and with Gabino having immunity; now even with his testimony against The Reaper, it's very likely that our friend Aronson can work a mental defect defense successfully."

Tom stops and thinks a little bit to himself without saying anything else to Garcia. "What does this all mean? Is there someone in Washington who wants The Reaper back on the street?"

"Or, could Mr. Impossible be the real leader after all?"

Tom looks up to Garcia, realizing he has created an awkward pause.

"So, has Daniel taken the mental defect strategy," Tom asks, "as we expected?"

'Yes, we received notice of it earlier this week." Garcia responds.

"How does he plan to back it up?" Tom asks.

"It's a sick irony really, "Garcia responds, "Aronson is using the bizarre behavior as proof that The Reaper is insane."

"All of the random kills. The apartment incident...."

"..Shooting his brother." Tom continues.

"Yes and jumping out of the apartment window. All of this is more than enough to constitute a pattern of irrational thought"

"There could be another side to this," Tom continues, "this could be jurisdictional. Washington might want our case to fail so that he can be tried in Federal court."

"You may be right," Garcia replies, "We had to drop the hotel bombing charges, and only focus on the apartment incident. Two witnesses, likely Repanelli lackeys, came forward and swore in an affidavit that someone else gave the order."

"I think that's it," Tom replies, "I think the Feds want this case to fail and then they will charge him for the murders of the eight agents."

"You're not hearing me; there is enough evidence to create reasonable doubt in that hotel bombing case." Garcia persists, "I mean, you know he is guilty and so do I, but proving it in court is going to be difficult with those two defense witnesses."

"Damn, then Washington must have another agenda altogether," Tom replies.

"If your hunch is right Tom," Garcia says, "then are we just wasting our time with this trial?"

Tom looks straight ahead and just shakes his head. "What is really going on here?" He wonders to himself.

"Garcia, what if it is actually Impossible that is behind all of this? If that is the case you have just made the clichéd 'deal with the devil'."

"That's the risk that they are willing to take," Garcia responds.

Tom looks very frustrated and does not approve, but it's out of his control and he realizes it.

***

Later that day, over at the Metropolitan Correctional Center, New York (MCC New York), this austere building is used by the Federal Bureau of Prisons to hold some of the most notorious criminals.

Since this case crosses jurisdictions, and because it is such a high-profile case, it was decided that both Mr. Impossible and The Reaper be kept here, in isolation.

Mr. Impossible has since been released because of his immunity deal and is being kept at a nearby midtown hotel under 24-hour police protection.

He doesn't care for it much.

The MCC New York is a fascinating building that once held such notables as Frank Lucas and John Gotti. The design of the building is such that for trials, prisoners must be led through an underground tunnel that links the prison to the adjacent courthouse.

This ingenious design prevents suspects who are well-connected, from having some type of street assault to free them while they are in transport from prison to courthouse. Sure enough, this was the original plan, until The Reaper and Mr. Impossible learned they would be going to the MCC. Now the plan had to change.

They needed to try another strategy, and soon.

Daniel Aronson is led through the basement and proceeds over to The Reaper's cell, where he is buzzed in by the three guards escorting him.

Daniel walks in and takes a seat at the table that has been set up just for this visit. The Reaper is across from him, handcuffed to the table, presumably for Daniel's protection. Two guards exit but one remains and stands in the room, his hand on his right holster to indicate he is there for protection.

Daniel is uncomfortable with this visit and does not speak first.

The Reaper senses Daniel being ill at ease so decides to speak first.

"So, counselor," The Reaper says, "what's the good word?"

Daniel stares blankly back at him.

"As we have discussed, the plan is to move forward with the mental defect defense," Daniel says.

The Reaper shakes his head.

"I am not...." The Reaper responds calmly, "Insane."

"You and I know that," Daniel persists, "But they don't need to know that."

"No, I want you to drop the mental defect defense." The Reaper continues, "We are not going to *need* it."

"Not going to need it, what are you talking about?" Daniel asks, completely surprised "you are on trial for multiple murders, you are facing...."

"I am facing *nothing*, counselor." The Reaper responds sternly.

"Again, could you please explain to me what the hell you are talking about?" Daniel says, starting to become irritated as if his client somehow knows the law better than he does.

"My contacts tell me that two of the jurors might be *sympathetic* to our cause." Reaper says, "If you know what I mean? It's not totally set yet, but I think we are good."

Daniel looks stunned, looking at The Reaper as if to say "shut the hell up" and then looking up at the guard who does not appear to be paying attention, indicating with body language the need for better discretion.

"Don't talk about jury tampering in here," Daniel says, "I cannot know about any of this. Don't want to be a part of it."

"But you *are* a part of it. You are a part of it now. You are a part of it, and thanks to privilege you cannot say a word about it to anyone."

Daniel just shakes his head, and cannot really respond.

"And I have two more favors to ask of you." The Reaper continues.

Daniel looks up and replies, "What would that be?"

"I don't want to risk my team having them, so I am sending you a few items that I need you to keep for me." The Reaper says,

"And what are they exactly?" Daniel asks.

"Nothing much, really." The Reaper responds, "Just a key and a flash drive."

"Flash drive holding what?" Daniel asks.

"Nothing much to worry about. It was just my insurance policy in case I really need some major help."

Daniel shakes his head. "Not sure if I should do this but I will do it, reluctantly."

"Fine, I will have them sent to your office today." The Reaper says.

"But I need you to keep them protected, don't keep them at your office, and put them at your house, in a safe or something."

Daniel stands up, and prepares to walk out of the cell, "I will do it, but next time when you come up with some 'brilliant' legal strategy maybe you should consult me *first*."

Daniel walks out of the call and is obviously incensed, feeling somewhat betrayed. He wonders what this key and flash drive could be? And should he even be keeping it, it feels wrong to him.

As Daniel walks away, and the guard shuts and locks the door behind him, The Reaper just looks straight ahead, a devious smile creeping over his face.

He has just made his lawyer a co-conspirator.

***

The next day at his office, Daniel receives a delivered package, and his assistant brings it in and puts it on his desk.

Taking a look at the package, he wonders whether he should have it examined or not. Surely The Reaper is not deranged enough to send Anthrax or some type of bomb to his own lawyer, right? Daniel wasn't sure but he proceeded to open the box anyway.

He opens the box and, just as The Reaper had said, there are three items within the box.

First there is a normal looking key such as for a residence, safety deposit box or anything else. Second, a flash drive and then finally, a device similar to a VPN Key Fob device with rotating codes on it. These are typically used for companies to provide secure remote access to their network. This Key Fob generates random number combinations, only one of which is valid at one specific time.

Daniel remembers what The Reaper told him, to not look at it, and to also keep it at home rather than at his office.

At this point, Daniel is truly confused, and if he had doubts about his client's guilt before, he has absolutely zero doubt about his guilt now.

But for the moment, he has a trial to finish.

***

For a month, in New York Supreme Court under Judge Hartwell, the trial proceeds as might have been expected. The prosecution, led by District Attorney Garcia himself along with a great deal of help from Tom Justice, appears to have a solid chance of winning.

A month after that and the trial has almost neared its conclusion.

Contrary to both the expectations of District Attorney Garcia and Tom Justice, Daniel Aronson has *not* taken an affirmative defense of mental defect.

In fact, for most of the trial, it has appeared that Daniel was not really trying all that hard if such a thing can be observed by non-legal experts.

The evidence that the prosecution presented was damning.

The testimony from multiple witnesses, including the sympathetic Frank Bourn, were especially compelling. Bourns' testimony, during which he described in great detail the pain at losing three of his officers, and then his own career-limiting injury.

The testimony about the fact that Repanelli had so coldly killed his brother and then used him as a human shield seemed like it was a complete win for the prosecution. Looking at the eyes of those in the courtroom and the jurors especially, one could tell that this simple fact was clearly indicative of a man who was guilty.

Still, Tom Justice could not shake the feeling, an intuition if you will, that something was out of place here.

He knows Daniel so well, and has watched many of his trials, but he cannot understand why the mental defect defense was not tried. In fact, many tactics that Daniel always used had simply not been applied in this very important case.

But now, the final witness for the prosecution, Leonard Gabino, AKA "Mr. Impossible". Impossible was provided full immunity in exchange for his testimony, and this should be the final nail in the proverbial coffin in this case.

District Attorney Garcia walks from the prosecution table over to the witness stand as the smug looking little man sits with a look of indifference on his face.

"Mr. Gabino is it true…" Garcia begins.

"Call me *Mr. Impossible*, bitch." Impossible replies.

The courtroom murmurs at this rudeness.

Not missing a beat, Garcia replies, "So, *Mr. Gabino*, please tell us everything that you know about Peter Repanelli, the so-called Reaper."

"Where do I begin? He's fucking crazy." Impossible says.

Again the courtroom murmurs amongst themselves.

"Just tell us about the incident at the apartment building, the incident with Repanelli's brother, the SWAT confrontation, etc," Garcia says.

"Oh yeah, well all I know is that The Reaper shot his brother, had me get those two people to hang on the door, knowing that they would have gotten shot, and they did, of course they fucking did."

"Objection, your honor!" Daniel says.

"Sustained." Judge Hartwell replies, "Mr. Gabino keep the language civil, will you please?"

"Sorry, your honor." Impossible replies insincerely and then resumes speaking to Garcia and continuing as if Judge Hartwell never said anything,

"So as I was *fucking* saying, I know that The Reaper was responsible for five deaths and whatever else you want me to tell you I will tell you."

"Mr. Gabino," Judge Hartwell adds, "final warning, enough with the language, just answer the question."

"Ok, your honor." Impossible replies.

Now, Mr. Impossible clears his throat and he shifts from defiant "criminal" mode to his suave, smooth salesman mode with his persuasive voice and tone, sounding almost like a voice-over commercial.

"So, in regards to the night in question, your honor, here is what happened. I was ordered to find two hostages, just two random neighbors in the building, actually a very sweet couple of newlyweds, and The Reaper forced me, forced me I say, to handcuff them to the front door of the apartment and then watch helplessly as they were shot to pieces by members of your SWAT team."

"You were *ordered*, but you still did it?" Garcia asks.

"I did, but I was under duress." Impossible replies.

"How so?" Garcia asks,

"You already know that he shot his brother, well guess who he threatened to kill first? That would be *me*. I think that it was just good luck that I came out of the door first, otherwise, it would have been me dead on the floor in that apartment."

"Is there anything else that you can tell us about Mr. Repanelli?" Garcia asks.

"Yes, what you need to understand is how organizations like this work. You see, the orders come down from the top and as soldiers we both follow and enforce them or we are cut out of the group if not worse." Mr. Impossible says.

Garcia nods, and replies, "Go on."

"And Mr. Reaper here is a sociopathic bully that loves to force others to kill for him. He truly *enjoys* it. Do you want to know how The Reaper initiated me into the crew?"

"Sure, please tell us," Garcia says.

Right here, Daniel Aronson should have objected, because this is prejudicial, but instead, Daniel says nothing.

Mr. Impossible continues, "He initiates me into the group by having me kill two young girls who just happened to see us leave the scene of a contract hit. No clue if these girls could have identified us, much less if they would say anything."

Mr. Impossible continues, "But no, it didn't matter, he had me shoot them both. Two girls, probably no more than eight years old, and he had me put a bullet in their heads. At night, on nights when I can't sleep, I still see their faces in my mind."

Mr. Impossible hangs his head and starts to cry. Then, he looks up indignantly and adds, as he stares angrily at The Reaper.

"I will never, never forgive you nor forget what you made me do, you psychotic, bullying motherfucker!" Mr. Impossible shouts.

The courtroom goes silent.

Garcia nods and says, "Good enough for me."

"No further questions, your honor," Garcia says as he returns to the prosecution table.

"Mr. Aronson, you may now cross-examine this witness." Judge Hartwell says.

Daniel Aronson stands up and says, "We have no questions for this witness at this time, your honor."

Tom Justice practically stands up and yells "Objection!" right then and there. He is no lawyer but he knows that Impossible needs to be cross-examined. He just made accomplice testimony that should absolutely be attacked, or else it could be the final nail in The Reaper's proverbial coffin.

But Daniel asks no questions.

"No questions for this witness?" Tom is outraged and thinks to himself, "Where would you begin? This man is a co-conspirator, this man was equally involved with the crime and was The Reaper's lieutenant and Daniel was not going to question that?"

Tom really knows something is out of place here, but he still does not know what.

Within the next few days, District Attorney Garcia presents his closing arguments and they are compelling. With the testimony of Mr. Impossible, the SWAT officers, Tom Justice and Shane McWilliams, it is clear that all of the facts are on his side and that a guilty verdict is an absolute certainty.

Daniel Aronson's closing arguments are not as strong. Only now does he attempt to challenge the testimony put forth by Mr. Impossible, but now it is too late. Daniel's best argument is the cryptic suggestion that Repanelli is only answering to a higher authority that he is protecting.

As Tom Justice watches the jury and tries to read their body language, he sees something that bothers him. Two women are not responding to Garcia's argument at all, and will not even maintain eye contact with him.

This case might be in trouble.

Juries normally deliberate major cases such as this one for several hours, if not days. The trial has gone on for only two months, and after closing arguments the jury is already prepared to return a verdict, and they have only been deliberating for two hours.

Inside the courtroom, the packed to capacity room waits in anticipation of what should be a controversial verdict, especially if a 'Not guilty' verdict is returned.

Tom and Shane sit in the back of the courtroom, nervously awaiting the outcome.

He does start to worry more, thinking how Daniel never used that mental defect defense that he was almost positive would and *should* be used in this case.

"What else could be going on?" He thinks to himself.

At the same time, Daniel sits at the defense table in the front of the courtroom with The Reaper seated next to him, who does not appear concerned whatsoever.

The jurors file back into the courtroom and each juror takes their respective seat in the jury box.

Judge Hartwell addresses the jury foreman.

'Mr. Foreman, as I understand it the jury has reached a verdict in this case?"

"Yes," The Foreman responds, "we have your honor."

"Very good, let us proceed." The judge says.

"For the first charge of murder in the first degree, how does the jury find?"

"We, The Jury, find the defendant *not* guilty." The Foreman says.

The courtroom is in pandemonium. Some people yell and others stand up in protest.

"Order!" Judge Hartwell exclaims, "I need everyone in the courtroom to be quiet and sit down!"

"On the additional two charges of murder in the first degree, how does the jury find?" The Judge continues.

"We, The Jury, find the defendant not guilty." The foreman says.

The courtroom again lets out a communal gasp, as a few on the row behind Daniel and The Reaper congratulate each other.

Tom and Shane just shake their head in disbelief, while The Reaper shakes Daniel's hand, but Daniel does not look particularly pleased. This is a bittersweet victory, to say the least.

Two rows from the back, ten federal agents express their frustration by screaming obscenities. They cannot believe that the man suspected to be responsible for the deaths of eight of their colleagues could be set free.

The Reaper leans over to Daniel and whispers in his ear, "Now, let me tell you what's next. I need you to bring the package to your office tomorrow and I will pick it up from you. Understand?"

Daniel shows a concerned, frightened look in his eyes, and just nods his head without saying a word.

"You never looked at the flash drive, did you?" The Reaper asks.

"No, you made me promise that I wouldn't," Daniel says.

"Ok, great. Well, see you tomorrow. Does 11 AM work for you?" Daniel nods.

"Great, well we will see you tomorrow." The Reaper replies.

Daniel and The Reaper walk off in different directions. As Daniel walks, the look on his face reflects one of significant concern. What on earth did The Reaper need to come to his office for? Did he trust that Daniel did not look at the files on that flash drive?

Now it was time to change course.

Seeing that Tom was still in the courthouse building, Daniel walks over to him and starts speaking. "Tom, can I speak to you for a minute?"

Tom has a disgusted look on his face, obviously still really angry about the verdict, "I am not sure if I want to talk to you right now."

"Tom, seriously, I think I may need your help." Daniel persists.

Tom motions for him to walk and talk with him down the hallway, as he responds, "Ok, Daniel what is it now?"

"I need to discuss two things really. I have an ethical dilemma and also I am a little bit worried."

"Worried about The Reaper? It's a little too late for that, wouldn't you agree?" Tom says dismissively.

"Tom, I know," Daniel responds with frustration, "Look, is now the right time for me to admit I made a mistake?"

"That time was about three months ago!" Tom replies. "That time was when you took this damn case."

"Man, could you just shut up and listen for a goddamn minute!" Daniel exclaims, as he reaches out to Tom and puts his hand on his shoulder forcefully for emphasis.

Tom's expression changes as he realizes that something must be seriously wrong for his best friend to speak to him like this.

"Alright, Daniel, what is the conflict?" Tom continues.

"I am fairly sure that The Reaper is guilty of jury tampering. He so much as admitted it to me a few weeks back." Daniel says, "I cannot prove it, he never actually gave me details, and he actually may not be the person who did it."

"Not surprising," Tom replies, "I knew something was wrong when you did not cross-examine Mr. Impossible."

"Exactly! He told me not to, against my objection." Daniel responds.

"But of course, that information is privileged since I am his counsel. I should not even be telling you this, and I realize I am risking disbarment for doing so."

"So why *are* you telling me?" Tom asks.

Daniel stops for a moment, looks around to make sure that no other people are listening and then adds:

"I think I know how you can put The Reaper away for good."

Tom looks up with a perplexed, yet interested look on his face.

"You have my attention, old friend," Tom says.

"Before the trial began," Daniel begins, "The Reaper sent me a package full of three items. One was a basic key, the other a Key Fob device, and finally there was a flash drive on which I believe he has all of his files and possibly his co-conspirators."

"Have you opened it?" Tom asks.

"No," Daniel replies, "I figured he might have some type of encryption on it or something."

"Here is what I propose Tom," Daniel continues, "He is coming to my office tomorrow morning to retrieve this package. Can we set up some type of sting to get him to confess to the jury tampering and you can arrest him on the spot."

Pausing to consider this proposal, Tom looks around and then responds,

"How about this?" Tom counters, "Do you have the files on you?"

"No, they are home in my safe." Daniel replies, "I wasn't sure if he might send one of his cronies over or something."

"What time are you meeting him tomorrow? " Tom asks.

"11 AM."

"How about Shane and I meet you at 8, see if we can open the file, I will even bring two of our techs to see if they can decrypt it or clear any other possible hurdles."

"That sounds good. Three hours should be enough." Daniel says.

"Don't know about baiting him into admitting jury tampering," Tom replies, "that part would be a little harder. Let's focus on the files. You said yourself that he might not even be the person who orchestrated the tampering."

"Good point. Tom, I think that's a great plan." Daniel says, his facial expression showing a little bit more relief than a few moments ago.

As Tom walks over to meet again with Shane McWilliams to discuss the plan for tomorrow, Daniel exits the courthouse feeling comfortable and maybe that he just might be finished with this Reaper drama once and for all.

8

Daniel paces around his Upper West Side Manhattan brownstone. The richly-appointed townhome is very upscale with mostly modern furnishings and artwork.

He is currently in the basement, lower level of the townhome, which he spent the past year having redesigned as his own personal sports bar.

It is a sports fan's paradise with wired surround sound and twin 4K 70 inch TVs on the main wall, currently showing a different baseball game on each. Mets-Astros are playing on the right and the Yankees-Red Sox on the left. The memorabilia collection is impressive. He has four framed jerseys, one of Nolan Ryan, one of Roger Clemens and two more with no names but from Yankees and Mets players. He even has a signed football from Super Bowl VII, the 17-0 1972 Miami Dolphins Championship, the only team to go undefeated.

Adjacent to these main televisions, Daniel has two smaller monitors on each side of the two main screens, each of which has a baseball game on it, except one that has the late CNBC market information.

Throughout the remainder of the large rectangular space, he has two more monitors on each of the side walls, and two televisions hanging from ceiling mounts. In the back of the room, he has a pool table, with a New York Jets pool light fixture hanging over it. He tries to practice his pool shots, but cannot focus.

Daniel continues to pace, majorly concerned about the meeting the next day. He thinks and hopes that Tom can get something off of the flash drive, but then again, wonders if it is being monitored in some way or another?

Violating the unwritten rule of the man cave, Carrie walks downstairs to the basement to speak with her husband Daniel. She intends to distract him in another way as she slowly walks downstairs at a model's pace wearing a form fitting, very complimentary Dream Angels Chiffon and Lace Babydoll to perhaps entice her husband upstairs.

Carrie senses her husband's stress, and walks over to him and puts her arm around him.

"How about this: we set the DVR to record the games, and we take our business upstairs?" Carrie says with a suggestive whisper. "..If you catch my meaning."

Daniel doesn't respond and continues to look straight ahead, as if in a fog.

"Daniel?!" Carrie exclaims, not believing that he is ignoring her.

Daniel slowly turns towards Carrie with an apologetic look.

"Oh, I am sorry Carrie," Daniel says, "I feel like an embarrassment to my gender but I am going to have to say 'no'."

Carrie looks as if her feelings have been hurt, not exactly being familiar with any type of physical rejection, but then quickly appears to understand.

"Do you mind if I ask why?" Carrie asks.

"This *case*," Daniel responds, "This case has been a nightmare for me."

Carrie looks surprised.

"This case? But you won." She asks.

"I won the case, sure," Daniel replies, "But at what cost?"

"What do you mean, 'what cost'?"

Daniel stands up and starts pacing around the room again.

"I mean…." He begins, "My best friend is pissed at me, I may have set a psycho killer back on the streets, and now this, this maniac wants to meet me at my office tomorrow morning. I don't trust this man."

Carrie gets up and again walks over to her husband to embrace and hopefully comfort him.

"I think after all of this stress, I think we have earned ourselves a trip to…." Carrie begins.

"Vegas?" Daniel finishes, his mood starting to slowly lift.

"You called it," Carrie replies.

"But how did you know that's what I was thinking?" Daniel asks.

"Are you serious?" Carrie asks, "Whenever you are stressed out, you want to gamble, and I know that you can't stand Atlantic City anymore, so there you go."

"Vegas!" Daniel stands up and shouts excitedly and repeatedly, channeling his inner Trent (Vince Vaughn character) from the movie *Swingers.*

"I am excited too," Carrie says, "Jill was just telling me that they have this new, ultra luxurious hotel on the Strip with the best private pool cabanas. I think she called it something like Cosmo or Sea breeze or something like that. We can get some sun, see a show…"

"And it's *football* season for me," Daniel says.

"Maybe it's time to take over the Sports Books just like the famous Vegas boxers do it."

"No, honey," Carrie says, "you are not betting a million dollars on a game."

"I would if I could," Daniel says with a smile.

"And it's funny dear," Carrie continues, "for all of your alleged gambling winnings, I never seem to see a dollar of that money."

"It is all strategically reinvested my dear," Daniel responds, "All reinvested."

The two laugh at Daniel's obvious bullshit but the laughter stops and they both freeze as they hear something above them, sounding like footsteps on the upper main level.

Sometimes they hear noises that appear to be in their townhome but the sound is actually the unit adjacent to theirs, so they aren't completely sure about the source of the noise this time, and therefore take no decisive action.

But then, mere moments later, they hear louder footsteps rushing down their stairs and a cryptic, sinister voice booming at them.

"That's the thing about Vegas," the faceless voice says, his face finally revealed to be The Reaper as he clears the stairwell and enters the living room, "you only remember the winners and conveniently *forget* all of the losers."

Carrie freezes, scared and silent, and Daniel starts to move towards The Reaper with a motion to indicate "be cool".

As he does so, three other men come down the stairs and into the living room. The men are Reaper henchmen Bippus and Mercado, and then the number two himself, Mr. Impossible. Bippus and Mercado hold their guns aimed at the couple, but Mr. Impossible has no visible weapon.

Seeing the additional men and realizing this is no social call, Daniel turns and makes a quick move towards a side table, where presumably he has a weapon of some kind stashed away.

"Freeze!" The Reaper shouts, "Not a single step for either of you!"

The Reaper walks in a little further and motions to Daniel and Carrie to sit on the leather sofa behind him. Daniel and Carrie comply without any resistance.

The Reaper walks over towards Carrie and stares at her outfit.

"I must say, counselor," The Reaper says, "you have done quite well for yourself. This is one fine looking lady. Based on the outfit, it looks like we may have interrupted *playtime.* Sorry about that."

"If this were another time, I might have to get a little....taste for myself, but this isn't that sort of visit." The Reaper continues.

At this point, Daniel rations that his best way out of this was to use his lawyer's wit and try to talk his way out of this.

"I don't understand. Weren't we supposed to meet tomorrow at my office?" Daniel asks,

"We absolutely *were* supposed to meet at your office tomorrow that **was** the plan." The Reaper says.

"Ok," Daniel says, acting confused, "so what is the problem?"

"The problem, good counselor," The Reaper says tauntingly, "the problem is that you had to go tell the police to come view the information first. Now, tell me why would anyone do that?"

"How did you…" Daniel tries to ask.

"How did I know about your little double cross?" The Reaper replies, "Well, computer techs have big mouths. That and you have to know that we have eyes and ears all over the department. A fact that you would have learned soon enough once you viewed my files."

Daniel realizes now that he is in big trouble. Even though he hasn't viewed it, they must assume that he has already read the files.

"Listen, I don't know what you think I did or was going to do, but I guarantee you that I have not looked at that flash drive. If it's money you need, just tell me; just tell me what it will take to get you guys out of here."

"Besides," Daniel continues, pointing at Mr. Impossible, "why is *this* guy even here, he testified against you. He was the prosecution's star witness."

Impossible walks over to Daniel, "All part of the plan, bitch. Personally, I thought it was one of my better performances. You might even say it was Oscar worthy."

"Impy, shut up and get out of the way." The Reaper says.

"Back to your comment about money. Money means nothing to me." The Reaper replies, "You betrayed me. That is what matters to me, and it is that which I cannot forgive."

The Reaper reaches into his jacket and pulls out a large .44 magnum pistol and aims it at Daniel's knee in a single unhesitating motion, firing one shot directly into Daniel's thigh, although he was aiming for his knee. Blood from the wound sprays on to Carrie's face which shocks her, and Daniel writhes in pain, screaming in agony.

"Daniel, No!" Carrie screams, as she reaches over to try to comfort and console her wounded husband.

As she does so, Mr. Impossible rushes over to her, grabs her by her arms, picks her up and shoves her on to the floor away from the sofa.

"Get the fuck out of the way!" Impossible shouts as he throws her down.

It is not addressed directly, but this action is apparently to shield her from whatever else The Reaper has in store for Daniel.

The Reaper pauses for a moment to enjoy and relish in the chaos he has created, before continuing.

"Did you bring the 'party favors'?" The Reaper asks Mr. Impossible.

"Yes, sir." Impossible replies, as he turns back towards Bippus and Mercado.

"Mercado, bring in the leather bag!" Mr. Impossible commands.

Mercado brings in a large leather bag and hands it to Mr. Impossible. Impossible walks over to the coffee table in front of Daniel's sofa and sets down the bag. One by one, he removes the items and places them on the table. It is a virtual torture chamber in a bag. First, a long knife with a scrrated edge, next a small drill, then an ice pick, and finally a small blowtorch.

"How would you like to hurt him, boss?" Impossible asks.

"The slower the better." The Reaper replies.

"I want something cinematic and epic."

"Cinematic?" Impossible looks up with a perplexed look and then asks, "Cinematic like *Braveheart* or more like *Hostel*?"

"Let's go with *Hostel*." The Reaper says.

Mr. Impossible follows his orders and picks up the small blowtorch and hands it to his boss. The Reaper walks over to Daniel, who is still shaking and trembling in pain from his gunshot wound.

As he walks over to Daniel, Carrie continues to sob and tremble at the peril that her husband faces. The Reaper takes the blowtorch and fires it up, holding it only inches away from Daniel's face.

Carrie cringes and covers her face, knowing that there is nothing that she can realistically do to save her husband from his fate. She then fears that they have something similar planned for her. Maybe, she thinks, they will just kill her quickly and not make her suffer.

Daniel can feel the flame but is not yet getting burned. The Reaper taunts Daniel cruelly, taking the blowtorch away and then placing it close again. Daniel trembles and sweats, the pain from his thigh and the agonizing anticipation of the blowtorch starting to take its full toll on his psyche.

Suddenly, and without speaking, The Reaper turns off the flame and backs away.

He walks back towards the stairwell, where Impossible, Bippus and Mercado are standing and he hands Mr. Impossible the blowtorch without saying anything else.

Mr. Impossible doesn't understand this odd turn of events and gives The Reaper a puzzled look.

"What is it, boss?" Impossible asks, "Do you want something else?"

The Reaper walks back over to Daniel at the couch as he continues talking.

"The more I think about it, I would rather he suffer a pain that he can never recover from, an eternal pain, a pain in his very soul."

The Reaper again raises his gun at Daniel, aiming it at his groin.

"I want to make it really hurt, really linger." The Reaper says, "But then again...the best way to do that...."

"*Change in plans.*" The Reaper says, his voice becoming even more sinister.

Suddenly, The Reaper turns towards Carrie, aims his weapon at her and fires three shots, hitting her directly in the chest and then forehead, killing her instantly.

Time stands still.

Daniel's face is frozen, and he cannot move.

Mr. Impossible's face reveals equal shock, revealing that he had no idea that this was coming either, an audible gasp escapes his lips as he looks to see Carrie's dead body.

Mr. Impossible is not a good person, but this disturbs him deeply.

The Reaper's smile conveys delight in the terror that he has inflicted, loving the fact that he is so unpredictable and that he has brought pain before what is Daniel's almost certain death.

Daniel is so shocked by this he cannot even think to scream. He is paralyzed, his mouth wide open and trembling, not believing what has just happened.

The Reaper then takes aim again upon Daniel and prepares to fire. As Daniel braces himself for the worst, he looks up and appears almost content, as if he realizes that he does not even want to live anymore and is resigned to his fate.

"Your turn," The Reaper says as focuses his aim, this time directly at Daniel's forehead.

"Bang!" The Reaper says as he continues to aim at Daniel, and then he slowly drops his gun to his side without doing anything.

Then without saying another word, he sets his gun down on the table and motions for Mr. Impossible to clean up all of the items on the coffee table and for them to leave.

A speechless Daniel attempts to crawl over to Carrie, but his bloodied thigh keeps him hobbled.

Coldly and quietly, Mr. Impossible packs the instruments of torture back into the leather bag and they all start to walk out of the apartment, looking back at Carrie's body and shaking his head. It is evident by his behavior that Mr. Impossible was not in on this little detail of the plan.

As The Reaper turns to leave, Mr. Impossible turns to him, puts his hand on his shoulder and turns him around.

"Boss, I was fine with killing the lawyer, but why the wife? That wasn't the plan. She's not even involved in this. And why in the fuck are we leaving the lawyer alive??"

"Don't ever question my tactics little man." The Reaper snaps, "I know what I am doing."

"But shouldn't we, at least, get the files?" Impossible asks.

"This was never *about* the files," Reaper replies, mysteriously, and without any further explanation as he looks at Mr. Impossible's hand on his shoulder. "And take your fucking hand off of me, you little weasel."

The Reaper storms off up the stairs, leaving Mr. Impossible behind.

Mr. Impossible looks back into the living room, and he sees a sobbing, screaming Daniel tend to his deceased wife.

Mr. Impossible just shakes his head in disagreement. For the second time, he senses a *disconnect*, a significant difference in opinion with his boss. Again, he has not been included in some very serious details in the plan and he has also again witnessed his boss kill someone without mercy.

Killing does not bother Mr. Impossible, but *senseless* killings do. He did not understand Phil when he impulsively shot the owner of the donut shop. He does not understand now the value or purpose of killing an innocent woman.

It's not necessarily the fact that he is suddenly becoming conscientious; if nothing else Mr. Impossible is a pragmatic realist. He is quickly realizing that if his boss is so willing to kill his own brother and then kill an innocent woman just to make a point, from that point where will it stop?

Mr. Impossible thinks to himself in his own unique voice,

"Who the fuck might The Reaper kill *next*?"

9

AFTERMATH

Inside Daniel's mind, the grief has become overwhelming. For most of his life, he really has not been that emotionally invested at any time, nor has he had any real tragedies to deal with. So for Daniel, the combination of losing Carrie and feeling partially responsible for the circumstances leading to her death leaves him an empty emotional shadow of his former self.

Daniel Aronson feels that his life has been completely torn apart. The funeral for his wife has come and gone, and he can barely remember a single detail. It is a week later, and he just sits in his home office staring at his computer, which has no files open, just a blank screen.

Tom and Jill had done everything that they could do to help out, coordinating the funeral, and hosting the post-funeral reception at their house. Jill took Daniel to the hospital to have his leg treated, and Tom and Shane McWilliams have coordinated police protective detail to be outside of Daniel's apartment.

The police still believe the attack was about the files, so it is expected that The Reaper will be back to retrieve his devices, but nobody knows when, where or how he might strike.

Daniel opens his Outlook file and checks his recent emails, mostly those from people with their sympathies, in addition to all of the flowers and cards that he has already received. None of it really helps, but he does appreciate the good intentions.

He looks at a recent email from Tom, and opens it, which is an email reminding Daniel that they had lunch planned for later that very day.

Daniel realizes that he hasn't even checked his phone in over a day and once he looks at his phone he sees over ten text messages from Tom as a reminder to their plans.

Daniel quickly types a response and prepares to get ready, although he is a man walking more like a ghost or a zombie, someone with no true purpose and no real passion.

Two hours later, they meet at the Riviera Maya restaurant on the Upper West Side. This festive Mexican, or more accurately Tex-Mex, restaurant has taken its inspiration from the tourist spots of its namesake region. Decorated just like something you would find in the hotel zone in Cancun, the Riviera Maya is known city-wide for its margaritas, sangria, and excellent Mexican food.

Daniel and Tom sit at one of the festively designed bench style tables in the back corner of the restaurant as a waiter rolls a cart over to their table.

The waiter starts to make table-side Guacamole as Daniel and Tom start to talk,

"Glad that you could join me Daniel," Tom begins, "under the circumstances especially."

Tom really doesn't know the right things to say, but who really does in this type of situation?

"Yeah, I know, less than ideal," Daniel replies, "Not sure why I had to come all this way for some Tex-Mex though, couldn't you have come to me?"

"I could have, but I thought that you needed to get out of that place" Tom responds,

"Yeah, it's safe to say that my man cave is somewhat *tainted* now,." Daniel says, "I may have to sell the place."

As they talk, the waiter continues to make the Guacamole, as Tom looks up to him, "No cebollas por favor." Tom says to the waiter who nods in acknowledgment.

Back on topic, Tom continues, "you don't need to *sell* your place, but it might be wise to go away for a while."

"What about those items that The Reaper gave you, did you still want us to look at them?" Tom asks.

Daniel shakes his head, "No, I don't think so. I am starting to think he has a tracker on it or something."

"Tracker?" Tom says, "I don't think that Repanelli has that kind of technical ability."

"It is not that hard to put a geolocator chip or some other type of mechanism. It is not hard at all, really." Daniel says.

Daniel continues, "That must be how he was able to track me at my house."

"I wouldn't assume that Daniel," Tom says, "There are easier ways than that to find out where someone lives."

"Good point," Daniel replies, "but somehow they knew I was going to show this to you and your team the next day, he so much as told me that one of your techs provided that information."

As they talk, the waiter completes the Guacamole and sets the molcajete (stone Guacamole bowl) down on the table along with two baskets of chips.

Tom motions over to Daniel.

"Here, you take the first taste," Tom says.

Daniel obliges, and dips a chip into the thick Guacamole and tastes it. His eyes light up like he is pleasantly surprised.

"See," Tom says, "is that not the best Guacamole that you have ever had? They tell me that the key is the right amount of cilantro and the right amount of lime."

"Its right up there," Daniel replies, "And I worked for a year in San Antonio."

"Sometimes we come here just for the Guacamole and don't even order an entrée," Tom says.

"Really?"

"Yeah, Jill and I will get the Guacamole and a pitcher of their Sangria, which will knock you on your ass by the way."

Daniel smiles as Tom describes his experiences here, but suddenly gets more somber. He looks around as if he is suddenly remembering something.

"I will tell you one thing that you don't know about this place," Daniel says.

"What is that, Daniel?"

"The owner of this place, Diego Orellana, uses this place as a front to launder for the Mexican cartels."

"How would you know this?" Tom asks.

"How else? I defended him."

"I don't understand, why wouldn't I know about this?" Tom asks.

"That is a great question. The unfortunate answer is that Orellana has connections above your pay grade."

"That would make sense," Tom concedes.

As the two men talk about him, his ears must be burning, as Diego Orellana walks over to greet the two men. Orellana is a mid 30's average height man who originally hails from Honduras but has lived most of his life in the United States.

He has bounced around from Miami to San Antonio to New York. As a Honduran, he did not want to work for the Columbian cartels, so instead aligned himself with the Mexican cartels, which has now become somewhat of a Mexican-Honduran alliance.

"Señor Aronson," Orellana begins, "How are you? Welcome to our fine establishment."

"Diego! ¿Cómo estás, Señor?" Daniel replies.

"Bien. Toda esta bien, gracias," Diego replies, "As a token of gratitude, how about a free pitcher of sangria to go along with your meal."

"Gracias Señor." Daniel replies.

Orellana walks away, presumably to get the pitcher of Sangria that he just promised.

"So his case looked like a no-win case for me, just like Repanelli," Daniel says.

"But you found a *technicality?*" Tom asks.

"That's just it, I didn't. I received information from an anonymous source that invalidated the initial search."

"Once the search was out…." Tom starts.

"Everything else was excluded, and bingo, no case." Daniel finishes.

"But Daniel, this happens a lot. That is part of the game."

"It does, Tom, and I get that," Daniel replies, "I also get that it has made me a rich prick, and I get that its part of the system we have. I don't really expect that to change."

"So what are you going to do, then?" Tom asks.

"I just don't think that I can defend people like this anymore."

Tom doesn't know how to respond.

"So you are out of the defense game for good?" Tom asks.

"As of now, I have stopped taking new cases and am only working the ones already in progress. Some of those I am looking to transition if I can get away with that. I will risk disbarment if I have to."

"Interesting," Tom replies.

Daniel picks his briefcase up of the floor, and retrieves a file folder from it and lays it on the table.

"Let me give you an idea of why I am walking away," Daniel starts, "this bookie that I have defended multiple times, now he tries to have me defend his friend Gordon."

"Ok and what is wrong with that?" Tom asks.

"Gordon is the man's 'muscle', whom he uses to collect, and by collect I mean breaking thumbs and the occasional cement shoes in the river old-school type job."

"Sleeping with the fishes?" Tom asks.

"Exactly," Daniel says, "That type of stuff."

"He admitted that to you?" Tom asks.

"Yes he did, but because of client privilege it is protected, and I cannot say nor do anything about it except provide the best defense that I possibly can. So, officially speaking, you never heard this from me."

As the two speak, Diego Orellana returns to the table with the previously promised pitcher of Sangria.

"Señores, here is your Sangria," Orellana says as he sets it down on the table, "I hope you enjoy it. Buen provecho."

"Thanks, Diego." Daniel says.

Tom takes his badge from his jacket pocket and sets it down on the table. Diego looks uncomfortable and awkwardly walks away without saying another word.

Daniel looks up to Tom and shakes his head as if to say "you prick."

"Why did you have to do that Tom?" Daniel asks.

"Just messing with him." Tom says, "I hate to be a jerk, but I just wanted to see his reaction. I still can't believe I come here all the time and didn't know about his true business. I must admit I am a little disappointed in myself."

"On another topic," Tom continues, "I assume that we are still on for golf Sunday at the club, right?"

Daniel has a blank look on his face.

"I am afraid not, Tom," Daniel says, "I think that I will need to take a break from golf, tennis, etc for a while. "

"Why exactly?"

"I just need to get my head right. I am even considering getting out of town for a few weeks; they say Miami is great this time of year."

Tom realizes something is really wrong here. Daniel has no interest in his work, no interest in sports, and generally no interest in anything.

He is no psychologist but realizes that these are some of the suicide warning signs.

"What can he do now? " Tom wonders.

Daniel continues talking about other ideas.

"Speaking about the flash drive earlier, I strongly suspect that someone inside your department tipped The Reaper off," Daniel says.

"What are you suggesting, Daniel?" Tom asks.

"What if there are leaks in the department, Tom?" Daniel asks.

Tom looks up and adds, "There always are leaks in almost every department Daniel, not much that we can do about this."

"You have to admit, *something* is out of place here." Daniel says, "for one thing, I should never have won the case. The only way to realistically win that case was with the mental defect defense, which I was told not to use. Then, after a 'miraculous' not guilty verdict, the attack at my home and Carrie's death."

"You think that The Reaper had help from the inside? That's a bold assertion," Tom shakes his head, "but having said that, if you are right it would actually explain a great deal." Tom concedes.

"I know," Daniel replies, "And with someone like The Reaper, who has already tampered with a jury, killed eight FBI agents and three SWAT officers, it is safe to assume that their reach goes further than the normal criminal enterprise."

"Probably," Tom replies, "but do you have any idea as to *whom?* Where do you think the connection points are?"

"That's just it, I don't know, could be local, it could actually be at the federal level. My primary point is that when you don't know where the corruption is, perhaps you need someone working on the outside? "

"Outside?" Tom asks, "What are you talking about?"

"I am talking about someone working in an unofficial capacity to gather information to then relay to you," Daniel says. "Someone outside of the normal chain of command. This way we could avoid any potential 'moles'."

"I don't totally follow. What do you mean by 'unofficial capacity'?" Tom asks, "What, some junior detective, private eye, Jim Rockford, kind of capacity?"

"Somewhat, but hear me out," Daniel continues, "this way there are no compromising connections. Think about it, if you don't know where the leak is how can you ever be sure where your investigation will lead? My investigators are completely outside of any chain of command and can operate without political connections. "

"They could gather information, research locations, key people, etc," Daniel says, "and then relay the information to you directly thereby passing any other points where corruption could hurt us. I could really help with this, it is the least I can do. My team of private investigators is top of the line; we can help outside of the restrictions of your department. Just think about it."

Daniel is on a roll and keeps going, "Understand that it is this team of investigators that have been the biggest key to my success. Trust me, these men can help find The Reaper and give us an opportunity to put him away for good."

"But that's the problem, isn't it? How fair of a trial do you think The Reaper would ever get seeing as how he has already tampered with one jury?" Tom asks.

"That's an outstanding point," Daniel concedes, "but we have to try every angle to find this man. He is simply too dangerous to be left at large."

Tom leans back in his seat and takes a serious position, as if he is contemplating Daniel's offer, which truly does intrigue him, and then leans back in to reply.

"Daniel, I understand your feelings right now," Tom says, "The idea is definitely outside of the box. But if you are suggesting that you help in some kind of off-the-books law enforcement capacity I have to stop you right there."

"But Tom," Daniel starts before Tom interrupts him.

"No Daniel," Tom says, "We have enough trouble now without other people getting involved in this. Besides, you are far too emotionally invested. Even if you were on my force we would remove you from this case because of what happened to Carrie."

"You make a good point," Daniel replies, "but I am not talking about some vigilante justice Tom. Again, all I am saying is that my team and I can do some research, some reconnaissance and feed that information back to you."

"No, Daniel," Tom replies, firmly.

"Okay, Tom, let's just agree to disagree then," Daniel replies.

"So do you think *now* you would be willing to turn the flash drive over to us?" Tom asks.

Daniel looks up as if he is not sure.

"Not quite yet," Daniel responds.

At this point, Daniel trusts Tom but not others in the department, and he is not willing to turn the files over to them. He also does not want to put Tom at risk.

Tom hides his frustration, but he knows that the flash drive is the best chance they have for any information that can lead them to The Reaper. As they continue to eat, he envisions the two strategies he has left. He knows that he could just subpoena the drive, but doesn't want to do that to his best friend, so he will try another tactic.

First, he will try to get Jill to persuade Daniel to turn it over. If this does not work, he will try the subpoena route, but he needs to find a judge friendly to his cause first.

Tom's problem is twofold: not only is he dealing with his best friend, whom he does not want to offend, but he is also dealing with a wealthy, well-connected, brilliant defense attorney who is more than cognizant of his legal rights.

"Well, I would be willing to make a deal for the flash drive if you are willing to listen," Daniel says.

"What kind of deal?" Tom asks.

"I want someone in your department, IAB or the DA's office to re-open the Martinez and Kinzer case," Daniel says.

"Oh God, not this again," Tom says dismissively.

"Yes, *this* again," Daniel says sternly, "Please tell me how those two bastards are still on the force after what they did."

"We have been over this several times, Daniel. Kinzer and Martinez were investigated, they were no-billed, we did not even bring this case to court." Tom says.

"They killed an unarmed 14-year old kid, just because," Daniel says.

"That's not true," Tom replies, "We have photos of Murphy holding a gun towards the officers."

Daniel just shakes his head.

"That gun makes no sense. His brother swore to me that Charlie never owned a gun, hell, had never even held a gun before." Daniel says.

"His brother may not have known everything about him," Tom says. "Sometimes people lead double lives, you know?"

"Besides," Tom continues, "you are forgetting one key fact."

"What is that, Tom?" Daniel asks.

"The boys' own parents decided not to pursue any criminal or civil charges," Tom says, "Do you really think they would be willing to drop it if there were any chance of impropriety? Furthermore, don't you think that activist groups would have been all over this one if these officers were really guilty?"

"I think there is more to the story than the official version," Daniel says, "I have my team looking into it now to find the evidence we need. And I think if the truth were to come out, these activist groups would rightly have had this case on the front page, but it has been suppressed for some reason."

"I just disagree with you on this," Tom replies. "The media would have been all over this one if there was any wrongdoing."

"So are these the types of cases you are going to pursue now" Tom asks.

"I think so." Daniel replies, "I don't think I can defend the very power elite that create this problem to begin with. I mean what kind of a world is this where a psychotic killer like The Reaper roams free and a young 14-year-old boy gets killed by two cops?"

"That's our system," Tom replies. "Well, not the 'cop killing the boy' part which I still don't believe, Daniel."

"Well, maybe the system needs a little tweak or hell, a big god-damned change is what it needs." Daniel replies, his tone starting to escalate.

"Okay, okay." Tom says, trying to calm his friend. "I will agree to your deal. I will ask Garcia and IAB to look into the Martinez and Kinzer case one more time, and then you will turn over the flash drive to me."

"Deal," Daniel says, reaching over to shake Tom's hand.

Daniel realizes that Tom will never hold up his end of the bargain. Tom does not want to see two officers convicted even if they are guilty. Daniel wants to make the suggestion but is fairly certain of the outcome.

Sure enough, Tom is thinking that at this point, given Daniel's emotional state, he needs to do and say whatever he can just to calm his best friend down.

As they finish lunch and walk outside the Riviera Maya restaurant, they say their goodbyes.

"Remember, "Tom says, "If there is anything that Jill or I can do for you please don't be afraid to ask."

"Thanks, Tom," Daniel replies, "and I really do appreciate all of your help with the arrangements and everything, if I have seemed distant, I hope you can understand."

"Of course I do," Tom says. "But you shouldn't be alone during times like these, I understand that you need a while to grieve, but don't let this consume you."

Daniel nods, and truly appreciates the message, but inside he feels differently as if he is already consumed by his grief and resigned to his fate.

***

At that same time, The Reaper and Mr. Impossible pace nervously in a home in suburban Westchester County. This nice house is in Tarrytown, New York, a pleasant suburban area near the Hudson River.

This gorgeous two story white wood and brick house with a red front door stands in stark contrast to the people inside. The front yard is impeccably manicured, with a nice stone driveway and an invisible fence of evergreen trees separating the home from neighbors on both sides. The neighborhood is located only a few miles away from the Hudson River and is at an elevation which provides a nice view of the river from certain angles.

Inside the home, Mr. Impossible and The Reaper pace nervously and discuss their next moves.

"In my opinion, we really need to hit the lawyer at his house again." Mr. Impossible says.

"We have been ordered to lay low for a little while." The Reaper responds.

"I cannot believe that you were stupid enough to give the lawyer all of our fucking files." Impossible continues.

"Man, it's not like I knew I was going to be acquitted." The Reaper replies, "I gave it to him before I was sure that the fix was in."

"I still don't understand why I was told to give it to him either." The Reaper continues, "Some of the orders that come down just don't seem right. I mean we should have destroyed the lawyer's place until we found the damn files, but instead we were told not to. I just don't get it."

"It would help to know who exactly is calling the shots; it's as if we are working for a ghost." Impossible says, "I just know that I have no complaints about the money."

"Well, I don't know who exactly, but I know that it is a high enough level that I don't want to ask any questions." The Reaper continues.

"I understand completely. Besides, I have our guy at Columbia monitoring the file and nothing has been transmitted yet." Impossible continues, "The minute he touches it we will know and can move in if necessary."

"Good." The Reaper continues, "If and when he opens that file we need to have the team ready to go."

"How much longer are we supposed to stay here in Westchester?" Impossible asks.

"Not much longer, they are supposed to have a new place for us in Manhattan in a week or two."

"Great, I am going stir fucking crazy in this place." Impossible says, "Besides it also makes me a little nervous."

"Oh, have you seen the blueprints to this place?" The Reaper asks.

"Yeah, I know you said that it was important to know how this place worked and you weren't kidding." Impossible replies.

"It's like something out of a James Bond movie or something," The Reaper says, "I was told that it was designed to be a final place for some 1980's Columbian drug lord or something, like Escobar," The Reaper says. "And this guy was *beyond* paranoid."

"Wait, Escobar, as in *the* Escobar, the cocaine guy?" Impossible asks.

"Not him specifically, but one of his lieutenants or something." The Reaper replies, "It was customized for his idea of a final confrontation with the FBI. I don't know, I guess when you have millions of drug money you can do whatever you want, although I must say this place is not all that isolated for someone so paranoid."

"I don't know about final confrontation," Impossible replies, "I just know it's fucked up, and I don't want to be here when the shit goes bad. If you asked me that guy watched *Scarface* just one too many times."

"What I cannot understand is why he would have a place like this in Westchester, and not Miami or hell Columbia." Impossible asks.

"Apparently he and Escobar had a falling out and he loved the New York lifestyle so he came here." The Reaper adds.

"I get it, because Manhattan was too dangerous, right?" Impossible concludes.

"Exactly, the same reason that we are here." The Reaper replies. "Let's just say that one of our superiors had connections that go all the way back to that guy."

"We still need to stay out of sight for a little while, and then we can move in on the D.A and the Captain," The Reaper adds, "as per our earlier orders."

"Not soon enough for me, Boss, we need to fucking end this." Impossible replies.

Impossible paces around the room, maintaining his best tough guy look and then turns back, changing the subject and his tone.

"In the meantime, do you think it would be too much to get some *bitches up in here*?" Impossible says, chuckling.

The Reaper pauses for a moment, initially taken aback by the sudden topic change, but then his eyes widen to the idea.

"I like the way you think, you little worm." Reaper replies, calmly as if they are discussing ordering dinner, "Shall we go Asian or Latina?"

"*Latina*, por favor." Impossible replies.

"Sounds good, consider it done," Reaper says.

"Muchas Gracias." Impossible replies, smiling. "Oh and see if you get one in yoga pants. Man, I love those yoga pants."

"Yoga pants?" The Reaper asks as he starts to dial presumably an escort service.

"Yeah, I love yoga pants. Let her have some of my 'downward-facing *hog*'." Mr. Impossible says, pointing at his groin.

The Reaper just laughs and shakes his head.

***

Later that night, back at Daniel's Upper West Side brownstone, Daniel sits in his office staring at a blank computer monitor. The computer is on, but no files are open or active.

His home office is gorgeous and spacious, with a large cherry wood desk, on which is a desktop computer with three monitors. A small leather sofa is off to the side, and there are nice black leather chairs both in front of and behind the desk.

On his desk, is a half-full bottle of Crown Royal along with a shot glass filled to the top.

In Daniel's mind, he keeps replaying the incident with The Reaper and Carrie over and over in his mind, almost as if it were in an infinite loop. He cannot understand why he was spared and she was killed. Survivor's guilt is one thing, but in this case, he knows that he himself was the target so still cannot understand why Carrie was killed and he was spared.

A series of questions repeat over and over in his mind.

What is the significance of that flash drive? Should he leave town to avoid any future incidents? He feels helpless as he realizes that he may be a target again, fears that the flash drive might have a geolocator on it, which Mr. Impossible just stated that it does.

Now Tom Justice has refused his idea of providing unofficial, off the books help. Daniel cannot understand why Tom is not accepting his help, considering the inside information that Daniel has being his former lawyer.

He cannot escape the darkness of this inner void that hangs over his mind and clouds every thought that enters it.

Now, Daniel's mind spins with guilt, fear, and feelings of utter helplessness. He failed his own wife, let down Richard Murphy by not preventing his younger brother's death, and now Tom will not allow him to help against The Reaper and Mr. Impossible.

He thinks about turning over the flash drive to Tom but fears for Tom's life if he has that file. It may be an irrational fear, but Daniel does not want to risk his best friend's life, especially after what happened to Carrie.

No, there was only one way to go now.

Daniel sits at his desk, and opens up a word processing application, and begins to type what appears to be a suicide note:

His message reads:

> *To all of our friends and family,*
>
> *I have come to the conclusion that I can no longer live with the guilt and shame of my connection to Carrie's death. Thanks to career mistakes and poor decisions on my part, my wife is dead and there is nothing in this world that I can do to change that.*
>
> *I was not directly responsible for her death, but if not for my poor decisions, and ignoring advice from my friends, my wife would still be alive today.*

I apologize for all of those that I have hurt, especially her parents Dave and Marie, who now have lost their only daughter, who was an angel.
--Daniel Aronson

Daniel opens one of the drawers in his desk, which has what appears to be a gun safe. He enters the combination code, and it opens. He removes the handgun from the safe and sets it on the desk. He takes one final shot of Crown Royal from the bottle on his desk, and hesitantly picks the gun up and puts it into his right hand.

Daniel pauses, but then presses the gun up to his temple, and prepares to fire.

As he readies himself for the infinity of the afterworld, or the numbing void of nothingness, he sees a framed headline on the wall of his office. Pausing, he sets the gun back down on the desk and then stands up to go look at the framed headline.

He takes the framed headline off of the wall and pauses to inspect it.

The headline reads:

Ballenger Acquitted in Wife's Murder.

This was the case that might have been the most egregious in Daniel's past before The Reaper case. This is the man who killed his wife and buried her on Staten Island. This was the first case in which Tom Justice tried to convince Daniel not to take but he refused.

It may have been five years ago, but the memories of this case are all too fresh.

This is that much more of a reason that he feels he should end it all.

Taking the picture frame over to his desk and setting it down in front of him, he takes yet another shot of Crown Royal and puts the gun back up to his head....

Shaking, trembling, not particularly convicted, Daniel pulls the trigger.

And the sound was "click".

No gunfire, no bullet.

Daniel is surprised, and actually somewhat relieved. He starts to lose his conviction more and more almost feeling like he has a second chance.

He looks at the gun and confirms that it is loaded, and once he confirms that it is, he decides to test it away from himself.

He goes and grabs one of Carrie's throw pillows from the bedroom, holds the gun over it, pulls the trigger, and the gun fires, blowing through the pillow and into the floor below.

Daniel then takes the gun and puts it back up against his temple, but suddenly he has lost his nerve. He looks at the headline about Ballenger again, and his mind starts to wander. His anger and frustration moves from being internally directed to outwardly directed.

Not being particularly religious, Daniel does not attribute this to some sort of divine intervention, but he recognizes that this does mean something.

He has no clue exactly what it means; maybe it was just a fluke, a chance occurrence. Most likely the gun just jammed or something, but he was not going to analyze this too deeply.

He then thinks, rather than take the coward's way out, maybe he still has some work to do.

If Tom won't accept his help, then maybe he can help in some other way.

10

DARK VENGEANCE

A gorgeous November evening, about 10:30 PM on a Thursday as the first snow of the year falls. It is a charming, atmospheric New York evening. Taxis rush by, steam rushes up from the manhole covers and couples walk hand in hand, all bundled up in their winter coats.

This is a week after Daniel and his suicide incident; we are in Midtown Manhattan where the atmosphere is significantly more festive than at Daniel's townhome. We are at Connolly's Pub in midtown near 54th street.

This festive, multi-level Irish Pub is a mainstay in New York with multiple locations, but most people claim this location is the best.

A large group of businesspeople has taken almost the entirety of the forty foot long wooden bar as they apparently celebrate something.

Their apparent leader is a boisterous blowhard named Jim. It is not completely obvious what he does but it clearly has something to do with money, as he is practically throwing it around, buying drinks for the entire group, and even some strangers across the bar.

You know the loud, obnoxious asshole in the bar at the end of the night?

He's that guy.

Jim picks up a bottle of Krystal champagne from the bar and holds it up to make a toast.

"Okay," Jim begins, "Everybody quiet down."

"Here's to another ass-kicking, great month!" Jim says, "Now drink up, tomorrow is another day! I don't need any of you slackers calling in sick with a hangover tomorrow."

The others all chant, "To Jim!!"

Jim revels in the moment a little bit and chugs the glass of champagne, and then another immediately after that.

Finishing his drink, Jim walks down the entire length of the bar, patting all the guys on the back, and patting the ladies on their asses. As he reaches the end of the bar, he reaches across the person sitting at the end of the bar, who is sitting there alone, nursing a draft Guinness.

"Yo, Yo, Anessa!" Jim barks, as the gorgeous red-headed bartender Anessa stops to listen.

"Can I get two more bottles of Krystal and six more Jägerbombs?"

"Sure thing, Big Jim," Anessa responds.

"But before I bring your drinks down, how about you ditch that god-awful scarf" Anessa continues, pointing at the multi-colored plaid disaster that Jim has around his neck.

"Yeah, I thought I could actually make this scarf work." Jim answers.

"You thought *wrong*, Big Jim," Anessa replies, jokingly.

As Anessa walks away, and Jim waits for his drink order, he looks again at the man at the end of the bar and thinks that he recognizes him.

"Hey, I think I know you," Jim says to the man.

"Sorry pal," Daniel replies, "your face doesn't ring a bell."

"No man," Jim continues, "I am positively sure of it."

"No clue, man," Daniel responds.

A look of revelation comes over Jim's face as he thinks he knows.

"I've got it, you were my lawyer!" Jim yells, "You look a little different, I don't remember you having that beard before."

Daniel finally turns to make eye contact with Jim, whom he had been ignoring up to this point.

"Maybe," Daniel replies, "still not entirely sure. You are right, the beard *is* new."

The two men talk a little bit more and Jim refreshes Daniel's memory about the case and they talk about ten more minutes.

Before they can talk much longer, the bartender Anessa finally comes out with Jim's drink order.

"Sorry about the delay," Anessa says, "but here is your Krystal and those Jägermeister and Red Bull explosions known as Jägerbombs."

"Thanks, Anessa." Jim says, "Tell you what, could you take them down to the other end of the bar and give them to my team there?"

"Sure thing, Big Jim" Anessa says with a flirtatious wink, as she walks down to the other end of the bar. As she does so, Jim is not so subtly staring at her assets.

"Damn," Jim mumbles to himself, shaking his head.

Now, turning his attention back to Daniel, Jim continues their conversation.

"Tell you what…sorry, what was your name again?"

"Daniel, Daniel Aronson," Daniel responds.

"Can you give me a little bit," Jim responds, "I need to circle back with my team but I would like to talk with you some more."

"No problem," Daniel responds.

Jim walks over to his team and continues their evening of drunken revelry. About an hour later, as the place has started to clear out, Jim walks back over to Daniel at the bar.

The two men talk for another hour, and Daniel opens up about his plans to quit his practice but does not say exactly why.

"That's too bad," Jim says.

"Why is that?" Daniel asks.

"It's too bad because you were a goddamned lifesaver in my case." Jim replies, "The D.A's office wanted me bad, the public was after me, everyone in the city thought that I did it."

Jim's tone is somewhere between playful and serious, but Daniel turns more serious as he looks at Jim in a serious, almost confrontational manner.

"Since you bring it up," Daniel says, "You never did tell me if you really did it or not."

"What?" Jim says, clearly taken aback by Daniel's blunt question, "What kind of a question is that?"

"As your lawyer, I could never say anything anyway. Besides with double jeopardy, nobody could ever touch you, even if you went to the courthouse with her dead body in your arms."

Jim pauses, confused by the direction that the conversation has just taken, and not feeling too comfortable with it.

"This," Jim starts, "this really isn't something we should discuss here. Besides, tonight is a night for *celebration*."

"True," Daniel responds.

"Tell you what," Jim says, "I know this special place about eight blocks away, really hot Asian girls."

"Oh yeah?" Daniel asks.

"Yeah, and let's just say it's a free for all in the VIP room," Jim says, smiling. "And since we're old friends I am buying!"

"Sure," Daniel replies, "I don't think the old lady will mind much. Split a cab?"

"Man, it's just eight blocks," Jim says, "I ain't that lazy, let's just hoof it."

The two exit Connolly's Pub, which by now is almost deserted, as are the streets outside. The streets, now covered with the snow that continues to fall, have very few people milling about.

Walking down these deserted, snow-covered streets, the two men resume talking.

"I cannot believe the Giants started so slow again this year," Jim says.

"Jets fan myself," Daniel responds, "Actually, my favorite team is whoever I have the most money on that week."

Jim laughs, "Ah there you go! You are a betting man just like me. I think I am really starting to like you, man."

"Maybe it's the Krystal and Jägerbombs talking, but I think maybe I want to tell you something," Jim says.

"What's that Jim?" Daniel asks.

"It *was **me**,*" Jim says.

"It was you...*what?*" Daniel asks.

"You are going to make me say it aren't you?" Jim says, "Okay, it was *me*. I killed my wife."

"There, I said it." Jim continues.

"Is that so?" Daniel asks as if he knew the answer all along.

"Yes," Jim continues, "but it's not that simple."

"Well, tell me Daniel" Jim starts, "how would you feel if you came home early from a business trip only to see your wife fucking someone right in your kitchen."

"I wouldn't like that at all," Daniel replies.

Jim continues, his speech becoming more of a rant, "And not just anyone, a fucking intern! Some college little schmuck, skinny piece of shit right there on my kitchen floor, on my kitchen floor screwing my wife!"

"Ouch." Daniel replies, "No I would not like that at all."

"So what happened then?" Daniel asks.

"Then I fired his loser ass!" Jim answers, "I had him blacklisted all over the city, that asshole will never work at any of the big firms, that's for damn sure."

"No, I meant with your *wife*," Daniel says.

"Well, I waited for a few weeks, then I strangled her cheating ass and buried her on Staten Island, near her fucking loser white trash family," Jim says.

"You killed her because she *cheated* on you?" Daniel says, seemingly really surprised.

"I mean, in this day and age of internet hook-ups, swing clubs, and Tinder, it's really not all that *uncommon*, is it?" Daniel continues,

"I mean, that doesn't justify it, not at all, but hardly a reason for murder, man."

"That wasn't the only reason Daniel," Jim says, "No, I killed her because she made me look bad, plain and simple. That intern had friends, that intern talked, and it has taken me almost all of five years of happy hours like tonight to get my reputation back."

"Not only that," Jim continues, "but as I was starting to almost be ready to apologize she told me that she had fucked him for months, that they had made sex tapes and that she was going to post them online if I didn't give her the divorce settlement that she wanted."

Daniel pauses for a moment, and then adds, "I must admit that it doesn't really surprise me."

"*What* doesn't surprise you?" Jim asks.

"I always knew that you killed her, Jim," Daniel says sternly. "But I must say I thought it would take a bit more to get you to *admit* it like this."

Jim is taken aback by the comment as he stops walking for a moment and looks directly at Daniel.

"What? What are you talking…..?" Jim speaks but is rudely interrupted by a sudden blindside right cross punch from Daniel.

The punch lands square and true and knocks Jim over on his ass.

As Jim lies on the ground grabbing his face in pain, Daniel stands over him and removes a handheld Taser from his coat pocket. He takes the Taser to Jim and shocks him three times with it, rendering Jim incapacitated.

This was the moment that Daniel was after. That headline, that damn headline lit a fire under him to find out once and for one what happened with this case. A full week of research and private investigative work led him to this situation where he felt that Jim Ballenger was vulnerable, and as you see it turns out that he was.

The plan was to track Jim down and hopefully at best elicit a confession from him.

Daniel actually never expected Jim to be this forthcoming. He had his private investigator lined up for another solid month of work just to learn the truth which Jim Ballenger had just so easily confessed to right now.

But now what can he do? He is guilty of assault already and with the Taser involved, he realizes it is already aggravated assault, Daniel feels that he has already gone too far to turn back.

Daniel looks around to ensure that there are no witnesses and no security cameras anywhere in the vicinity. He takes and drags the much larger Jim Ballenger into the alley and back behind two garbage dumpsters and props him up against the brick wall.

As Jim starts to recover, Daniel takes his handgun out of his other coat pocket, the very gun he had held to his own forehead just a week earlier.

"These bullets were supposed to be for *me*," Daniel says, "I had all but given up on my own life, my own purpose."

"I made mistakes before and you are one of the worst." Daniel continues.

"Now maybe I can make things right in some small way or another."

Daniel raises the gun and aims it at Jim. His hand trembles with a combination of rage and fear. He hesitates, as he is still not completely convinced that this is the right move, but slowly, Daniel fires twice and misses.

The now-alert Jim sees the bullets miss, and replies defiantly as he tries to stand, "You can't do it, can you? It takes real guts to be a k...."

Four more bullets rain and Jim is struck twice in the head and twice in the chest, and cannot finish his sentence.

Silence.

For an odd eerie moment, especially for Manhattan, there are no sounds, no sirens, no shouting, no drunk pedestrians, nothing.

The rising crescendo of anger that Daniel has felt for the past month starts to fade, but as that fades, the mind takes over and the dark reality starts to take hold deep within.

Now, Daniel realizes that he is a murderer and a cold blooded one at that…what can he do?

Panic and fear start to set in as Daniel starts to realize the complicated web that he has now created. He realizes that anyone at that bar could identify him, especially Anessa the bartender. Luckily no one really saw them leave together, but still this could be something from which he could not return.

He hides Jim's body behind one of the dumpsters in the alley as he goes to get his car, parked back behind Connolly's. He is gambling that nobody discovers the body in the meantime, but no one does, and he is able to put Jim's body in his trunk and drive away.

A two-hour round trip later; he is driving back from the Greenwich, CT area at which he dumped the body somewhere in the Long Island Sound. This is a location that was given to him by one of his many shady clients.

As he is driving, feeling somewhat relieved that the worst is over, he has a thought that makes his stomach sink.

That *scarf*. That scarf that he noticed earlier, but in the chaos of all of the activity he forgot about it.

That ugly and ridiculous scarf was not on Jim's body when Daniel put the body in the Long Island Sound.

It must have fallen off back in the alley, but there was no way to go back now.

11

FIRST SUSPICION

Snow continues to fall on what has become a fairly early winter in the Northeast. I say winter but it is still only technically late fall. Two days have passed since Daniel killed Jim Ballenger, and he has been reported missing by his firm after missing the closing bell on Friday.

Two of Tom Justice's detectives have been sent to Connolly's Pub to speak to the bartenders there. Connolly's being the location at which he was last seen, as reported by his staff that accompanied him.

The two police detectives are Juan Parra and Cliff Barnes. Parra, 35, is a bronze- skinned, dark-haired, handsome man originally from Santiago, Chile. He is laid back, calm, smooth and intelligent. In his partnership with Barnes, he is clearly the brains of the two, whereas Barnes is the muscle. Muscle might be giving him too much credit, as Barnes 6'4" 260-pound body indicates that he is not exactly a gym rat.

Barnes is the designated interrogator, and he absolutely loves grilling both suspects and witnesses. He is adept at making them uneasy and getting them to volunteer information that you would think that they would not provide.

Parra is on the fast track to a promotion. He plans to take the Sergeant's exam in the next few months, and it is not improbable that he would be the man taking Tom Justice's captain position in the next several years. If Tom considers anyone to be his protégé, it would be Parra. Shane McWilliams is more of a number two, but Parra could one day lead the entire department.

Parra and Barnes walk into Connolly's Pub and up to the front of the bar where a middle-aged male bartender wipes down the counter.

"Excuse me, sir," Barnes says, "Detective Barnes, NYPD. We called earlier about a missing person case."

The bartender looks up, confused at first, and then nods as he remembers.

"Oh yes," the bartender says, "yeah, you want to talk to Anessa, she is down at the other end of the bar, the redhead. Oh, and, it's 'Anessa', not 'Vanessa'. There is no 'V'. Just saying, she hates it when people call her 'Vanessa'."

Parra and Barnes both nod as Parra says "Got it."

Parra and Barnes walk down and begin speaking to the attractive, red-headed bartender who is dressed even more revealingly today with a low cut top, accented by her long flowing crimson hair.

As Anessa talks, she continues to lean over to put glasses below the bar, exposing more and more of her cleavage.

Yeah, both men look.

"So what time did you say he left?" Barnes asks.

"Not entirely sure," Anessa replies, "but it was somewhere between 1:30 and 2, really late."

"Okay and I understand that he left with another man, is that correct?" Barnes says.

"Yes, sir."

"Can you describe him for us?"

"Hot, really hot. Good looking." Anessa replies, "Old, old like you, but waaaay better looking."

"Thanks," Barnes replies sarcastically, "always great to hear."

Parra leans over to join into the conversation.

"Okay, is there anything more specific that we can actually use?" Parra says.

"Look," Anessa replies, growing agitated, "I don't really want to talk any more about this. If you want I can come down and talk to one of your picture guys."

"Do you mean 'sketch artists'?" Parra asks.

"Yeah," Anessa replies, "Sketch artists, picture guys, what's the difference?"

Before another word can be said, a uniformed officer, Officer LeCorgne, comes through the front door holding a piece of clothing in his right hand. He walks down to Parra and Barnes and presents the item to them.

"Not sure if it's relevant, detectives," Officer LeCorgne says, "But we found this a few blocks down in an alley, has what appears to be blood on it."

He holds up the item and it is the plaid scarf that Jim was wearing two nights earlier.

Anessa gasps.

"I would recognize that scarf anywhere," Anessa exclaims, "That's the scarf Jim had on two nights ago. Hideous, just hideous."

"Maybe we should go see that sketch artist now," Parra says, motioning to Anessa.

"Don't you mean 'picture guy', partner?" Barnes says smugly.

Anessa doesn't laugh and flashes Barnes a dirty look, then sticks her tongue out at him like a six-year-old kid.

***

At that same moment, back at the precinct office, Shane McWilliams walks across the busy precinct floor towards Tom Justice's office. As he walks, he carries a file folder in one hand and a cup of Dunkin Donuts coffee in the other.

Reaching Tom Justice's office, he knocks and Tom acknowledges him and motions for him to come in.

"What's new Shane?" Tom asks.

"I may have at least some kind of lead on The Reaper," Shane says.

"Really?" Tom responds, "Tell me more."

"Yeah, well Parra was telling me that he had from a very reliable source the name of a former hitter that worked for The Reaper for years."

"And?" Tom prods.

"And they had a falling out about a year ago, and apparently this guy is more than happy to share anything and everything that he knows." Shane continues.

"Sounds good," Tom replies, "Let's check it out this might be the lead we needed."

"I already ran it by the Chief of D's and Agent Poer with the Bureau, they are fine with it," Shane says.

"Excellent work, man," Tom says.

"See," Shane responds, "I told you they should have made me Captain."

The two men laugh at Shane's favorite line and then Tom rolls his eyes.

"Any other leads beyond this one, Shane?" Tom asks.

"No, nothing. As we discussed, we can most likely safely assume that the entire crew will lay low for quite some time." Shane replies,

"What about your contacts at the bureau?" Tom asks.

"No," Shane says, "Nothing. No word."

"How about on your side, Tom?" Shane continues, "Did you make any progress getting the flash drive from Aronson?"

"No," Tom replies, "I tried, but no luck on that front."

"We could always try to get a warrant," Shane says.

"I thought of that," Tom responds, "But for a few reasons I dropped the idea. First of all, Daniel is a friend, but second and, more importantly, he knows every judge in town and practically all of them love him."

"And he has the sympathy factor," Shane adds.

"Precisely," Tom says, "How could I persuade any judge to give me a warrant under the circumstances? Daniel is a grieving husband and a man who everyone loves. Yeah, fat chance on that one."

"Good call," Shane says.

"I do have one other angle to play," Tom says.

"What is that?" Shane asks.

"I am having a lunch date with Jill tomorrow, and I was going to ask her to visit Daniel at his house and do some snooping."

"Ouch," Shane replies, "Getting your wife to do your dirty work for you?" Shane says, laughingly.

"Actually, I just want to know if it is there," Tom says, "Most likely he has moved it or it's in his safe or something protected."

"And let's step back a second. " Shane says, "You said that you and Jill are going on a lunch 'date' tomorrow?"

"Yeah?"

"Why didn't you just say you were meeting your wife for lunch?" Shane says.

"It's this stupid trial separation, man," Tom responds.

"The counselor suggested that we approach these meetings as less routine, and more like we are dating again." Tom continues.

Shane tries to play along but it's more like he is playfully mocking his friend.

"So tomorrow is sort of like your 'first date' again?" Shane says.

"I guess you can say that," Tom replies.

"Okay," Shane says, "but hopefully it won't end up like your real first date with you puking all over the steps at Woodrow's"

Tom looks away and says, "Yeah, not exactly my finest hour. But thanks for reminding me."

"See, I told you they should…." Shane starts.

"Oh, shut the hell up!" Tom interrupts, as he smacks Shane with a playful right to the shoulder.

***

The following afternoon, it's a gorgeous and clear Mid-December day. Temperatures in the high 40's, no wind and the bustle of the holiday season in full force. Jill Justice walks hand in hand with Tom after their "lunch date" and they are crossing Central Park west to go and walk a little bit in the park.

Walking down the snow-covered paths, down and around the area known as the Pond, Tom thinks of all of the many holiday seasons they had spent together, and all of the good times. The ice skating, the walks, the hot Chocolate, just fun times.

"You know," Jill starts, breaking the silence, "That really did hit the spot."

Jill is looking especially fashionable today with a very sharp casual black winter dress and covered by a stylish white winter coat.

"I know," Tom replies, "It really was great, wasn't it. I mean, we have been to Serendipity several times but I don't think I have ever seen you eat so much!"

"I know," Jill says, "I almost finished the entire thing, too!"

"It's really never fair when you drag me to that place; I mean, I know it was your pick and everything..." Tom says.

"Hey, don't hold it against *me* just because you are lactose intolerant." Jill counters.

"Yeah," Tom says, "but all of those gorgeous looking sundaes, all the ice cream, it's almost too much to bear."

"You had your lemon cake," Jill says.

"Oh right," Tom replies, "my freaking cake was about one-tenth the size of your colossus of a sundae!"

Jill laughs.

"I know, right?" Jill says, "I mean they bring out the huge sundae first, and then you expect your pie to be at least proportionate, but then this little bitty piece of pie comes out." She says, laughing.

"Yeah, I think I got cheated," Tom says.

Jill stops smiling, and there is an awkward pause for a moment, and then she speaks again.

"Maybe **you** shouldn't use the word '*cheated*' for a while, right?" Jill says.

Tom can't respond, and there is again a moment of awkward silence.

Tom finally decides to break the silence.

"Oh well, I guess I really screwed that one up," Tom says, as if conceding defeat for this date.

"So, anyhow, I was planning on watching the Knicks game tonight in my basement 'apartment', and then passing out," Tom says.

"Not necessarily," Jill says flirtatiously.

"Not necessarily what?" Tom asks.

"I was thinking," Jill says, "I was thinking… well, maybe you can sleep upstairs tonight."

"You mean just…..*sleep*, right?" Tom asks.

"Not necessarily," Jill replies, this time, flashing an inviting grin.

Tom looks up and flashes a sly dog smile as if he thinks he is getting lucky tonight.

"How about right now?" Tom says, "I have Shane and Parra both visiting with the Feds so I have three hours free right now!"

Jill hesitates for a moment, and then looks up and smiles but doesn't say another word.

She doesn't have to.

An hour later back at their home, Tom and Jill enter the front door with their hands all over each other. They seem like two teenagers on prom night whose parents are out of town for the weekend. Items of clothing drop little by little as they make their way through the house.

Upstairs, as they near the bedroom, here in the absolute peak of passion, Tom has to speak, not knowing when to shut up and go with things.

"Wait," Tom says, "are you really sure we should be doing this?"

Jill looks up with a complete look of shock.

"You *really* want to have this debate at this moment?" Jill responds, clearly taken aback.

"Yeah," Tom says, "I think sometimes I need to know when to…"

Jill interrupts, whispering sweetly as she moves in for another kiss.

"...when to *shut the fuck up,*" Jill says with a smile.

As she finishes her playful comments, she kisses Tom like she hasn't in over a year. The passion, the kissing, the romance feels far more like a date, almost like an illicit love affair but in a positive way. The intensity is far greater than either of them had felt in five years, and it is electric.

12

THE ATONEMENT

We shift from a scene of a couple in renewed love over to the brooding, dark thoughts of Daniel Aronson.

Only a few days removed from his first murder, Daniel sits expressionless at his home office desk with a glass of Crown Royal in his right hand and his gun again on his desk.

Has he come this far only to again attempt to end his own life?

The full gravity of what he has done has been processed and evaluated, but Daniel is wondering to himself why he doesn't feel anything.

"Shouldn't I feel some guilt?" Daniel wonders to himself.

But he doesn't.

The more Daniel thinks about it, Ballenger had it coming. Not only was he an admitted murderer, but Daniel had extensively reviewed Ballenger's business dealings and seen his corrupt deals. The more Daniel learned about Ballenger's insider trading and his firms' connection to the bailouts of 2008, Daniel was convinced his course of action was the correct one.

According to Daniel's files, Ballenger had single-handedly deprived over 500 people of their livelihoods via insider trading and fraud. As his lawyer, Daniel knew all of this, but for these crimes, these transgressions there were never any charges brought, nor would there ever be.

"But am I really able to make these moral decisions on my own?" Daniel again wonders to himself, "The key point here is that what is legal is not necessarily what is moral. Morality is a tricky thing."

He continues to drink his Crown Royal, and then he opens up his files in which he has stored critical information on all of his cases, a handful of which he has recently flagged for further review.

As he reviews these files and copies the flagged records into a brand new directory, he comes to a conclusion as to what his next course of action will be.

These men, he reasons, were clearly guilty of their crimes and only freed because of his own legal trickery.

Now the idea was that much clearer.

If Tom Justice will not accept his help, then he will still continue to work from outside of the official investigation. Daniel will do whatever he can to help to locate The Reaper, Mr. Impossible and all of those soulless lackeys that do their dirty work.

Daniel realizes that his will take some time since not even Tom Justice and the FBI can find these men. On the other hand, He knows that he has the resources and the connections to get this done along with one piece of information that Tom Justice does *not* have.

Daniel has the flash drive.

A colleague has already arranged for someone out of state to decrypt the files in a manner that should be untraceable. After the Carrie incident, Daniel does not want to take any chances, and will need to go to Atlanta to meet this man. This way, if there is some tracker on the device, he will be long gone and in another state before anyone could get to him.

So, then if it works, the information on this file will provide him the information to locate this organization and provide two opportunities for action.

The first option is that he can provide the information to Tom and his task force and they can act on it. The second option would be for him to take action himself, perhaps using some for-hire contacts he has made in his many defense trials for mafia soldiers. With his team of private investigators coupled with these other, more off-the-books connections, he could get something done.

The risk with involving Tom, the police, and the FBI is the simple risk that there could be some informant or leak in the department. From Daniel's experience defending several bad, bad men, he knows firsthand that there are plenty of corrupt cops in the NYPD.

He realizes that the frightening truth is that he may need to use this information and then take on the organization by himself. For this task, he realizes that he is clearly under-prepared.

He knows full well that at his most basic, he is a privileged, spoiled lawyer, not a one- man vigilante crew. He has no intention of becoming the next masked vigilante but realizes that he can help in his own way.

This will likely take some time and research by his team before any kind of move could be made against the organization; in the meantime, he looks at the list of names on his new file of marked cases. For each of these five names, he will need to visit and attempt to make right what once went wrong.

So, he makes the decision, he will work on three fronts: first, he will utilize his private investigators and sources on the police force other than Tom to find out as much as he can about the whereabouts of The Reaper and his organization.

Next, he will go to out of state to have the file decrypted and act upon what hopefully is useful information. And finally, he will start working his list, not out of revenge but out of the attempt to correct wrongs that he helped to perpetuate.

Then, Daniel rationalizes to himself, "if all goes well, I will turn the file over to Tom, and then turn myself in for the Ballenger murder and others that I decide to harm. And that will be that."

Daniel doesn't expect to emerge from this mission or quest without being either dead or in prison.

But, he realizes, nothing can happen until he has more time to work this list and find out about The Reaper's plans. It is a risk to take these actions which could easily get him arrested, but for each situation, he devises a defense strategy of plausible deniability that should keep him free, even if he becomes a suspect.

Still, it is a very significant risk.

It is a risk that he is willing to take.

But now, Daniel thinks to himself, "Let's work the list."

The first name he marks as being completed, that is the nearly departed Jim Ballenger.

The next name on the list is Gabe Gomez, a recent Cuban immigrant who was arrested for killing two teenage girls. Actually, to be more specific, Mr. Gomez did not just kill them, he raped and sodomized them and then slit their throats. Daniel was hired to defend them by the agents of the cartel for whom Mr. Gomez worked.

Daniel, being the excellent lawyer that he is, succeeded in obtaining an acquittal.

How was this man acquitted of such a brutal and heinous crime?

The answer is quite simple, really. No witnesses were willing to testify against Mr. Gomez, and Daniel was a genius at attacking the validity of forensic information.

The third name on the list is Bruce Stephens, a known pedophile, and pornographer. Stephens is known to participate in illegal sex trafficking of underage girls from Latin America and Asia. He has been tied by multiple witnesses to also participating in the murder of at least three girls who were trying to escape.

Rumor has it that Mr. Stephens also participated and filmed a so-called "snuff film", which is a pornographic S&M film in which one of the participants is actually killed on film. What made this crime particularly horrific and list-worthy is the fact that the participants were two elementary school girls, both under the age of 10.

The fourth name on the list is Will Harrison, the man from the trial earlier with the "Professor Light" devices. Daniel realizes that the recently-acquitted Harrison is actually quite the danger to society. He knows that Harrison's name has been linked to multiple terrorist organizations, and fears that if even **one** of Harrison's inventions got into the wrong hands, it could be a huge tragedy along the lines of 9/11 or Oklahoma City.

And the final name on Daniel's list is Kyle Yancy, the bookie that Daniel had discussed with Tom Justice a few weeks back. This man was responsible for five deaths, but they were all committed by his hit man known only as "Gordon". Daniel knows that Yancy is connected to even more murders, however, Daniel was able to get Yancy acquitted by attacking the credibility of the prosecution witnesses. Therefore, Yancy received an acquittal he did not earn nor deserve.

On a subsequent, "maybe" list is the man whose hospitality Daniel had enjoyed a few weeks back at the Riviera Maya restaurant, Diego Orellana. Orellana leads the regional drug trade as a primary point man for the Honduran-Mexican cartel. They are linked to about a dozen murders in the area, and Daniel suspects Orellana has ordered or, at least, knew about these murders.

He is on the so-called "maybe" list because Daniel does not have enough evidence to make a case. He realizes that he cannot bring a trial against Orellana again, especially not having been his defense attorney in an earlier trial. His private investigators are currently doing their research on Orellana to see if there are any other concrete bits of evidence that he can use. If he can go the trial route first, he would prefer to go that way.

And finally, rounding out the list in the "maybe" category are NYPD officers Martinez and Kinzer. These two men were never charged with the killing of young Charles Murphy, but Daniel has multiple sources that substantiate their guilt. Daniel's problem with this is the fact that police are protected, and he does not necessarily want to commit a capital offense.

Guilty or not, Daniel does not want to become a cop killer. This one will have to wait because to accomplish this might mean that he and his best friend Tom Justice are forever enemies.

He has plans for all of the others to deflect guilt, and even has devised clever defense strategies for each case if and when he is ever arrested. This plan had to be developed first before any of this could ever begin.

What is paramount for this plan to work is that he must remain off the radar and not a suspect as long as is necessary to complete the work. Even if he is arrested for any of these crimes, he knows full well that he would be able to negotiate bail and then keep on working.

No time better than tonight to start from the top, it's time to speak to Mr. Gabe Gomez. Thanks to his Private Investigator's file on Mr. Gomez, Daniel knows exactly where he will be tonight.

***

Across town, it is closing time at the Habana 1957 restaurant, a small and quaint place known for having the best mojitos and Cuban sandwiches in town. This lively place has had a great night and made a great deal of money, but now it is time to close up.

Two people remain at this lower east side institution, Mariana Vasquez works behind the counter processing all of the credit card transactions and collecting the remaining cash from the front registers. Across the restaurant, Gabe Gomez wipes down the tables and does the final sweeping for the evening.

Mariana is a strikingly beautiful Latina with long black hair, bikini model body and a smile that would stop almost any man in his tracks. Gabe Gomez is a large, muscular, light- skinned Cuban with a scar over his right eye. He is still working for the cartel, sheltered here at this location where in theory he can lie low for a while.

"Do you mind finishing up by yourself, Gabe?" Mariana asks.

"Si, Amigita." Gabe responds, "No hay problema."

"Gracias," Mariana responds, "I really appreciate it. I have to watch my roommate's kid tonight."

"I am happy to do it. No problem." Gabe responds, in a thick Cuban accent.

Mariana walks by Gabe as he continues working.

"Maybe you make it up to me some time. No?" Gabe says, playfully patting Mariana on the ass as she walks by.

She turns, and flashes a look of mock surprise or offense, but then says in a flirtatious whisper as she smiles.

"Maybe I will do that," Mariana says with a wink.

"Mentira. Mala." Gabe says, "Always the tease. But I think this time you might be for real."

Mariana does not respond, instead, she flirtatiously flips her hair and flashes Gabe a teasing smile.

She leaves through the door extra slowly on purpose so that Gabe can take in her view from behind, and he does.

Mariana laughs, as she looks back and notices him staring and as she walks out the door, Gabe continues to sweep the floor.

"Chingada," Gabe says to himself, as he shakes his head and smiles.

About a minute or so later, the restaurant door opens slowly.

Looking up, Gabe thinks and hopes for a moment that maybe Mariana has decided to come back and give him a kiss…or better.

Instead, Gabe sees Daniel Aronson standing there, clad all in black, and not speaking.

"Sorry, amigo guero," Gabe says, "We closed."

"Gabe Gomez," Daniel responds cryptically

Stunned that this unfamiliar "Guero" (Spanish slang for 'white guy') knows his name; Gabe looks up with a puzzled look on his face.

"Gabe Gomez, we need to talk…" Daniel continues.

Gabe continues to not fully understand what is going on, but his puzzled look changes to one of defiance as clearly he believes that this man cannot be any threat.

"Talk about what?" Gabe says, cocking his head in a defiant manner.

Daniel removes his gun from his jacket and points it directly at Gabe's chest, and says menacingly.

"Your confession."

***

The next day, it is a completely different mood back at the 17th Precinct, where Tom Justice, Shane, Parra and Barnes all sit in the precinct game room.

The 17th Precinct game room is a converted locker room that Tom Justice had re-purposed in order for his people to relax, play games, eat, and generally foster communication that cannot always happen out on the busy precinct floor.

He added a refrigerator, microwave oven, card table and foosball table, and has made it into quite a comfortable space, one that the entire precinct loves.

Although the game room is open to all members of the precinct, for two hours every Wednesday this is reserved exclusively for Tom, Shane, Parra and Barnes for their slightly-illegal but fun game of poker.

At the moment, the loud-mouthed Barnes is telling one of his many Texan anecdotes.

"So, I see this couple park in a handicapped spot," Barnes says, "and they are both mid-40's and in obviously good shape so I walk up and I say to them, 'Hey, you aren't disabled, you can't park here.

So, before the man can say anything, the woman quips with perfect comedic timing, 'Oh he's *not* disabled?' she says, 'you haven't seen his **dick**.'"

The guys burst out laughing.

"Straight up, happened just like that." Barnes continues, "I swear I thought the guy was going to have a stroke right then and there his face was so red. Of course, I had to let them off without a ticket that was too good."

The four of them like to meet in here to discuss the case while also playing their game of poker (not for money, of course, that would be wrong.) Along the way they love to discuss several other types of topics, as they call it the weekly debate topic.

This topic could be anything from a deep concept as the meaning of life, to as superficial and juvenile a topic such as *"who would you do?"*

"I still can't believe you got them to approve the game room," Shane says, "much less the card games."

"Game room yes," Tom responds, "but not the card games and definitely not poker. Guys, if anyone asks we are using this table to review *crime scene photos*, right?"

The four men laugh and go on with their game.

"And remember," Tom continues, "we can only play for about two hours per week, or however long it takes for me to end up ahead."

"Less talking, more dealing," Barnes barks, "So, where are we so far on this week's 'great debate'?"

"I still say it is 'I Ran' by the Flock of Seagulls," Parra says, "If nothing else for that whack hairdo."

The men laugh.

"No way, man." Barnes counters, "It has to be 'Relax' by Frederick goes to Hollywood."

"*Frankie*, you dumbass." Shane corrects, "*Frankie Goes to Hollywood.* Frederick is the lingerie store, sort of like a 'Victoria's Secret' for rich people."

"Frankie, Frederick, whatever." Barnes replies, "All I know is that I loved that scene from that movie…what was the name of that?"

"*Body Double.*" Shane replies,

"Yeah," Parra says, "The porn scene with Melanie Griffith. Man, really hot. I like it hot, real hot." Parra continues, emulating the line from the film.

"What about 'Walking on Sunshine' by Katrina?" Shane asks.

Tom, who hasn't really been engaged in the conversation, finally looks up and has to ask:

"What are we talking about here?" He asks, "Nobody told me the topic of the week yet."

"The weekly 'Great Debate' topic," Shane replies, "This week it is *'what is the cheesiest Song/Video combination of the 80's?'*"

"What happened to the government conspiracies and assassinations topic?" Tom asks.

"That was last week, boss," Parra replies, "And the fake moon landing was the winner."

"I still say that is horseshit," Shane says, "like we never really walked on the moon. You guys are way off on that one."

"Buddy of mine worked at NASA," Barnes says, "and he tells me there is no footage of it anywhere. One of the most significant events in our history, yet all of the original footage is just *gone*."

"I didn't believe him either," Barnes continues, "but then I checked with other friends of mine in Houston and they told me the same thing."

"Conspiracy nuts, all of you, I swear," Tom says, dismissively.

As these great debates rage on, Officer LeCorgne walks into the room looking for Tom Justice.

"Captain, sir," Officer LeCorgne says, "You've got a call. It's your wife, and she says that it is urgent.

"Fine. Just tell her I will be there in a minute," Tom says as he starts to get up.

"Damn," Tom continues, as he looks at his cards, "and I had a great hand, too!"

Tom walks towards the door, exits and prepares to close the door behind him. He mostly closes it but then pokes his head back into the room to make one more comment.

"*'Take on Me'*" Tom screams, "By A-HA with the cheesy black and white. That's your winner!"

The other guys crack up and burst out laughing as they continue to play cards and Tom exits the room.

Tom walks into his office and picks up his desk phone and sits down.

"Yes, Jill," He says.

"Hi, Tom," Jill replies, "Were you able to see Daniel at his house?"

"Not yet," Tom replies, "But I finally got him to agree to play a round of golf with me at the club this weekend."

"Good," Jill responds, "Maybe then we can get a feel for what he is thinking."

"When is your lunch with him?" Tom asks.

"Tomorrow," Jill replies.

"Tomorrow? I thought it was next week." Tom says, "Well if you are meeting him tomorrow, try to size him up then."

"Okay," Jill responds, "Anything specific?"

"Yes," Tom replies, "We really need for him to turn over this flash drive to us."

"Flash drive?" Jill asks.

"Yes, we think it has significant information about the organization and hopefully enough to get us on their trail again."

"Why hasn't he given it to you already?" Jill asks, "That doesn't seem right to me."

"He has some wild idea that the file might have a tracker on it," Tom says, "He fears that once it is opened, men might be coming there to shoot whoever has the file."

"Well isn't that kind of what happened with Carrie?" Jill asks.

"We think," Tom says, "We still don't know why Carrie was even involved, that's one main part of this case that hasn't fit."

"Okay, well let me see if I can persuade him to turn it over," Jill says.

"Okay, talk to you later, 'bye," Tom says as he hangs up the phone.

As Tom hangs up the phone, Shane walks into his office and resumes a conversation that they began a few days prior.

"All done with the game?" Tom asks.

"No, just taking a break. I thought I would follow up with you about something." Shane says.

"What's up?"

"Now would be a good time to check out that lead that I was telling you about earlier," Shane says.

"Oh, you mean the former hitter that worked for The Reaper?" Tom asks.

"Exactly," Shane says, "Did the Chief give us the green light to proceed?"

"He did, what about Director Maxwell?" Tom asks.

"Yes, Maxwell is on board," Shane replies, "His only instructions were to keep the meeting on a need to know basis."

"Meaning what?" Tom asks.

"Meaning no Parra, no Barnes and no members of the Bureau, just us," Shane says.

"Okay," Tom responds, "Can't say that I love it, but, at least, they are letting us do something instead of just waiting around."

13

CONFESSIONS

The next day is a gorgeous winter Friday afternoon; a light snow falls on a bustling late December day. Jill Justice crosses the street at Park Avenue and 28th as she proceeds to her favorite Midtown restaurant.

She walks in where she is immediately greeted by the host who knows her well and who seats her at her normal table.

She loves this place, Park Avenue Winter, and comes here at a minimum once per season. This intriguing restaurant changes its décor and its menu each season and since we are in late December, they have just opened up their winter menu, which Jill is just dying to try.

The dining room is a fairly small room, typical Midtown Manhattan-sized restaurant with white walls and the effect of bare winter trees hanging down from the ceilings. The effect successfully creates a very cozy and warm atmosphere, which is why Jill prefers winters here the most.

As Jill sits and soaks up the ambiance at one of her favorite restaurants, Daniel walks in the front door and the host brings him over to Jill's table to be seated.

Jill stands up to greet him, and the two take their seats.

"Thanks for joining me Daniel," Jill says.

"No problem, I always have time to meet with a great friend," Daniel replies.

Jill realizes that she needs to be a calming influence on Daniel, and needs to feel him out first to see how he is handling things.

"So how have you been doing these past few weeks?" Jill asks.

"Not bad," Daniel responds, "All things considered."

"Did Tom tell you about my plans to quit my practice" Daniel continues.

"Yes," Jill responds, "and I can honestly say that I completely understand your decision based on what happened."

"I may decide to come back at some point," Daniel continues, "but it will have to be a little while later."

"Well, you should stay social at least...what about joining us over at the club this Sunday?" Jill asks.

Daniel hesitates before responding.

"I don't think so, Jill," Daniel replies, "I am just not up for a big scene right now. Meeting you for lunch is one thing, but the full country club scene? No thanks." Daniel concludes as he shakes his head.

"Okay. I understand." Jill says.

"Can I tell you something, Jill?" Daniel asks, his mood continuing to be somber.

Jill looks up with comforting and attentive eyes.

"Anything, Daniel," she replies, "What is it?"

"And can you promise not to tell Tom?" Daniel continues.

Jill wonders what he could be thinking.

"Yes, of course, Daniel," Jill replies.

Hesitantly, Daniel finally begins to respond.

"Well, quite frankly, I wanted to kill myself." Daniel says softly, "And that's not being truly honest. I actually *tried* to kill myself."

"Oh, Daniel, no," Jill responds.

"I just felt," Daniel continues, "I just felt so much guilt over Carrie's death."

Jill interrupts, "But it wasn't your *fault* Daniel."

"Not directly," Daniel responds, "but Jill you cannot possibly argue that I was not *indirectly* involved in it."

"Still…" Jill starts, as Daniel then interrupts her.

"We could debate this point forever, but I still think that now, now maybe there is something else that I can do to make up for it," Daniel says.

"And what is that exactly?" Jill asks.

"I cannot get into that right now, Jill," Daniel responds.

"Ok," Jill replies, "well I don't want to pry."

"On another topic," Jill continues, "let's not forget about our mixed doubles match next Sunday."

The mood starts to lighten, as the topic turns to tennis, where the two have been mixed doubles partners for years.

"Are you kidding me?" Daniel continues, as a smile creeps across his face. "Mixed Doubles City Finals, yes I think I might be ready."

"Tom still gives me grief over partnering with you, even though the whole thing was his idea," Jill says.

"Well I understand," Daniel replies, "and it probably doesn't help that I tell him how much I like you in those short tennis skirts that you wear," Daniel adds with a wink.

Jill reaches out and slaps Daniel's hand playfully,

"Daniel!" She exclaims, with a face of mock offense, secretly loving his observation.

"Hey," Daniel continues, defending himself, "if Tom can comment about Carrie's boob job, I think I can comment on your short little tennis skirts."

"Good point," Jill says, "and as Tom said himself, and it's all about the level of the friendship as to what is and what is *not* appropriate."

Jill smiles, "Well and there is that one difference between you and I as opposed to Tom and Carrie."

Daniel's face lights up and he smiles.

"Yes, you are exactly right, they weren't college sweethearts."

Daniel continues, "I must admit, I have often wondered how things could have turned out if we had gone down that path."

Jill smiles, and replies, "Remember the tennis skirts that I used to wear back in *college?*"

"Are you kidding me?" Daniel responds, "Of course I do. What I really remember was the time you didn't wear anything *underneath* your skirt and we only got through two games before we…"

Jill interrupts, "*Daniel!!!*", and Jill and Daniel both smile at each other.

"I *do* remember," Jill continues, provocatively, "and I also remember how close my parents were from catching us."

"Ha!" Daniel replies, "Yeah that was fun, really fun."

Daniel starts to feel better, and Jill realizes that she has been successful in elevating Daniel's mood, which had only recently reached suicidal depths. Hopefully, she feels, more days like this will lure him back to his normal life and he will resume his career.

That's an example of friends looking out for each other.

Jill reaches out to touch Daniel's hand, which is now on the table. She touches it lightly at first and then caresses it.

Daniel is a great friend who needs her help but is also a former lover and someone for whom she felt love for the first time. The feeling of her touch evokes some comfort for Daniel and then the feelings shift to guilt and memories of Carrie, and that sinking, destructive and inescapable feeling that he was somewhat responsible for her death.

But at the same time, Jill's touch feels nice, feels comforting, and makes him feel alive again, at least in some small way.

***

The following day, Saturday, Daniel is consumed by more guilt as he maintains the conflict in his mind over his current behavior.

Daniel was raised in a mixed religious family, not so affectionately called a "Cashew" by some, which is a combination of Catholic and

Jewish. Daniel always found a great many of the biblical stories too far-fetched to be believable.

As he grew up, his struggles with his faith led him to the ultimate understanding that a majority of the scriptures were meant to be allegorical, and that the important thing was to focus on the similarities between religions rather than the differences.

Being exposed to both Catholic and Jewish traditions, he was impressed by the number of similarities yet also intrigued by the differences. And as a child, he rather loved the combination of Christmas and Hanukkah, which was a virtual bonanza in presents for 9 days.

As a pragmatic person, Daniel learned to take advantage of the best that each religion has to offer and that is what he plans to do today.

Walking into the B'nai Jeshurun synagogue to attend a Saturday morning Shabbat service, he sits down and feels comfortable and relaxes to enjoy the service, which he has been absent from for many years.

After the service ends, he feels better but still not altogether clear mentally. Walking down a few blocks, he still feels like he needs some additional help so he sees a nearby church and walks towards the St. Regis hotel where he sees St. Patrick's Cathedral.

He has made the short walk many times to this New York City landmark when his conscience had gotten the better of him, and today is one of those occasions.

As a child, he had always preferred the Shabbat service to Catholic mass, which he found too ritualistic and boring. He, however, never felt comfortable speaking with rabbis directly and rather liked the anonymity afforded to him by the Catholic penance sacrament, otherwise known as the confessional.

He knows that the Saturday afternoon confession times are currently available, and chooses to take advantage of them.

After it is his turn, he proceeds into the confessional and takes his position on the kneeler.

"How can I help you, my Son?" The priest asks, his face concealed by the privacy screen to protect the anonymous nature of the confessional.

"Forgive me father for I have sinned," Daniel says.

"And how have you sinned, my Son?" The priest asks.

"I have had impure thoughts," Daniel says.

"I see, so thoughts such as those of a *romantic* nature, I presume?"

"No, far worse than that, Father." Daniel continues.

"Please tell me these, these thoughts that you are having." The priest says.

"I have thought about killing people," Daniel says.

There is a noticeable pause.

"I understand, that is not altogether unusual my Son, but what is important is that you not act on these impulsive, not act on these thoughts." The priest says.

"I see," Daniel replies.

"Can you tell me *why* you are having these thoughts? That is if you even *know*."

"I do know why, Father. My wife, my wife was killed by gunmen right in front of me and I want to see them and others like them brought to justice." Daniel says.

Again, there is another pause.

"What you seek my Son, is nothing more than *vengeance*." The priest says, "And only The Lord should have the power of vengeance, not any of us. It is out of our hands. In the Bible it says 'Vengeance is mine, I will repay, says the Lord'."

"I am not seeking *vengeance*, Father." Daniel says, "I seek *atonement*. I seek a correction for the mistakes in my own life, something that I fear that I cannot rely on either the Lord or the police to handle."

"What do you mean by mistakes in your own life?" The priest asks.

"I am the one responsible for these men being free, so I am trying to correct those mistakes and bring them to justice. Well, in my own way." Daniel replies.

"Again, my son, what you are talking about is vengeance, and it is one of the deadly sins."

"I see." Daniel replies, "I understand your point, but at this point, I cannot agree with you."

"Answer me one more question, my Son." The Priest asks, "Have you yet acted upon these thoughts, these impulses."

There is a moment, a pause as Daniel hesitates before responding. He then realizes, but he really knew all along, that anything that he tells this priest is protected just like attorney-client confidentiality. The words of the penitent cannot be used in court.

"Yes, Father," Daniel finally replies, "I have already killed one, and I *plan* to kill several more."

Silence.

The Priest does not respond, and Daniel does not utter another word as he lets himself out of the confessional and exits the Cathedral.

***

A few hours later Daniel walks into the lobby of the St. Regis hotel and walks over to the lobby bar.

Already there waiting for him at a table inside the lobby bar is his former adversary in The Reaper trial, District Attorney Garcia.

As Daniel approaches, Garcia stands to greet him and the two men shake hands.

"Daniel, it's good to see you. Although I must admit that I was surprised that you called me." Garcia says. "I have tried to reach you several times since Carrie's funeral, but we haven't been able to connect.

Daniel nods, as the two men sit down.

"And I appreciate you being willing to meet with me, considering our recent trial," Daniel replies. "I never like having to face my former mentor as adversaries."

"Daniel, I will admit that I was disappointed, but that is just business. You and I have been friends for too long for me to forget all about that because of this, this 'Reaper' trial."

"It's actually that trial that I want to talk to you about," Daniel says.

"What about it?" Garcia asks.

"Well, not the Reaper trial specifically, but several cases *similar* to this one," Daniel says. "Cases for people that I would like to see corrected."

"What exactly do you mean by corrected?" Garcia asks.

"I have reviewed my case files and found about twenty cases in which my client's guilt was obvious and complete. But, because of varying reasons, these men were never convicted." Daniel says.

"That is how the system works, whether we like it or not," Garcia replies.

"I understand. But, what if I could turn these files over to you, would you be able to charge these individuals with different crimes other than those which they have double jeopardy protection on?" Daniel says.

"Most likely not," Garcia replies, "and I would have to reject any information provided by you, which any judge would quickly rule as inadmissible because of the source of the information."

"What if it came from one of my investigators and not from me directly?" Daniel persists.

"It would be a long shot, Daniel. I have to be honest." Garcia says.

Daniel just shakes his head.

"Then, there is nothing else that I can do, I suppose," Daniel says.

Garcia hesitates for a moment, looks around to make sure that no others are close enough to be within eavesdropping range, and then continues the conversation.

"There is something being planned now, something really interesting, but I cannot divulge any details at this time," Garcia says.

"I don't understand," Daniel says as he looks back at Garcia with an intrigued and focused look.

"Several individuals at top spots in both the state and federal government realize that there is a major problem with the system," Garcia responds. "Low-level criminals and the underprivileged being arrested and sometimes killed when the men responsible for it, the truly *powerful* men, serve no time at all."

"What about cases like the Charles Murphy case, bad officers hurting and sometimes killing suspects?" Daniel asks.

"That would be another function of this group, to improve the process altogether and make the legal system fair on both sides, the upper and lower spectrums. We cannot have anymore Charles Murphy type incidents or this city won't survive it."

Daniel nods his head, "Exactly."

"But making a change like this is not something that happens overnight. It is in the works, I can assure you, but I just cannot tell you when." Garcia continues.

"The problem is that in many ways, the law and the system is designed to enforce the status quo, not really execute justice." Garcia finishes.

"The Charles Murphy case is only one example of the problem. How about pedophiles that get released only to continue to stalk kids?" Daniel adds.

"Yes, we simply need to do a better job protecting our children, protecting and improving our lower classes such that they can get out of this negative cycle," Garcia says.

"I must admit that I am stunned to hear a District Attorney saying this," Daniel says.

"Ten years ago, I would not even have had a *thought* like this, but from what I have seen, and from what several contacts of mine who are in the Federal government have told me…"

"It's at *all* levels, isn't it?" Daniel asks.

"Yes, and that is why a core group of people across multiple agencies want to make changes, but they have to be *careful*." Garcia finishes.

"To whom exactly are you referring?" Daniel asks.

"I cannot say. In fact, I probably have said too much *already*." Garcia replies and looks nervously over his shoulder and around him.

"I need to leave, but I will be in touch soon." Garcia says, as he gets up uncomfortably and then leaves the hotel bar.

Daniel barely has time to tell him goodbye before Garcia is out the door, and Daniel is left at the table all alone, more confused than ever.

As District Attorney Garcia walks back out into the winter cold, he removes his mobile phone from his jacket as he continues to walk.

He begins to speak into the phone.

"I think we have one other person that we need to concern ourselves with," Garcia says.

There is a brief pause as Garcia listens to the other line on the phone and then he responds.

"Aronson. Daniel Aronson. I will have his file sent to you first thing Monday."

14

TARRYTOWN

The following Monday, Tom Justice and Shane McWilliams stand in a Midtown South apartment speaking with one Bill Tucker. Tucker was once in the employ of The Reaper and admitted to being involved in multiple shootings and contract killings for The Reaper directly, and also for other members of the organization.

Bill is a very gruff, unpolished man. Tall and athletic looking but with an icy, cool stare almost as if a man with no soul.

"Tucker," Tom says, "This is completely off the record. There will be no charges brought against you. It's not you that we are after, only The Reaper."

Shane continues, "Yes, Bill, anything at all no matter how trivial."

"We really need some help, Tucker," Tom says, "We are struggling here. I can guarantee you that if you help us I will give your name to the Mayor for special consideration."

"You just need to know that I will not testify if you catch him," Tucker replies firmly.

Tom nods, "Nor would I expect you to."

"With his actions, we really don't need any more corroborating testimony. We plan to just hold him indefinitely without a trial if we can get away with it." Shane says, "This time the FBI is pressing to try him for the hotel bombing charges and it should be an entirely different outcome in federal court."

"You know he doesn't leave witnesses alive, right?" Tucker says,

"I once saw him kill a two-year-old kid." Tucker continues, "I mean as if that little booger is going to identify him in a fucking lineup or something. It was just crazy!"

"No court, no witness, I promise," Tom responds.

"Not only will I not testify, but this entire conversation has to stay off the record," Tucker says, "Because if word gets out on the street that I talked to you, then I would be suddenly ventilated in my head."

"We understand," Shane says.

"Or he slits my throat." Tucker continues, "I once saw him do that, he takes the knife, cuts the guy's throat all the way back to his spine, made like a 'pez dispenser' out of his fucking head, man."

"Completely understand, Bill," Shane says, "This is partly why we are meeting at your place and not at the precinct."

"I don't know how much I can help," Tucker says, "One thing I do remember is that The Reaper would always refer to his 'Boss'."

"Anything specific?" Shane asks.

"I remember the name 'Angel Oscuro'. Wait, wait… it was 'Ahente Oscuro' I think or something like that. I never got a description of this Oscuro guy, but this might be worth checking out."

"Anything else specific that we could use?" Tom asks.

"I know that when things get too hot, they like to stay outside the city," Tucker says.

"We figured that, but where?" Tom asks.

"It used to be Jersey, but Jersey City got too hot" Tucker responds, "Then they have a supplier in Connecticut so they like to stay within about 30 minutes of Greenwich."

"Specifics, Bill." Shane persists, "Do you have the address, or, at least, the city?"

Bill Tucker thinks for a minute.

"White Plains, no, Tarrytown, that's it, yeah Tarrytown." Tucker continues.

"They have a small house right near the Hudson River that is convenient enough to get into the city by train but away from the majority of police pressure. If you saw it, you would not look twice because it's a totally middle-class, white-collar safe neighborhood." Tucker says, "But if you go there be prepared, from what I was told it has some fairly unique defenses, some serious James Bond-type shit."

Shane looks back dismissively, "I think we can handle whatever they have in store for us."

"I don't have the address, but I always make sure I take photos of any location that I visit. Let me get those to you." Tucker says, "And maybe you can derive the address from that."

As Bill Tucker goes to retrieve the aforementioned photos, Shane and Tom look at each other and nod, thinking that this might be it.

***

Four hours later, in an almost world record for efficiency, Bill Tucker's photos have been processed, evaluated and the location identified as being the house that Mr. Impossible and The Reaper had been staying at weeks earlier.

Tom coordinates with the local Westchester County officials, making them aware of what will happen next. Shane McWilliams works with the bureau and they coordinate with SWAT again, with Frank Bourn set to take the lead. For Frank, this is absolutely a personal mission, having lost several men to The Reaper's fury a few months prior.

Barnes and Parra work with the FBI who sends two of their most senior agents to serve as the negotiators and be on the front line. It is decided that Barnes and Parra will stay back behind the SWAT team where Tom Justice and Shane McWilliams also will be situated.

An additional two hours later, right as darkness starts to fall, the entire team gets into place. In a similar formation from the apartment incident, the SWAT truck is in front with four police cars surrounding it. The FBI specialists take point going in front of everyone else, with Frank Bourn and his SWAT team standing close behind.

Any element of surprise that they may have had is long gone, but they hope that by surrounding the house on both sides that they have eliminated any realistic escape avenues. Perimeter containment is in progress, with three SWAT officers going around the back of the house to prevent an escape in that direction, and two officers on each side of the house, which is located almost in the exact middle of this quaint Westchester County town.

Also, the "capture alive" mandate has been lifted for this mission. At this point, these two men have been identified as being too risky to capture alive. They are not to be shot in cold blood, per se, but the idea is to not take unnecessary risks like the first time when three SWAT officers were killed.

The house stands on the corner of Grove Street, a small cozy looking two story home, with a balcony garage and a slightly cracked driveway. Cement steps lead from the street level up to the front door, which is adjacent to a nice little front patio that has an outdoor sofa and a small rocking chair.

They recognize that the approach might be difficult because of the way the steps lead up and narrow, almost forming a bit of a potential "death tunnel" if someone is watching from upstairs.

Directly above the first floor, there are two main windows on the second level, one of which is currently open. The windows on the right side of the house are visible, but a large oak tree obscures the window on the right of the house, which will look down right on anyone approaching the front door. The biggest problem with this approach is the height and slope of the house, it is only two stories, but with the street level garage it is effectively three levels, and on a fairly steep hill.

Before they move in, Frank comes over to discuss the situation with Tom and Shane.

"So, is this the same situation as before?" Frank asks.

"Not at all," Tom replies, "We do not believe that there are any hostages, just our guys."

"How many?" Frank asks.

"At least two," Shane responds, "but there could be as many as six."

"And these are the same assholes that did this to me, right?" Frank says, pointing to his leg.

"The very *same* assholes," Tom responds.

"Is it safe to say that we will approach it differently this time?" Frank asks.

"We have to approach it differently," Shane responds, "Shoot at the first sign of a weapon, and take them dead or alive, no quarter this time!"

"...and no more traps, no benefit of the doubt this time," Frank adds.

"Frank, the FBI guys want to take point on this and I have told them to," Tom says, "I know last time you ran it, but I would rather expose you to as little direct fire as possible."

Frank nods his head.

"Four months ago, I might have fought for it, but not today," Frank says. "Not to at all suggest that I am scared, only *wiser.*"

"Frank," Shane interrupts, "Agent Brooks tells me that they are ready to move in when you are."

"I am good now." Frank replies, "I have my men spread out to prevent any possible escape, and now I am ready to follow the Feds wherever they want me to be."

Agents Brooks and Olson motion to Frank to start moving in, they approach the front of the house and call to the house.

Brooks and Olson move to the front of the house, Olson has his weapon drawn, and Brooks is preparing to use the megaphone to call to the house.

As they move towards the door, Frank Bourn holds his position back at the sidewalk which is at the end of the front yard, a rectangular spot of grass about thirty feet wide.

To Frank's side, his second in command holds a Blackhawk Monoshock Battering Ram, which is a hand-held battering ram very effective at knocking down all types of doors regardless of how supported they are.

To their left, Tom Justice and Shane McWilliams hold their positions behind the SWAT truck. As noted earlier, the SWAT officers are in various positions on each side of the house, situated to prevent an escape on any side.

And finally, there are two snipers perched atop the house across the street in case a firefight starts out the front. Agent Brooks is fairly well covered.

"This is Agent Jim Brooks of the FBI," He broadcasts, "We need you to come out with your hands up and nobody needs to get hurt."

They wait for several minutes and there is no response.

They maintain their position, but at this point are not sure exactly what they should be doing.

They wait for approximately fifteen minutes, and after no response and no movement is noticed inside the house, Agent Brooks walks back to confer with Frank Bourn.

"Well, what now?" Brooks asks.

"I say we go in." Frank replies, as he motions for Tom to come over.

"How long should we wait before we go in?" Frank asks

Tom hesitates as he considers his options.

"If we go in and there is nobody there," Tom says, "then we may have wasted our best opportunity."

"But Tom," Shane counters, "if this is the wrong place, no harm, no foul. But if it *is* their place, certainly they have left something behind that we can use."

"Good point," Tom says, "I really hate to get this wrong, though."

"Frank, what is your opinion?" Tom asks. "And what about infrared? If we had that, we could verify how many people are in there."

"I agree with Shane, we cannot wait for the infrared to get here." Frank replies, "Let's go in, take the door down, and if we have made a mistake, worst case scenario we buy them a new goddamned door."

"Okay," Tom says, "I still disagree, but I will go with majority vote."

Frank walks back to his position and walks up with his second in command with the battering ram, and they establish their positions. The battering ram will obviously be used first, and then Agents Brooks and Olson, followed by Frank and SWAT Officer Stalzer.

Agent Brooks once again calls out on the megaphone to warn them of the impending attack.

"Final warning, either come out now or we are coming in!" Brooks shouts.

Five minutes later, no response, so they move in. Pulling back the Blackhawk Monoshock Battering ram, the door is smashed open in seconds, as the agents rush in quickly, in less than three seconds they are all inside the house.

They are stunned to find that there are no people at all inside the house but do notice a great deal of what appears to be incriminating evidence such as five laptops, some scattered liquor bottles, a few ladies' undergarments, and several lines of what appears to be cocaine.

It looks like The Reaper and Mr. Impossible have been partying.

Frank communicates with Tom and Shane via radio while this initial team continues to investigate inside the home.

"Frank, any sign of them?" Tom asks via radio.

"No, no, false alarm I am afraid," Frank responds.

"Hold on, Frank, we are coming towards you," Tom says.

Shane leans over to block Tom's movement.

"Tom, not quite yet," Shane says, "let them, at least, get some evidence that we can use and then secure the perimeter."

"I did find a number of laptops that might be useful." Frank continues, via radio "Let me see if I can get anything off of this one."

"Frank, you are no computer tech," Tom says, "Leave it alone until we can get the techs inside."

"No, I think I know how to open a laptop," Frank insists, "I will just disconnect this one, and bring it out."

Frank directs the other individuals to get the laptops and secure them.

"Agent Brooks and Olson," Frank says, "get those two in the living room." "Stalzer, you and Taft get those two in the kitchen."

As Frank disconnects the one laptop, the other agents remove the four other laptops and prepare to remove them from the house. As they remove all of the laptops they notice a strange red beeping light.

"Tom, I think we may have a slight problem he....." Frank starts to speak but cannot finish his sentence.

Tom hears nothing but screams and the sound of gunfire and explosions on the other end of the radio.

"Frank!!!!" Tom screams, "What's happening! Frank, speak to me!!"

Tom's words echo in vain.

When the red light completes its ten-second safety delay, in the office where Frank is standing, panels in the wall open up revealing programmed automatic .50 caliber M2 machine guns on both sides, which each fire about thirty rounds, shredding Frank Bourn to pieces and cutting through the walls of the house.

"Get Down!" Several officers yell as the bullets clear the house and ricochet above the area where the officers are standing. They are only saved from certain death by the fact that the ground level is one level below the first floor of the house, and the bullets fly over their heads.

At the same time, in the living room where Agents Brooks and Olson are standing, panels open up in the ceiling above them dropping pure sulfuric acid on their heads, causing a lethal burning reaction, and essentially melting half of their faces off.

Their screams are almost unbearable.

Then, on the north and south walls of the room, side panels open up revealing stainless steel blades that are three feet long, these blades are launched outwards by spring-loaded mechanisms, striking the agents, finishing the job, cutting down what remains of Agents Brooks and Olson.

The agents are, quite literally, cut in half.

The SWAT officers in the kitchen, Stalzer and Taft, hold the final two laptops, which do not trigger any reaction in the house. No, instead they were designed to self-destruct and that is exactly what they do, the two laptops blow up while the officers hold them, exploding and killing the officers instantly.

This is a disaster.

Five more men are dead, the laptops are all destroyed and the entire house is in ruins.

The remaining SWAT officers all close in and what they find is sheer carnage. Three of their own, along with two federal agents dead, and the house destroyed beyond recognition.

Tom Justice and Shane McWilliams move in as well, but at this point, there is nothing that they can do.

Tom looks around at the scene with the smoke and the fire from the explosions, the chaos of removing the fallen officers from the home and thinks that he is partially responsible for leading them into this trap.

Tom shakes his head and puts his hands on his hips in a display of significant frustration.

"Damn you, Frank," Tom says lightly, "why didn't you just retire when you had the chance?"

Tom's facial expression changes from a look of horror and outrage, to one of extreme anger.

Tom motions for Barnes and Parra to move in and then he directs them,

"Parra, Barnes," Tom says, "work with these guys, get them anything they need and let them know I will be right back."

Tom motions for Shane to come with him as they head towards Tom's car to drive away, "Shane, we have somebody that we need to talk to right now!"

"Wait," Barnes shouts, stunned that Tom and Shane are leaving such a sensitive scene, "where the hell are you two going, this is kind of serious!"

"I am going to find the man that sent us into this deathtrap!" Tom replies.

The drive from Tarrytown to Midtown Manhattan is normally about 55 minutes, but Tom Justice makes it, police lights flashing the entire way, in less than 20.

"Tom you really need to calm down, no need to get us killed here!" Shane yells, trying to calm down his irate friend.

"Tucker sent us right into a trap man!" Tom replies, "This was a goddamned setup, and Tucker needs to pay for it!"

Seemingly teleporting up to the apartment where Bill Tucker sent them on this fatal wild goose chase, they do not hesitate, kicking down the door and rushing through to the back living room where last they saw Bill Tucker.

Sitting in his recliner with his back to them, Tom Justice yells out to Tucker.

"Bill Tucker," Tom yells, "you need to come with us. You are under arrest for conspiracy to commit murder."

There is no response.

Finally, and very slowly, Tom and Shane walk over to Bill Tucker and tap him on the shoulder to get his attention.

As they do so, they spin him around and then they see what is left of Bill Tucker. His throat had been slit from ear to ear and is quite obviously very dead.

"Oh shit!" Tom exclaims.

"Man, like a 'pez dispenser' just like Tucker said," Shane says.

"Oh, I don't get this," Tom says,

"What do you mean, Tom?" Shane asks.

"So, explain this to me: Tucker warns The Reaper, so then The Reaper escapes and sets a trap for us, and then as a reward, The Reaper kills Tucker as some warped form of a thank you?"

"It just doesn't make any sense." Shane concurs. "But then again, this is the same man who killed his own brother as a human shield."

"Great point."

"Tom, you have said this all along," Shane continues, "it is as if Repanelli loves to be unpredictable just for the sake of doing it."

"Like we keep saying about the flash drive," Shane continues, "why would he let Daniel keep that? I would have thought that The Reaper would have attacked Daniel again by now, but nothing."

"I still scratch my head over that one." Tom agrees, "But I think you just told me our next move."

"We need to get the flash drive from Daniel," Shane says. "it's simply our best chance."

"Exactly, if nothing else before The Reaper gets it." Tom replies, "Best friend or not, at this point it is the only thing left for us to do."

"Well not quite yet, Tom," Shane cautions, "Now we have a whole lot of cleanup to do in Tarrytown. You might want to call the Mayor before he hears it from someone else."

***

Back at the precinct 17 office the following day, in the normally jubilant and fun game room, instead hangs a dark aura somewhat like a tomb.

The four key individuals, Tom, Shane, Parra and Barnes all sit around the card table and nobody talks.

They don't look happy.

Finally, Shane breaks the awkward and uncomfortable silence.

"What did the Mayor have to say?" Shane asks.

"About what you might expect." Tom replies.

"I half expected him to fire or suspend me on the spot."

"Did they recommend suspensions for any of us, Boss?" Barnes asks.

"No, not as of yet, but there will be a full investigation led by the Feds," Tom responds.

"But they already had their chance, Tom" Shane protests, "and they botched it."

"I understand their position, being former Bureau," Shane continues, "but after the hotel disaster and the fact that two of theirs led the Tarrytown mission, why are they getting this case?"

"They have already lost ten agents!" Barnes adds, "In my mind they haven't earned the right to decide anything."

"I agree," Parra adds, "I also don't see how anyone could hold it against us because Tarrytown was a trap."

"I went against my own instincts." Tom admits, shaking his head. "Something felt off about the whole thing and I still agreed to let them go in."

"Tucker actually even said something about the house being protected," Shane adds, "I thought he was just exaggerating. He wasn't."

"That doesn't matter guys." Parra replies, "We did everything by the book, besides it was Agents Brooks and Olson that had the call whether to engage or not."

"But Mayor Lockhart doesn't see it that way," Tom says.

"It's most likely Washington and not Mayor Lockhart," Shane adds, "If I know how they think, and I do, then they feel that because of the jurisdiction crossing three states, they should own this case and they have always felt that way."

"Bullshit!" Barnes exclaims, "They just want as many cases they can claim so the Feds can muscle us out."

"The problem is" Tom replies, "Shane and I got the tip from Bill Tucker and ultimately led us to the Tarrytown house."

"And you said that when you found him his throat was slit?" Parra asks, curiously.

"Like a Pez dispenser," Shane replies, "His head barely hanging on to his body."

Parra makes a face as if to say "nasty".

"Why did they kill Tucker, if he was successful getting us into what was basically a trap?" Parra inquires.

"Shane and I were wondering the same thing," Tom replies.

"This is about the third or fourth move that they have made that defy logic," Shane says,

"Which is why I say that there has to be more to this, there must be some bigger plan."

"But what?" Tom asks.

"We don't know," Shane says.

Barnes leans forward defiantly.

"If *we* don't know, then the Feds abso-fucking-lutely don't know!" Barnes says.

"No argument here," Tom replies.

"If the Bureau follows protocol," Shane says, "they will want to come in and set up a base of operations here at our precinct and then will want to debrief us about Tarrytown and everything else."

"How should we play this?" Parra asks.

"Be cooperative, and give them whatever they need," Tom says.

"We don't want any more trouble from Washington."

"Is there anything else we can do on the case?" Parra asks.

"Not officially," Tom responds. "But Shane, I would like for you to coordinate with one or two officers of your choosing to continue to work 'off book' on this if you follow me."

"I need to figure out how to get that flash drive from Daniel, I think that file is the key to putting these pieces together," Tom says.

Suddenly there is an awkward silence in the room, and then Shane breaks the momentary silence.

"Parra," Shane says, "you and Barnes should tell Tom about the Ballenger case."

"Right, that major player, the energy trader-hedge fund guy that disappeared," Tom replies, "Any luck, any leads?"

Barnes nods and then says, "Parra and I went to the Pub where he was last seen and interviewed the staff."

"Was a body ever recovered?" Tom asks.

"No, but the man has been missing for over a month now," Barnes responds.

"It's odd," Tom responds, "Daniel and I were just talking about this guy. He was one of Daniel's most controversial clients."

"And by controversial, I mean guilty as hell." Tom continues.

Parra and Barnes look nervously at each other.

"It might not be just a coincidence, Boss," Barnes says.

Tom looks at him with a look of surprise.

"What exactly do you mean?" Tom asks.

"You want to take it from here?" Barnes turns and asks Parra.

"Sure," Parra responds, as he reaches down to the floor and retrieves and opens his briefcase. He pulls out a manila file folder and takes a piece of paper out of it.

"Are you guys holding out on me?" Tom asks, half jokingly.

Parra continues to avoid eye contact as if he was very uncomfortable about the conversation, but he finally looks up at Tom and continues.

"You see," Parra begins, "After we interviewed the bartender we brought her in to give a description to our sketch artist."

"The 'picture guy'," Barnes adds, trying to lighten the mood.

"The what?" Tom asks, not getting the joke.

"Never mind that," Parra says, trying to continue, "So after she provided her description this is what our sketch artist came up with."

Parra hands the paper over to Tom who takes a look at it and sees what is essentially a photo of Daniel Aronson, the resemblance is that close.

"This is the last person that was seen with Ballenger before he disappeared," Parra says.

Tom cannot say anything right away and just continues to look at the sketch.

"Son of a bitch!" Tom says, as he finally speaks and slams the picture down on the table.

"What should we do now, Boss?" Barnes asks.

"Nothing yet," Tom replies, "We have too many problems, not the least of which is the fact that there is no body and no murder weapon. Hell, there is not any proof that the man is even dead, right?"

"We found his scarf in an alley a few blocks from the pub," Parra adds. "and there was blood on it. We did a DNA check and it matched Ballenger."

"Okay, fine. That is all circumstantial." Tom says.

"You're right" Shane interjects, "Mostly circumstantial, but maybe we should bring Aronson in just to talk to him."

"Not now, Shane," Tom says, "And that goes for all of you. Let me handle this and that is an *order*."

Tom gets up abruptly and leaves the game room, his week getting worse and worse by the minute.

As he walks back across the precinct floor towards his office, in his mind he plays back the conversation that he had with Daniel at the Riviera Maya restaurant. Sure, maybe Daniel wanted to leave the profession and start over, but this?

No, maybe all of this was just coincidence.

Then again, he wonders to himself, maybe not. Either way, he is not ready to bring in his friend in any kind of official capacity right now.

15

MISDIRECTION

Sunday Morning, 9:30, Trump Westchester Golf Club. Tom and Daniel are riding in their golf cart on a truly cold, dreary and generally unpleasant day for golf. The two men pull up and stop their carts at the green for the thirteenth hole.

As the exit the golf cart, they take their putters with them as they approach their respective golf balls on the green, and set up in position to putt.

Tom violates one of the unspoken rules of golf etiquette by talking right as Daniel is about to putt.

"No pressure man," Tom says, "but if you sink this putt you take the lead, 8 holes to 5, for almost an insurmountable lead."

Daniel looks up indignantly.

"Thanks, schmuck," Daniel says, "I can keep score just fine by myself."

Daniel re-focuses and draws the putter back, swinging smoothly and sinking the nine-foot putt.

It is Tom's turn, and even with a much shorter six-foot putt, Tom somehow manages to three-putt, meaning that it takes him three shots to sink it.

"Nice putting form," Daniel says sarcastically.

"Shut up," Tom replies, apparently not having much of a witty comeback.

Tom retrieves his golf ball from the hole and re-tends the flag in the hole and the two head back to the golf cart.

As they begin the fairly distant ride to the next tee box, the conversation turns a little more serious.

"Awkward topic time," Tom begins, "I really have to ask how you are doing, you know, with the Carrie thing and all."

Daniel hesitates.

"Oh, you know," Daniel says, "it's not as bad as maybe it could be."

"I mean it definitely hurts," Daniel continues, "But a little bit less each day."

"That is to be expected," Tom replies, "I don't think that it will ever go away completely."

"What about you, Tom?" Daniel asks, "How have things been going with Jill? She seemed a lot happier when I met her for lunch a few weeks ago. For a few months, it seemed like you two were always fighting."

Tom hesitates and wonders if he should confide in Daniel, ultimately deciding to do so.

"Actually, and this is a complete secret Daniel," Tom says.

"Yeah...yeah," Daniel responds as if to say "on with it".

"Jill and I are in the middle of a trial separation," Tom says.

"Oh no," Daniel says, "When did this happen?"

"About five months ago," Tom responds, "I am optimistic, though. As you said, Jill has been a lot better in the past few months. I actually got to sleep in my own bed for the first time in months."

"What happened? I mean, what caused this, did she find out about your Texas thing?" Daniel asks.

"Yeah she did," Tom exclaims, "And I still have no clue, how, although I think Shane, Parra, and Barnes all knew about it."

"Well you *did* screw up, you know?" Daniel says.

"No shit," Tom replies, "I just can't believe a stupid one-night stand in Houston is putting my marriage in jeopardy."

"You can't think negatively, though," Daniel replies, "this is just another challenge, and Tom Justice is always up for any kind of challenge. Right?"

"Right," Tom replies.

"I have learned that many times women just want to be appreciated, other times they like a little bit of drama, some tension when things have gotten stale or boring," Daniel says.

"You make a good point, Daniel."

"And I know that Jill really loves you. You *did* betray her trust, and now you just need to build it back up little by little. Once you regain her trust I think you two will be that happy, charming, almost *disgustingly* happy couple again." Daniel says playfully with a smile.

"Another great point, Daniel" Tom says.

As Daniel stops the cart at the next tee box, he turns towards Tom and flashes a sly smile.

"*The Defense Rests*," Daniel says.

The two men laugh and then get out of the cart to retrieve their golf balls and driver for the tee box approach.

"You and your stupid catch phrase," Tom says, "You do realize that you are not Bruce Willis or 'Ah-nold' in an action movie, right?"

As the two men approach the tee box, Tom thinks to himself that this is a perfect opportunity to discuss the Ballenger case, but he simply can't do it.

That will have to wait for another day.

***

A few hours later, as Daniel and Tom finish their round of golf, back in Manhattan at P.J. Clarke's restaurant on West 63rd street; Jill Justice sits in one of the rear booths with another man.

The other man is none other than Juan Parra, one of her husband's detectives and close confidant.

P.J Clarke's is packed to capacity with this Sunday brunch crowd ready to get their fill of the Em's Breakfast Sandwich or Caramel

Apple pancakes. The lousy winter weather serving only to drive more people indoors to enjoy the red and white tablecloths, the great food and the lively atmosphere. Glasses rattle, servers bustle between the tables, and the mimosas flow freely.

Parra and Jill Justice sit as they await their check to be delivered, having just recently finished their brunch.

"We really need to keep this quiet," Parra says.

Jill continues to look down at the table, continuing to avoid eye contact.

"I am not really sure about this. One time, maybe but I just don't know about continuing." Jill says.

"Maybe," Parra responds, "but we have come this far, I don't think that there is any going back for either of us."

"This could really end badly for both of us," Jill says, "You still have your career to think about you know."

"And I have my marriage to consider of course." Jill continues.

"If Tom found out…." Jill starts.

"..He won't Jill" Parra interrupts, "I have everything covered, I promise."

"As I was saying before you *interrupted* me," Jill says, "if Tom finds out you can kiss your career goodbye."

"At this point, this is simply a risk that I have to take," Parra replies.

The waiter returns from the kitchen and sets the bill folder for the check on the table.

"I can take that whenever you are ready." The waiter says.

"I've got this," Parra says.

Jill does that semi-awkward "reach for the check but you know you are going to let the other guy pay for it" move, but ultimately lets Parra pay.

"Thanks for the lunch Juan," Jill says, "I need to rush, Tom and Daniel are likely heading back from Westchester about now."

"My pleasure, Jill," Parra responds.

Jill exits the side exit of the restaurant onto 63rd street.

Parra remains behind to pay the check, the entire process of which takes approximately 10 minutes to complete considering how the place is packed to capacity. Finally, Parra completes the transaction, gets his credit card back and then heads towards the exit.

As he walks away, down on 63rd street he fails to notice that he is being watched. No, he is not being watched by Tom Justice, a jealous husband stalking his wife, but rather Lieutenant Shane McWilliams.

McWilliams shakes his head as he fears that his suspicions have been confirmed. Now he faces a personal and professional crisis.

Do you tell your boss and good friend about this? Or do you wait until you have more substantive proof?

***

Daniel and Tom return from their golf round, Daniel having won as per usual. Tom returns to his loving wife and they watch the NFL Playoffs as Daniel sits in his lovely townhome all by himself, in silence. Even though his beloved Jets are in the playoffs for the first time in a decade, Daniel couldn't care less and is not watching.

As Tom and Jill enjoy watching the Jets crush the Colts in the playoff game, Daniel sits in his office drinking his Crown Royal. He looks over his key files on his computer, one of which is the file listing his targets, those men he has marked for vengeance. Somewhat tired from the golf round, and maybe from the Crown Royal, Daniel is not sure about making another move tonight.

He opens the specific file for Kyle Yancy, and reviews the information gathered for him by his private investigation team. According to this information, Yancy lives only about fifteen blocks away, and since he is a bookie and this is an NFL day, odds are good that the man is home.

It might be time to pay him a visit.

***

Later that night, at approximately 10:30 P.M, a nice apartment on the Upper West Side on the 44ᵗʰ floor, sits one Kyle Yancy.

Kyle is a mid-30's, unkempt blonde man who sits back on his couch in his bathrobe. On the table in front of him is a pizza delivery box, opened to reveal a half-finished cheese pizza. Next to the pizza box, are five empty longneck Miller beer bottles. Kyle's table looks like half of America's on a football Sunday.

Kyle, who looks as if he has never worked a day job in his entire life, sits in his sparsely-furnished apartment watching the late Sunday NFL playoff game on his 70+ inch HD TV.

As he watches the game, gulps his Miller Genuine Draft beer, and takes the occasional bite of pizza, he answers his mobile.

"No," Kyle says on the phone, "Have you gotten any word from any of the other books?"

"Off-shore books have it going up a half point." Kyle continues.

"I think that the Seattle game should move a full point, because so many dogs have covered this weekend."

"That matters because all of the suckers who only bet favorites will be looking to make up for a bad weekend by doubling down next week. They follow the same formula every week, year after year. Plus, with Seattle winning in a blowout, the public will move the line."

"Right, this means that the line will go up immediately after this game is over."

Unnoticed by Kyle, Daniel has let himself in through the unlocked front door and has started walking through the entry way towards the living room located towards the back of the apartment.

As Kyle continues his phone conversation, he finally sees Daniel, but does not panic, or even really react in any way. Instead, he rather coolly and calmly ends his phone conversation.

"Yo man," Kyle says on the phone, "let me hit you back, something just came up."

Kyle disconnects from his mobile phone and puts it down and looks up at Daniel.

"Kyle Yancy," Daniel begins in his trademark cryptic manner, "we need to talk."

Kyle continues to stare at Daniel, defiantly not standing up, and not really even moving. He does not at this point perceive Daniel to be a threat that he cannot handle.

"Okay," Kyle says smugly, "big man says we need to talk, we need to talk."

Suddenly, with a look of intense aggression, Kyle reaches down between his sofa cushions, feeling around for something that he expected to be there. His pale face lightens by another shade once he realizes that the item for which he is looking is no longer there.

Daniel reaches into his winter coat and removes a handgun that Kyle quickly recognizes as his own damn gun.

"Looking for this?" Daniel asks, playfully. "Sorry about that, I had one of my investigators search your place and retrieve that for me."

Kyle shifts around on his sofa a little bit, *now* he sees Daniel as a threat.

"What the fuck do you want?" Kyle yells, his tone quickly changing as he realizes that the tables have turned badly against him.

Daniel starts to raise his gun up and points it at Kyle.

"This is for all of the poor souls you had Gordon put away," Daniel says.

"Man, I never did any of that." Kyle yells, now trembling in fear "It was Gordon, man that is who you are after not me."

Daniel moves a step closer.

"It doesn't really matter who does the grunt work, does it?" Daniel asks.

"You gave the order, and so you pay the *price*." Daniel finishes as he prepares to fire.

Kyle raises his hands to protect his face, because as we all know hands can stop bullets, right?

Daniel fires twice at Kyle, hitting him twice in the chest and apparently killing him instantly.

As Kyle lies dead on the sofa, Daniel takes the gun over to the kitchen, wipes it down and makes sure that there is no other forensic evidence that can lead back to him.

Daniel walks over to the sofa and puts the gun in Kyle's right hand.

He has no intention of making this look like a suicide. He realizes there is no realistic chance of that. Daniel is just trying to make it as difficult for the police as possible so he can stay free and complete his mission of atonement.

Daniel realizes that no realistic suicide would feature a person shooting themselves in the chest, much less twice, but Daniel just wants to make it as confusing as possible.

He knows that he just needs to create reasonable doubt.

Daniel walks calmly outside of the apartment, and a neighbor a young college-aged woman comes by and speaks to him in the hallway.

"Did you hear that?" She asks.

"Hear what?" Daniel replies.

The young woman looks scared.

"It sounded like, sounded like gunfire..." She continues.

Daniel replies coolly, "No, no gunfire, that dumbass in 4413 was actually setting off fireworks in his kitchen."

"Fireworks?" She asks, not particularly buying this explanation.

"Yeah, I already called the Super," Daniel responds, "I wouldn't be surprised if they evict him."

Daniel walks down the hall towards the elevator, and the woman walks back to her apartment, apparently persuaded by Daniel's argument.

***

The next day, it is early morning on a cold and dreary mid-Winter day. A large haze hangs over the city and there is very little sunlight. This is one of those types of days that Jill Justice would describe as gloomy days or "go-nowhere" days.

Jill feels rather gloomy as she approaches Dr. Elsbury's office and enters.

Minutes later, Jill and Tom sit on the sofa across from Dr. Elsbury, who begins the counseling session.

"So, how do you two feel that the experiment is working so far?" Elsbury asks.

"I would say fine," Tom says, "Considering that I wasn't sold on the idea from the beginning."

Dr. Elsbury nods and then turns to Jill to get her opinion.

"Jill, how about you? Do you feel the same way?" Dr. Elsbury asks.

"Do you think that this is working?" Dr. Elsbury continues.

"I *think* so," Jill replies, rather meekly and not at all convincingly.

Dr. Elsbury nods. "Great," He says.

"Do you think that the two of you are more committed to your relationship?" Dr. Elsbury continues.

"And what I mean by that," Dr. Elsbury continues, "is that should we stop the trial separation now, or continue it for the optional additional six months?"

"I think six months has been long enough," Tom responds, "I know that I feel further committed and this has certainly helped me to re-focus my priorities."

"Great to hear, Tom," Dr. Elsbury says.

"Jill, what about you?" Elsbury continues.

Jill hesitates for a moment and does not respond.

Dr. Elsbury asks the question again.

"Jill. Do you feel that we should *stop* the separation or continue for an additional six months?"

Jill finally looks up and responds.

"I actually think that we should stay on track and go the additional six months," Jill says.

Tom turns and looks directly at Jill as if he has been completely blind-sided by this comment. In his mind, and based on her recent actions, they were on the path to recovery.

"Okay," Dr. Elsbury continues, apparently surprised by Jill's response, "understand that with this additional six months, I do not recommend going any longer than that. At this point, once this period ends, the decision has to be made whether to continue the marriage or not."

"Yes, I understand that," Jill replies.

Tom cannot say anything and just shakes his head in obvious disagreement.

Dr. Elsbury continues, "Okay, and what about dating? Have either of you started seeing other people during this trial period?"

"No, absolutely not," Tom replies, "I learned my lesson in Texas, made my mistake, and just want to move on."

"Good, and what about you Jill?" Elsbury asks.

Jill doesn't respond, and in fact, she keeps her head looking straight at the floor as if ignoring the question.

Noticing the hesitation, Tom turns towards Jill to repeat the question.

"Jill? Could you please answer the man's question?" Tom asks.

Jill raises her head and finally replies.

"Yes, okay, yes I *have* been seeing someone," Jill replies.

"It has only been a few times, but…" Jill continues.

"But what?" Tom interrupts.

Jill looks up rather harshly at Tom for interrupting.

"But as I was saying, I am not sure if I want to move forward with it," Jill says.

There is a momentary pause and then Dr. Elsbury continues.

"This is somewhat uncomfortable for me to ask," Elsbury says, "you would think I would be used to it in my career but I am not. Anyhow, there is no easy way to ask this so here goes. Jill, have you been, have you been intimate with this man yet?"

Jill looks straight at Dr. Elsbury without responding, turns to Tom and sees his curious gaze, almost as if his life and future depended on her answer. Jill then looks back at Dr. Elsbury and responds rather guiltily,

"Yes," Jill says, "He and I *have* been intimate."

Tom cannot say a word. He turns away from Jill and looks as white as a sheet. Inside he feels as if he has just been hit straight in the gut by a Mike Tyson punch. He starts to feel a little queasy. For all of his own indiscretions in the past, he was not expecting this.

After the appointment has ended, Tom and Jill walk outside discussing these latest developments.

"Just a *few times*, Jill?" Tom asks as the two walk down the street away from Dr. Elsbury's office. "What is that? And you already sleep with the guy? Nice."

"Look," Tom continues, "I understand you wanting to get back at me after the Houston incident, I really do. I screwed up and maybe you deserve your little payback. But, I thought this trial separation was just a formality."

Jill turns to Tom.

"Maybe it's not just a formality, Tom," Jill says.

"Oh, I see," Tom replies, "It's just like I thought, this is your first step out the door."

"That's not what I want Tom," Jill replies.

"If it's not what you want, then why are you screwing some other guy!?" Tom says, his anger starting to crack through.

"You should *know* what I want by now, Tom," Jill responds.

Tom looks back at Jill with a stern expression and continues,

"I get so frustrated when women expect us guys to be smart, no not just smart, but mind readers. You think that we should somehow be psychic enough to know what you are thinking, know what is going on in your minds...." Tom says.

"I will let you in on a precious little secret about men," Tom continues, "we are just not that fucking *smart!*"

Jill stops walking and turns to face Tom directly and almost confrontationally, poking him in the chest to make her point as she speaks.

"Maybe the sex *was* payback after your fling, maybe you are right," Jill says, "But maybe also I just thought you might try harder if you felt like you had a little competition."

"You men love to compete," Jill continues, "golf, tennis, stupid fantasy fucking football. Well, how about competing over *me* for a change?"

Jill starts to lightly sob as Tom moves towards her to comfort her, but Jill turns abruptly and storms off away from him, leaving him standing alone in the street.

Tom watches her walk away, the full impact of all of this sinking in slowly as he says softly to himself.

"Maybe you *do* understand men after all."

16

REVELATIONS

Tom Justice does what he can to recover from the emotional shot of what Jill told him at Dr. Elsbury's office.

He makes the twenty block walk from Dr. Elsbury's office to the 17th precinct office on 51st. The entire walk it is as if he is sleep-walking, as he is completely lost in his thoughts. For the first time, he really feels that his marriage is in deep jeopardy.

He almost gets hit by a bus as he crosses a street without looking, fortunately, his quick reflexes save him from a premature death. You could say that Tom is in a heavy funk right now, both personally and professionally.

Walking up to the steps of the precinct building, Tom enters the precinct office and then heads towards the back in which his office is located. The rectangular main office is wide open and a flurry of activity. Phones ring, detectives cross the floor, and it is generally a very frantic day.

As he nears his office, he looks up and notices that Shane McWilliams and Detective Barnes are already in his office waiting for him.

Tom is surprised and more than a little irritated by this and he enters his office with his eyebrows furrowed and looking ready for a fight.

"Gentlemen," Tom says with hostility as he enters his office, "something that I can help you with?"

Shane stands up as a sign of respect, and Barnes does as well…. slowly.

Tom walks around his desk and motions for them to sit back down.

"Sorry to be so presumptuous, Tom," Shane says.

"We really thought that this was too important to wait."

"No problem, Shane," Tom says, now trying to mask his initial frustration.

"Don't mind me, Shane," Tom continues, "I think I am letting other things bleed over into my work. I apologize."

"So, Boss what we have is this," Barnes interjects, "a murder victim found shot in his apartment."

"Okay. Not that unusual for New York. And your point is?" Tom asks.

"Well in our questioning of the neighbors we found a woman who was able to provide a description," Barnes replies.

"Apparently there was a man seen leaving the hallway at the approximate time of death." Barnes continues.

"Oh don't tell me…." Tom says.

"Yes, Tom," Shane interjects, "Daniel Aronson. For the second time, the description is spot-on"

"Oh my God," Tom says, starting to pace back and forth around his desk.

"It gets worse, Tom." Shane continues, "We also have an unsolved case on the Lower East side. This man who disappeared, Gabe Gomez, was another client of Aronson's."

"Disappeared? Have they found a body?" Tom asks.

'No, not this time, Tom, and no witnesses in this case." Shane says.

"Are we sure that foul play was involved?" Tom asks.

"No, but the man disappeared when he was supposed to be closing up the restaurant," Shane says, "the door was left wide open and unlocked and the broom right in the middle of the floor."

"Any forensics, any evidence to speak of?" Tom asks.

"I need to check with the 5ᵗʰ and see where they are with the investigation," Shane says.

"Please look into that and let me know as soon as you can."

Shane continues, "I felt like we needed to talk to Aronson, so I coordinated with Parra and sent him over to see if he can get Aronson to come in voluntarily."

Now Tom's facial expression changes from a look of shock, concern, and surprise for his friend. His expression shifts to a look of anger over this breach of professional protocol.

"You did *what* now?" Tom asks, growing more and more agitated.

"Who authorized that?" Tom continues.

"I did Tom," Shane says.

"I felt that you are too personally biased to be objective in this case." Shane continues.

"You didn't have to do that," Tom responds.

"Tom I realize that he is your best friend," Shane says, "and I get that he is likely had some type of psychotic break or breakdown, but..."

Tom interrupts, "He's not having a breakdown."

"Whatever it is, we simply have to..." Shane starts.

Tom interrupts again, "We have to *what*? I guess now you are going to tell me what I have to do, is that it? Did I miss an email? Are you now Captain of this precinct, or am I?"

Tom slams his fist on his desk and continues with his tirade.

"'*See, I told you they should have made me Captain.*'" Tom says sarcastically, mocking Shane's expression, "Your stupid catch phrase, well you're *not* Captain, Shane, but can you tell me who is?"

"*You* are, Tom," Shane says.

Tom looks at Shane and Barnes intensely and continues.

"I damn sure don't need you two insubordinate assholes telling me what to do!"

"Here's what you are going to do now, Shane," Tom says, continuing his angry tirade, "I want you to stop Parra right now, and if Daniel is with him, tell him to go back home otherwise I want you to cease and desist and let me handle this."

Shane abruptly gets up, turns and prepares to walk out.

"Did I say that we were done here, Shane?" Tom asks.

"Not sure about *you*, but I am done," Shane replies, "I will be happy to talk more about this when you are ready to listen to the goddamn facts that are in front of you. Until then, you are on your own."

Shane walks out of the office and slams the door behind him.

Barnes still remains in the office, and the normally boisterous big man sits quietly and avoids any eye contact with his captain.

"What about you, you got anything else to say?" Tom asks Barnes.

"No Boss, I think I'm good," Barnes replies nervously.

Tom motions for Barnes to leave, so the big man slowly gets up and very quietly exits the office and shuts the door nice and softly.

Tom sits there and looks down at his desk, and speaks quietly to himself.

"Damn it, Daniel, what have you gotten yourself into now?"

***

Later that same afternoon, across town in a recently gentrified warehouse building Bruce Stephens stands with a large HD camcorder in his hand, apparently filming something.

This 40-ish, harmless looking man in his white dress shirt, khaki pants and old school eyeglass frames is not as harmless as he appears.

He currently stands in his nicely appointed loft in front of his sofa looking over a large king sized bed in the main floor. On the large bed, two late teen Asian girls are in the early stages as Bruce Stephens films the "action".

The younger looking petite woman, Mai, with her long black hair and cute schoolgirl face, starts to softly kiss her partner Sunny, with her much shorter black hair and a little rounder body.

"No, come on!" Bruce commands, "This has to look real! I am just not buying this, and I don't think anyone else will either."

At that moment, the front door opens as Daniel slowly walks in and closes the door behind him, the large steel door makes a loud slam as it shuts.

Mai stops what she is doing and looks up, as do Bruce and Sunny.

Daniel slowly and calmly walks further into the loft, towards the rear of the loft where all of the "action" is taking place.

As Mai looks up in Daniel's direction, Bruce continues to film but also aims his camera towards Daniel, catching Daniel on film.

Bruce puts down his camcorder and remains speechless as Daniel slowly moves in their direction.

"Bruce Stephens, we need to talk," Daniel says in his typical cryptic manner.

"What the hell is this?" Bruce asks, completely taken aback that some stranger would approach him in his own home. "Do I know you, man?"

"Ladies, would you please leave?" Daniel asks, very coolly.

Mai and Sunny quickly put their undergarments back on and then grab their bathrobes and don't hesitate to get out of there. They don't really have a clue what is going on but they know that it is time to leave.

As Mai and Sunny rush towards the door, Bruce calls out for them to stop.

"Bitches, wait!" Bruce shouts.

"If you want to get paid, you better come back here." Bruce continues, "I am in control here!"

Daniel takes out his gun from his jacket and points it directly at Bruce.

"I think the man with the *gun* is in control here, don't you?"

Bruce backs away from Daniel, as he only now starts to realize his danger. He backs up and does not notice the sofa behind him, which trips him and causes him to fall backward and unintentionally take a seat upon it.

By now, the girls are long gone and the steel door slams to confirm their exit.

Now, Bruce realizes that he should try a different tactic since he is obviously in a disadvantageous position.

"Look, man," Bruce says, "I don't know if you are some frustrated street cop, maybe you are a Fed or 'Jack Fucking Bauer' for all I care. Whoever you are, you need to know that these girls are completely legal. I have their IDs, and a photocopy of each are on my desk if you need to see them."

"I am not here because of them," Daniel says, "I am here because of all of the others that you filmed, that were not exactly legal."

"No way, man," Bruce responds, "I was charged with that crime once before, and was cleared of all charges."

"I *know* you were," Daniel replies.

"In fact, I don't know much about the law," Bruce continues, "But I know enough to know that I cannot ever be tried again for that crime, something called 'Double Jeopardy'."

"Very good," Daniel responds, "maybe you could be a lawyer some day. Although I am betting this little enterprise of yours is *far* more lucrative."

Bruce starts to look closer at Daniel, and a slight glimmer in his eye indicates some type of recognition. Slowly, and finally, it registers as to how he knows this man, this assumed "stranger" in his home.

"*Lawyer*, that's it!" Bruce exclaims, "You were my lawyer, you defended me. What are you doing here, is this some type of sick joke or something? What did I not pay my last bill or something?" He says with a slight, uncomfortable laugh.

"No joke," Daniel replies.

"Okay, let's just cut the mystery please," Bruce says, "Stop the intimidation tactics and just tell me what you want from me, please."

"All I want," Daniel says, "is for you tell me where you keep your illegal, underage, kiddy videos. Don't pretend you don't *have* any because you and I both know better. I need both the physical and the virtual servers, plus information on any cloud servers that you have used."

"Is that all?" Bruce replies sarcastically, "I won't be giving you any of that, especially now that I know that all you are is a fucking lawyer!"

"That's *not* all," Daniel says, "I also need you to tell me if you killed those two elementary school girls in that video."

"Why would I even tell you *anything*?" Bruce asks, defiantly.

Daniel waves the gun around playfully. This gun is recently provided to him by his chief private investigator, Alex Martin.

The Smith & Wesson .500 Magnum revolver features a barrel that is ridiculously long and packs a punch like few other handguns out there. Bruce doesn't know it yet, but Daniel really just wants to scare him. Daniel has no real plans to shoot him, at least he didn't when he first arrived here, anyway.

"Again," Daniel reiterates, "man with the gun over here."

Bruce just shakes his head as if to indicate that he is not impressed. His eyes sharpen with a strong, stubborn defiant look as he casts his gaze, almost looking like an "evil eye" upon Daniel.

"I am just not buying any of this," Bruce replies, in a very dismissive tone. "You are a lawyer, not law enforcement. You have no real authority over me."

Bruce hesitates for a beat and then adds, with escalating intensity.

"Now, get out of here and go fuck yourself!"

Daniel quickly raises his weapon, takes aim and fires one shot, hitting Bruce in the kneecap which has the effect of practically blowing Bruce's leg off. The impact from a .500 Magnum is so severe as to likely have partially severed the leg.

Bruce Stephens will never walk again.

Bruce screams in pain, more of a piercing wail, as Daniel races over to him in a rage that he has not previously shown. Sweat drips from his forehead, as he stands over Bruce Stephens taunting him, demanding that he get the information he earlier so politely requested.

Daniel has deviated from the plan, he has caved in from emotion and he is not sure why. It actually starts to feel good to him, like a rush or infinite high that somewhat scares him.

But he was not *supposed* to do this, and he knows it.

"Answer my questions, you little, perverted, weasel, douchebag!" Daniel screams, "I want an answer, like *now* before I lose what is left of my patience."

Bruce's stubborn resolve is now gone.

Bruce responds, in what is more of a stammer than real speech, clearly in agonizing pain.

"I....I have about ten servers, all in a climate controlled storage unit ten blocks away in Chelsea." Bruce whimpers, "All of the addresses are listed under C-10 on a black notebook on my desk."

"I have all files uploaded to multiple cloud servers, several of which are on the dark net. There is nothing you can do about any of this anyway. It's all on the Internet, what are you going to do shut the Internet down? Once the material is out there man, it's out there forever."

"I am aware of that. What about local files?" Daniel asks,

"Yes, yes," Bruce replies, "I have some of my newer files, most stored on a drive I keep in a hidden compartment in my credenza."

Bruce points in the direction of his office towards the front of the loft apartment behind Daniel.

"My office is just down that small hallway to your left."

Daniel starts to walk away from Bruce back to where he was initially standing, as he has started to calm down.

Bruce doesn't yet understand it, but Daniel is not here as some sort of pornography/morality police. Even if he were, as Bruce noted, once the material is on the Internet it is out there forever.

But Daniel is not here because of that, rather he is here to have another more important question answered.

The real question, the one that earned Bruce Stephens a spot on Daniel's list, has still yet to be answered.

"Okay, that was the easy part," Daniel says.

"Easy?" Bruce whimpers.

"Now, to the *other* question," Daniel says.

"What other question?" Bruce asks.

"What about the elementary school girls?" Daniel asks again, "Were you responsible for their deaths? Please don't pretend you don't know what I am talking about."

Bruce continues to clutch his knee, hesitates for a moment, and then answers.

"No, no I didn't kill them. I have never killed anyone." Bruce says, continuing to grasp his bloodied knee in obvious pain. "That's not my thing man, I am at my core an artist."

"Thanks," Daniel says, "That's all that I needed to hear. Although I must say that calling this shit art is a bit of a stretch."

Daniel raises his gun, this time aiming at Bruce's head. Bruce trembles and tenses up his body in anticipation of the inevitable.

Daniel just holds his pose for about thirty seconds, continuing to point the gun at Bruce. Bruce covers his face in preparation.

"Bang!" Daniel says as he drops his weapon to his side, imitating what The Reaper had done to him months earlier, and then he turns to walk out of the loft apartment.

As Daniel walks out and is almost to the front door, maybe two steps away from it, Bruce defiantly yells out to him, not content to leave well enough alone.

"No, like I said," Bruce shouts, trying to make sure Daniel hears him before leaving.

"I didn't *kill* the girls, but I did *film* them being killed." Bruce continues.

Daniel stops in his tracks and then he turns to approach Bruce, walking back into the apartment to about the same spot where he was standing before.

"Oh please, *elaborate*...I am all ears." Daniel says.

Bruce's tone starts to become even more indignant, possibly the shock of adrenaline after the gunshot, his knee pain, possibly some poorly-timed ego, but for whatever reason he starts to get hostile with Daniel.

"I just had a thought as you were walking away," Bruce says, "That since you were my lawyer, whether current or prior, anything I have told you is *protected*."

"Maybe," Daniel replies.

"Yeah, I think it is." Bruce continues, his confidence growing into borderline cockiness. "I could admit to being the shooter behind the grassy fucking knoll and you couldn't testify against me because of privilege."

"Right," Daniel says as he nods, "Go on..."

"So now that we have that straight," Bruce says, "if this is what you want to hear, I will tell you. I filmed them, sure, I filmed them as two of my guys took turns strangling them, never stopping as the girls begged...no... *pleaded* for their lives."

Daniel shakes his head in disgust.

"I don't do any killing, but I had no problem breaking those two in." Bruce continues.

"I liked that, okay, but what I really liked was the begging, their pathetic cries for help, that I knew we wouldn't listen to."

Daniel cannot say anything, but feels like throwing up.

"Breaking them in?" Daniel asks.

"Do you want me to paint you a picture?" Bruce replies, "You should be able to figure out what 'breaking in' means."

"You see, people pay really good money for kiddy. There are some sick fucks out there." Bruce continues, "But kiddy *snuff* videos, those are a bonanza. You would not believe the number of hits we got on those."

"You said 'those', so there are more? And you made big money on this, I assume?" Daniel asks.

"Oh yeah, big money. Especially overseas. I think those guys are even more whacked out than we are. And yeah, there are dozens of these."

"So you said that you enjoyed the begging?" Daniel asks.

"You know, I really did. Some guys really love fucking them, but for me, it's all about the pain, the control. I guess I just love to see them hurt."

Daniel starts to pace a little bit, his mind very conflicted. He is at once disgusted by what he has just learned and simultaneously truly shocked that Bruce Stephens would volunteer all of this information.

"Why are you telling me all of this?" Daniel asks, stunned at Bruce's overt confession, answering questions that were not even asked.

"I am telling you this because I know you can't *get* me," Bruce says, "You can't do anything about it."

"What do you think about that?" Bruce finishes with a sly grin on his face as if he has won the debate.

"Well, I think a few things actually," Daniel says.

"First, I think you are a sick, sick man. Secondly, I think you did not need to tell me all of this. I think that you didn't really think this all the way through, and by this I mean this one key point. You might be protected legally, but did you really stop to consider this fact."

"What fact is that, counselor?" Bruce says, maintaining his defiance.

"Did you consider the fact that I am a man with a gun in your apartment who has *already* shot you in the knee? Do you think I am really here as an agent of the law? Do you really think that I am all that worried about what is legal and what is not?" Daniel says, "I have already committed aggravated assault. Assault with a deadly weapon, and I could possibly even be charged with attempted murder."

Bruce's facial expression goes from a cocky smile to a concerned, serious look bordering on panic. The actual reason for Daniel's visit is only now starting to sink in.

Only now does Bruce become truly worried.

Daniel continues his diatribe, "And finally, I think that I was only six feet away from the door and out of your life forever, but then your ego made you have to get the last word in."

Daniel finishes, "And as a good friend once told me, sometimes, man, sometimes you just need to know when to *shut the fuck up.*"

Daniel raises his gun and fires at Bruce and hits him square in the groin. Bruce screams from unimaginable pain, but rather than let him suffer anymore, Daniel ends it with one final shot to the chest.

Daniel should leave right away, but instead, he walks over to the bed and sits down. He drops his gun on the bed and puts his head in his hands in an act of despair and starts to shake, starts to tremble.

He feels like he is going to throw up.

"What am I doing?" Daniel thinks to himself, as his rage starts to dissipate. "I just brutally and cruelly shot and killed a man, and a groin shot??"

He realizes that this might have been the point of no return. This was not his original plan, he did not suspect that Bruce Stephens was involved in the killings; he was just hoping to find out who *was*. Even once Bruce admitted his involvement, the plan was never to kill him.

His primary rule, which he has now violated, "*Only those who confess to murder deserve to die.*" He knows that he is not supposed to be some sort of avenging angel, some *vigilante* that was never the idea.

This mission was never about true vengeance, it was about atonement.

Yes, Daniel realizes that he has gone too far and now will need to stop. This will be the final atonement. Instead of atoning for previous mistakes, Daniel realizes that he is really just changing himself; he has become just as bad as the people that he has killed.

This rage has cost Daniel his faculties and any tactical advantage that he once had with the police. He was careful before to not leave any evidence behind nor get anything that CSU could find on his body, clothes or anything else for that matter.

This time, the blood will be difficult to hide. Sure, he can get rid of the coat and he will, but blood traces can linger and this could be dangerous.

As Daniel walks out of the apartment and the emotional strain starts to somewhat wear off, Daniel realizes why this man bothered him more than any of the others. This is not some type of devolution as the criminal profilers would describe it.

This was a personal response due to the personal loss in his life. The two elementary school girls reminded Daniel of the two lives that were taken from him.

Yes, *two* lives.

He reaches into his coat pocket and removes the photo that he has taken with him on all of his many visits. This wrinkled, weathered black and white photo is that of an ultrasound image.

This ultrasound image is that of Daniel's unborn son.

Daniel's rage and guilt and all of the emotions related to that are more due to this loss than even that of his beloved wife. It is one thing to lose a child or a spouse, but to lose both and also feel *responsible* for it also is Daniel's proverbial cross to bear.

As Daniel walks out of the loft apartment and he starts his drive home he remembers one little detail. These details, these oversights convince him that his little vendetta needs to come to a close. He is just not made out for this type of work as he is just simply not good at it.

He remembers that Bruce Stephens had aimed the camcorder at him as he walked in the door. If the police view the tape, then that will be the first *concrete* evidence that they have against him.

Now, is the right time to get out of town for a while? It's time to get that flash drive decrypted and to see what secrets it has to offer.

The list has been completed, and there is nothing left to do but decrypt the files, and then he has to determine the best time to turn himself in. There is no escaping that fact.

He will be arrested and spend the remainder of his life in jail, but that can wait, first he has to do what he can to help Tom and the authorities find and capture The Reaper.

But for now, he needs to safely have the files decrypted, and that means using an old friend's contacts out of state.

Daniel's next stop: the Georgia Tech campus, Atlanta Georgia.

17

THE A-T-L

The very next day it is 12:30 PM and Daniel Aronson crosses the extremely frantic and crowded Terminal B at Hartsfield-Jackson International airport in Atlanta, Georgia.

Daniel has been to Atlanta's airport multiple times but never has he seen it as chaotic and busy as it is today. This airport is not only the busiest airport in the nation but is the busiest airport in the entire world. This stands in stark contrast to what he is used to, flying out of almost a barn-sized airport terminal in Westchester County. From the intimate simplicity of HPN Westchester to ATL, which is an airport so busy and large that it has its own mini subway and seven total terminals within its vast complex.

Daniel takes a seat outside Gate B-4 and checks his text messages, confirming the time for his afternoon meeting.

After retrieving his bags, he gets on the local Atlanta mass transit system known as MARTA. This extremely convenient setup enables him to take the train to the Midtown station, and then from there it is a short four block walk to his hotel, the Renaissance Midtown.

This hotel is perfectly situated only two blocks away from the Georgia Tech bookstore and computer center. This is where a key colleague has arranged for him to hand off the flash drive and to have it decrypted.

Originally, the plan was to have the file decrypted locally in Manhattan, but Daniel is extremely cautious after what happened at his house with The Reaper and his team. There is a good chance there is a tracker on it, and it simply was not worth the risk to open the file in New York.

So, the plan that Daniel and his friend developed was to have two trusted resources decrypt the file here in Atlanta in a public area that hopefully could not be traced to any one person. This way, if the flash drive were being monitored, it would be very unlikely that anyone to get to them here in Atlanta, at least not immediately.

After hotel check-in and a quick Grey Goose and Red Bull in the gorgeous hotel lobby bar, Daniel takes his briefcase and heads out for the short walk to the Georgia Tech campus area. He crosses Fifth Street to the row of restaurants and shops, enjoying the pleasant midwinter day, which hints at the possibility of an early spring.

He thinks to himself that this is definitely an afternoon to sit outside and enjoy the unusually warm winter weather.

He heads over to the previously-arranged meeting location, Ray's New York Pizza, where he is scheduled to meet the two men.

As he approaches, he looks out on the patio and recognizes the two men immediately based on the descriptions he was given.

Already seated at the table on the nice outdoor patio are Bill Sykes and Minh Wynn. Bill Sykes is a short, white, bowl-haircut-having odd-looking fellow. His colleague, Minh, is a young Korean gentleman and is more polished in his appearance.

Minh makes the initial introduction, "Mr. Aronson, I presume?" Minh asks politely, as he stands to shake hands.

"Yes, sir. I assume you are Mr. Wynn?" Daniel replies, shaking his hand.

"Yes, and I am Bill, Bill Sykes," Bill says, as he also shakes Daniel's hand.

The men all sit down at the table, Daniel puts his briefcase on the empty fourth chair at this "four-top" square table.

"I hope you don't mind but we took the liberty of ordering a pitcher of Sweetwater," Bill says,

"Sweetwater?" Daniel asks, not knowing what that is.

"Yeah, it's a local Atlanta beer," Minh replies, "I think you will love it."

"I trust you," Daniel says, as he pours a glass from the pitcher and then takes a sip. His eyes widen with approval and he nods.

"Not bad," Daniel says, "Actually pretty damn good. It tastes like a great IPA, one of the best that I have had, to be honest with you."

"Thanks for the beer." Daniel continues, "Should we get down to business?"

"Please," Bill responds, "Where should we start?"

"Do you have the flash drive with you?" Minh asks.

"Yes, right here in my briefcase," Daniel responds.

"Great, well I have the decryption program ready," Bill says, "of course we will have to open the file to know which specific encryption we are dealing with and which decryption algorithm to apply."

"So what are the next steps then?" Daniel asks.

"Well, we finish our beers here, and then we go to work, and then we give you a call once we are done," Minh says.

"Just like that, seems almost too good to be true," Daniel says.

"What outputs do you want from this?" Bill asks.

"I want three things," Daniel replies, "first, print all text files and put them into a binder notebook that I have in my briefcase. Secondly, make a full copy of the file onto a separate flash drive, and finally, destroy the original and return back to me."

"Not a problem," Minh responds, "Anything else?"

"It should be about two hours, three hours at the very most," Bill adds.

"Great, that should be around dinner time," Daniel replies, "Once you guys are done we will meet for dinner, anywhere you want, you call the place."

"How about the Alluvia restaurant?" Bill asks.

"Sure, any place that you want," Daniel responds.

Minh and Bill look at each other and share a nerdy laugh.

"Did I miss the joke?" Daniel asks.

"You will understand when you are there," Bill says, smiling his geeky smile.

Daniel opens his briefcase and removes the flash drive and the notebook binder and hands them over to Minh.

"Is there anything else, did you have any other questions?" Minh asks.

"Well you already understand the risk," Daniel replies, "Do you feel that you have adequate protection? If you want, I can be there to be another set of eyes."

"Yes, we have campus security situated outside of the lab," Minh replies, "and we also have an APD officer escorting us."

"Do you trust him?" Daniel asks.

"I have to," Bill replies, "He's my brother-in-law."

***

About three hours later, Daniel has texted the young gentlemen and received the good news that they had completed the file decryption with zero ill effects.

As promised, he was to meet them in thirty minutes at Alluvia restaurant. He is extremely excited and a little bit impatient, so he arrives about fifteen minutes early.

As he walks into the Alluvia restaurant, which from the exterior appears to be a nice, Midtown Atlanta five-star restaurant, Daniel finally understands the joke.

Alluvia restaurant is a fine dining restaurant located in a strip club, The Cheetah.

"Just the type of place two *college nerds* would pick," Daniel thinks to himself.

The hostess escorts Daniel to his table, and as Daniel walks towards it, he observes a place, unlike anything that he has seen before.

"This place is like a cross between a Capital Grille restaurant and Scores." Daniel thinks to himself, "I have heard that Scores in Manhattan is similar, but not sure if it is quite like this."

Daniel reaches his table and takes a seat. His table is directly adjacent to the main stage, on which two gorgeous nude women dance, playfully messing with each other's hair. The blonde waves to Daniel and he very awkwardly waves back.

Daniel orders a glass of wine and sits back to relax. This place more amuses than arouses him, he just finds the thought of a fine dining restaurant and strip club to be quite an unusual combination.

About fifteen minutes later, Bill and Minh walk in, appearing to be visibly uncomfortable in this location, especially the more socially awkward Bill.

Minh and Bill take their seats at the table, and Minh places a binder notebook and a flash drive on the top of the table. The binder notebook appears to have about 50-75 pages of printed material in it.

Daniel picks up the binder notebook and looks at it.

"Quite a bit of material I see," Daniel says.

"There was definitely a lot to it, just like you thought, Mr. Aronson," Bill says.

"What about the original?" Daniel asks.

Minh hands Daniel a small manila envelope such as a coin envelope used in banks. Daniel opens the envelope and then empties its contents on top of the table, which are five separate pieces of the disintegrated original flash drive.

"Good work," Daniel says, "Did you encounter any issues with anything?"

"Not really," Minh replies, "But you were definitely right about there being a tracker on it."

"Isn't that bad?" Daniel asks.

"Normally yes," Bill interjects, "But before we started the decryption we added a modification to the geolocator program and reset the location."

"Not speaking my language, man," Daniel says.

"Let's just say as far as anyone could tell we opened the file on a European train somewhere between Amsterdam and Cologne, Germany," Bill replies.

"Nice." Daniel says, "But does this mean that I took unnecessary precautions coming here? It sounds like I could have done this in New York."

"Not necessarily," Minh adds, "some geolocator programs cannot be fooled. We just happen to be pretty good at this."

"Right," Bill adds, "plus if it didn't work you could have been killed and besides what was the downside for coming here other than having to work with us two losers?" Bill says, self-effacingly.

Daniel laughs and smiles at the two men, whom he is slowly beginning to like.

"Nothing of the sort, I think you guys are great." Daniel says, "or should I say *y'all* since I am in Georgia?"

"'You guys' is fine," Minh says, "We don't all talk like rednecks down here," He adds, jokingly.

"Well since you guys did such a great job, and you set me up with that nice Sweetwater beer allow me to return the favor. Sitting in front of you are the favorite beverages of a former....associate of mine, Jägerbombs. Drink up, Gentlemen!"

Minh and Bill quickly drink their beverages, and Daniel kicks back and enjoys the sight.

Bill makes a wincing expression as the full flavor of the Jäger gets to him and Daniel smiles.

"Gentlemen, you have more than earned your fees, which I had wired to the accounts you provided. Feel free to use your phones to check your balances, I won't be offended." Daniel says.

"Thank you, sir," Minh responds, "No need to check, we trust you."

"This was actually kind of fun," Bill adds, "It was like some James Bond, 'cloak and dagger' type stuff."

"Yes, I suppose it was," Daniel replies with a laugh.

"Not all that normal for Georgia Tech," Minh adds, "This was definitely more fun that prepping for my quarter exams or pretending to care about the football game."

"Well I am glad you enjoyed it," Daniel says, "And to further show my appreciation, and just because you guys seem cool to me, you know…. in your *own way*."

Daniel laughs, as he removes two envelopes from his briefcase and places them on the table.

"I have two thousand extra in cash for each of you, and then I have another surprise, since you brought me to a place like this." Daniel continues.

Behind Daniel, slowly walking with sort of a sashay over to their table are two of this club's most in-demand dancers: Melinda and Stacie.

Melinda is a statuesque blonde with a nice California tan, pouty lips, and round sexy blue bedroom eyes. She stands about 5'7 and is dressed in a black lace bra, combined with black lace panties and black garter.

Stacie is a model gorgeous African-American petite woman with dark brown skin and dazzling green eyes. Stacie's long brown hair cascades along her gorgeous form-fitting, sexy, yet professional black dress.

Melinda moves over to Bill and without saying a word sits upon Bill's lap. Bill's eyes widen with surprise and shock.

At the same time, Stacie approaches Minh and asks, "May I join you?"

Minh says nothing but merely nods sheepishly, as Stacie sits on his lap.

Daniel smiles as he enjoys the fact that the guys are pleasantly uncomfortable, if such a duality is possible.

"Before you arrived, I took the liberty of booking the remainder of the evening for both the lovely Melinda and Stacie here." Daniel says, "So unless you have any objections, they will take you to the V.I.P room for the remainder of the evening."

Still speechless, Minh and Bill just nod as the ladies lead their willing patrons into the adjacent V.I.P room. "Deer in the headlights" does not begin to describe the look of excited apprehension on Bill and Minh's faces.

"Behave yourselves, Gentlemen," Daniel says with a smile as the two men are escorted back to the V.I.P room.

"Ah, stupid youth," Daniel thinks to himself, "is it wrong that I envy their naiveté?"

Daniel puts cash on the table, retrieves the flash drive and the notebook binder and prepares to exit the restaurant/strip club. As he walks out of the club, he wonders if this all was a waste of time, but remembers that his trip to Atlanta had multiple goals.

The objective was not only to get the file decrypted, it was also to get out of New York because Tom and the NYPD by now had surely detected a link to him and his recent killings. He also sought to build a rapport with these two men Bill and Minh, because he views them as them being strategic allies in the future.

Daniel realizes that if he has any prayer against an organization as strong as he is facing, he needs allies everywhere, especially those with specific skills that he does not have.

But that is the distant future, for right now, this file and notebook binder is all that he is worrying about. He needs to review the contents, see if there is any information that he can use, and then determine his next steps.

***

While Daniel plans his next moves in Atlanta, back in New York, the impact of Daniel's latest victim is becoming apparent to the NYPD.

Bruce Stephens' loft apartment is covered with police officers investigating the grisly scene. It is a fairly busy scene with four CSU investigators reviewing the scene and taking photos, two uniformed officers, and Detectives Parra and Barnes. Tom Justice walks in the front door and sees Shane McWilliams waiting for him.

"What do we have here, Shane?" Tom asks,

"Guy took three shots." Shane responds, "The knee, groin, and then the kill shot to the chest."

"Obviously personal," Tom replies.

"Can't get more personal than groin shots," Shane adds.

Parra and Barnes walk over to Tom and Shane and joins the conversation.

"Might be some additional significance to the groin shot, Boss," Barnes adds.

"How is that?" Tom asks.

"Well, we haven't checked all of it yet, but from what we have found already, this guy was into some really warped porn."

"Warped? Define warped." Shane asks.

"Bad stuff, man," Parra says, "The office desk had apparently been ransacked, and all types of media, photos, videos, magazines were spread across this man's desk. We are talking kiddy stuff of the most heinous nature."

"And we know this is one of Daniel's clients?" Tom asks.

"He's near the top of our list, Tom," Shane responds.

"I went to his house again this morning and he wasn't there," Tom says, "There is no answer on his mobile, literally no sign of Daniel at all."

"I think we need to proactively warn others who may be on his list," Shane says.

Tom shakes his head in disagreement.

"Now that's an *awkward* conversation, Shane," Tom says dismissively, "How exactly do we begin that conversation? 'Hi, oh hey, just be on the lookout, your former lawyer may be trying to kill you.'"

"I know, Tom, but I don't know what else we can do."

"We have a video camera also," Parra adds, "Based on the setup it suggests that he was filming something when the attack occurred. "

"Can you two bring the camera and all of the material to me? I will have the techs analyze it and bring it to me personally." Tom orders.

Barnes and Parra nod, as Parra moves over to get the camera and Barnes walks towards the office to retrieve the other media.

Tom turns to Shane to resume their conversation.

"I have another parallel approach idea," Tom says, "I will ask Jill to reach out to Daniel. Maybe he will open up to her like he wouldn't with me."

"Anything at this point is worth trying Tom," Shane replies.

"Tom, on the subject of Jill," Shane begins, thinking that now might be the opportunity that he was waiting for,

"I saw...." Shane starts but is quickly interrupted as Parra and Barnes walk back to where Tom and Shane are standing interrupting the conversation's flow.

"Saw *what* Shane?" Parra asks.

Barnes interjects, "Here is the material we were discussing, Boss. I have to say, that is some of the most disturbing shit I have ever seen, and I have seen some shit."

"Thanks, Barnes. Shane you were saying?" Tom says.

Shane is obviously caught off guard here.

"Nothing, Tom, it can wait," Shane says.

"Tom, I have an additional lead on The Reaper case that I want to pursue," Parra adds.

"We can't, Parra." Tom answers, "We can't do anything for that case that could be on the record."

"We have a meeting set up with the Mayor to get some clarification of our role, but as it stands we have been ordered to stand down."

"This is bullshit!" Parra exclaims.

"Also," Shane adds, "any information that we do find we need to turn over to the Bureau before acting on it."

"Here is the video camera," Parra says, "Barnes and I are heading back I think you guys can handle this for now.

Parra storms off with Barnes behind him, clearly unhappy that his hands are tied in regards to The Reaper case.

"Tom, about Parra..." Shane begins.

"Not now, Shane, please," Tom responds.

"No, Tom you really need to hear this…"

Tom starts to get agitated and puts his hand on Shane's shoulder in an aggressive posture.

"Listen, Shane, I do not have time for this right now, do you understand?"

"I understand," Shane says reluctantly, as he walks away, extremely frustrated at this communication breakdown.

Tom holds the video camera in his hand and takes a quick glance at the material that Barnes brought him and agrees that this is indeed some of the most disturbing material that he has ever seen.

***

Back in Atlanta, Daniel receives a call from his private investigator, Alex Martin.

Alex Martin is retired NYPD and one of the keys to Daniel Aronson's success as a defense attorney. Through Alex, Daniel has been able to collect precious evidence that has made his career so successful.

Alex Martin is an expert at finding any type of information on any witness, police officer, prosecuting attorney. His connections in the department, FBI, and the State Department are almost unlimited, and this has, one could argue, made Daniel's career.

Alex can learn almost anything about anybody, and his tactics are definitely grey-area if not illegal. He does not mind dealing with criminals or paying people off if it means getting the information that he needs.

Alex Martin's team is the single reason that Daniel has been able to find all of the people on his list, to know exactly where they would be at any given time, and also know when they were at their most vulnerable.

The connection to Alex Martin is one key fact that he even hides from his best friend Tom Justice.

Alex informs Daniel that Daniel is now being very actively pursued by NYPD in a string of recent missing person's cases and is also a suspect in two murders.

"One bit of positive news," Alex adds, "I was able to find the address of a location in Manhattan where Bippus and Mercado are operating. My team checked it for three days and has identified solid patterns of their comings and goings."

"Oh that's excellent," Daniel replies, "What about our other two?"

"The so-called 'Reaper and Mr. Impossible'?" Alex asks, "Unfortunately no sign of them yet."

"Okay, well risky or not, I am coming back to the city, can we meet later this week?"

"When are you flying back?" Alex asks.

"Too risky to fly," Daniel responds, "I will get a car here in Atlanta and drive back so let's meet in two days."

"Don't use the same car," Alex adds, "it's a good bet they already know you are in Atlanta using your flight records."

"Go from Atlanta to Washington, and I will have one of my guys there get you another car," Alex says.

"I can do that," Daniel says, "And I will register the car under that alias that you gave me."

"Okay, anything else that I can help you with in the meantime?" Alex asks.

"Not yet, but be ready as I have a data file for you to examine and a bunch of names and addresses that make no sense to me but hopefully you can make something out of it."

"Okay, you know that we can handle that, just nothing too technical." Alex responds,

"Technical stuff has all been handled," Daniel replies.

"Good news. But, there is one other bit of information for you, Daniel, and it is something we are continuing to monitor but I wanted you to know," Alex says, "There is some chatter that an outside team is being brought into the city for a large operation."

"Do you have any idea for what purpose?" Daniel asks.

"Still trying to figure that out," Alex replies, "maybe it's nothing, but it could also be reinforcements for your guys. If that is the case, then it could be a serious problem."

"Okay, well there is a good chance they could come after me again, and with Tom and his team surely on to me by now; I have to consider my home off –limits," Daniel says.

"Where will you go? You can't check into a hotel, all of that will be monitored also." Alex says.

"I have a place that I keep under a corporate name; I usually let my clients stay there before trials for any last minute preparations," Daniel says, "Not even Tom knows about this place, and neither do you.....well I *hope* not anyway."

"No, believe it or not, I don't," Alex replies, "As far as you *know* anyway." Alex finishes with a laugh.

"But I think that is the plan," Daniel says, "For now, drive back, lie low, and then figure out a way to talk to Tom directly. Not that I will be able to explain any of this, though."

"Sounds like you have it figured out then," Alex replies, "Alright, I will see you in two days. But before I go, I need you to look at one more item of business."

"What's that, Alex?" Daniel asks.

"Open your laptop and look at the file that I just emailed you," Alex says.

Daniel walks over, opens his laptop and opens the email from Alex.

"Okay, I have it, what now?" Daniel asks.

"The video file, play it," Alex says, "This was provided to me by an anonymous source from Kinzer and Martinez's precinct."

Daniel plays the video, which shows young Charles Murphy in the back of the police car, sitting there crying. All of the sudden, he looks up and then he is shot twice without any provocation, and none of the alleged resistance or trying to get a gun.

This is the evidence Daniel needed.

"This.…..this is what we needed to put those bastards away for good," Daniel says.

"Not so fast, Daniel," Alex says, "I have one piece of bad news to go along with this. You should know that I really debated whether or not I should even show this to you."

"What is the bad news?" Daniel asks.

"My source for the video, he insisted that this evidence not be used in court against either Kinzer or Martinez," Alex says. "He fears some type of reprisal."

"Well that's too bad, Alex, this is something that I need to bring Charlie's murderers to trial." Daniel says.

"Daniel, you can't do that. I gave my word." Alex says. "You know you need my information and I know that I can trust you not to violate our partnership."

Daniel hesitates for a long moment, before relenting.

"I will respect your wishes," Daniel says.

"Thank you, Daniel, I know this is difficult for you."

"Okay, Alex, I will talk to you later," Daniel says.

Daniel disconnects the phone.

Then he launches the damn thing across the room as he curses at the top of his lungs.

***

Back in New York at Tom Justice's office at the 17th precinct, Tom sits at his desk reviewing the files on his computer screen, specifically the files related to Daniel Aronson's clients.

The camcorder recovered from the apartment sits on his desk, and he debates whether he should view it or not.

Making sure that nobody can see what he is doing, Tom walks over to close his office door and also closes all of the window blinds.

He starts the video camera and begins to watch. The film starts predictably enough with the erotic parts featuring our girls Sunny and Mai.

Moments later he sees that there is a disturbance, and then the camera moves to notice a man standing in the front of the apartment. Now there can be no mistaking it, this is absolutely Daniel. This is the final bit of evidence that will put him away for life.

Tom realizes that he is bound by duty to turn over this bit of evidence. The camera and recording must be turned over to D.A Garcia immediately and Daniel will be arrested. Instead, in a total violation of personal and professional ethics, Tom hides the camera in his desk drawer and locks it.

Tom walks out of his office and makes it halfway across the main precinct floor, and then he starts to doubt himself.

He realizes that this move will put his career in jeopardy and ruin any chances of a political future. He thinks to himself that this loyalty might be misplaced, and then he realizes what he must do.

Daniel might be his best friend, Tom reasons, but if Daniel is truly a murderer, then he must be arrested.

18

BETRAYAL!

Tom Justice realizes that his best friend Daniel Aronson is a killer, and must be found, tried and convicted. The video camera that can put his friend away is on his desk, and he is prepared to present this to Mayor Lockhart and District Attorney Garcia at their meeting today.

Shane McWilliams walks into the office looking for Tom.

"You said you wanted to leave a little early, how about now?" Shane asks, "We have two hours until the meeting."

"Now is good, I want to walk it and it's an hour walk, at least," Tom says.

"That's a crazy far walk, Tom," Shane says, "But if you insist."

"I had some ideas that I want to run by you also," Tom adds.

Tom and Shane proceed to leave the precinct house and stop at a local burrito chain, think Chipotle, and grab a burrito for the walk and talk lunch.

It's a great early spring day, the type of day that New Yorkers call in sick for and go lay on the grass in Central park. Ladies walk the streets in their new spring clothes, and there is an electric energy in the city. This is part of the reason Tom insisted on walking the significant distance between the 17th precinct and the Mayor's office.

"By the way Tom, I have been meaning to ask," Shane begins, "how is the trial separation with Jill going?"

"Man, where did *that* come from?" Tom asks.

"Sorry, but there is no easy way to bring that up. It's not a topic that flows organically from any conversation." Shane replies.

"Oh, it's okay," Tom replies, "It's just still uncomfortable to talk about."

"Well, we don't have to..." Shane concedes.

"No, we can. Okay, well, you see....she admitted that she is seeing someone else during this separation."

"Ouch!" Shane exclaims.

"Yeah, and also that they have already *slept* together."

"Double ouch!" Shane says, "Is that supposed to be a part of the trial separation?"

"Oh yeah, shocked me also," Tom replies, "But it's only as if we were just dating, with free reign to date, and apparently *screw*, other people."

"What about you?" Shane asks, "Have you seen anyone else?"

"No, I think since I was busted from that Texas incident, I have learned my lesson."

"Well to be fair it wasn't only that one time, right?" Shane adds, "Don't forget the strippers from Connecticut and the pharmaceutical sales girl that you met."

"Yes, I know" Tom replies, "I am mostly good, but I have that one weakness, and I guess now I am paying for it. Jill has been very patient in putting up with me for several years."

"Karma is a bitch as they say," Shane says, "That was just messing around, though. This does sound like it might be an actual relationship."

"That's my bigger concern," Tom says, "I can deal with the sex part, but the idea of Jill being in love with someone else is almost unbearable."

"Well of course," Shane replies.

"On the topic of Jill, I have already asked her to do what she can to find or contact Daniel." Tom adds, "But no luck as of yet. She said she had one other place to check and would get back to me later today."

"While we are on the topic, Tom," Shane adds, "There is something I have been trying to say and I am just going to say it now before I lose my damn nerve again."

Tom stops walking, and motions Shane to stop and walk over to an adjacent park bench at Union Square Park and they sit down.

"Tom, there is no easy way to say this," Shane starts, "but I believe that it is *Parra* who Jill is seeing."

Tom looks up with a 'deer in the headlights' look. He is confused because Parra and Jill hardly know each other, although Parra is considered handsome and the two couples have met for dinner on two occasions.

"It's not just a hunch, Tom. I actually had this idea weeks ago, and then followed them to a restaurant where they met for a Sunday brunch." Shane continues.

"Brunch?" Tom asks.

"Yes, at PJ Clarkes a few weeks back," Shane says, "My question to you is, does she even know Parra?"

"She does." Tom answers, "We have had dinner with him and his wife Cyndi, but only a couple of times."

"This is just brunch, right?" Tom rationalizes, "this doesn't mean anything in and of itself."

Shane looks up with a serious look.

"By itself, no, but combined with Jill's admission that she is dating someone else, I think it doesn't take a detective to put two and two together."

"Son of a bitch," Tom says softly under his breath.

***

Two days later on East 55th street, between Madison and Fifth Avenues, Jill Justice walks through the 55th street entrance of one of the most prestigious hotel addresses in all of Manhattan.

The St. Regis Hotel is known for its attention to detail and the highest definition of luxury. The hotel's very enviable address puts it mere blocks from such landmarks as Rockefeller Center, the Museum of Modern Art, and Central Park.

Jill walks into the ornate lobby, looking every bit as if she fits in with her impeccable outfit and confident manner. She bypasses the front desk and walks towards the elevator.

As she boards the elevator and begins her ascent upwards, her mind takes her back to the many good memories and thoughts of enjoyable times that she has had at this amazing place.

She remembers most specifically the wedding reception for Daniel and Carrie in the room known as the Regis Roof. How perfect that night was, even better than her *own* wedding reception.

The gourmet food, the slow dancing, the excellent band that had played for two presidents and one prime minister. Wealth is nothing foreign to Jill and her family, but there was something about that gathering and the amount and sheer degree of wealth in that room that actually made Jill Justice uncomfortable. She actually recalls how she felt as if she did not *belong* in the same room as a Senator, Mayor, and two Congressmen.

Then there were the lighter moments of that evening such as Tom's best man toast that somehow managed to embarrass Daniel, Carrie and *himself* all at the same time.

Jill laughs and thinks to herself, "Tom never could handle champagne."

As she exits the elevator and heads down the hallway, she realizes that this type of meeting is not quite as joyful as the wedding reception and starts to feel just a little bit guilty about it.

Tom has asked her to check on Daniel and see if she can get information about where he has been. Tom didn't even know about this place, but Jill was playing a hunch and just crossing her fingers that she might be right.

Tom didn't tell her the entire truth, however, not wanting to tell her that their close friend is also very likely a killer and also possibly not thinking clearly.

Jill has no idea that she might be in danger.

Jill knocks at the door of unit 1719 and after a slight delay, there is an answer at the door and Daniel Aronson opens the door.

"Jill?" Daniel says, obviously very surprised to see Jill there, "I wasn't expecting you."

"Actually, I wasn't expecting *anyone* to be honest with you." Daniel continues, "How did you know where to find me?"

"May I come in?" Jill asks.

"Oh, of course, sorry…." Daniel says, still acting uncomfortable with this turn of events, "I don't mean to be rude, it's just that you surprised me."

Daniel steps out into the hallway, looking nervously around, to makes sure that nobody else is there waiting for him. He is not sure what to make of this visit and does not know if he is in trouble or not. He knows that he is wanted by the police, and wonders if Tom has sent Jill there to get him to come in voluntarily and turn himself in.

Once he sees that the hallway, at least, appears to be empty he walks back into the residence and speaks with Jill again.

"Again, sorry to act so standoffish," Daniel says, "I just got back into town, and haven't spoken to Tom in days."

"I didn't even think that he knew about this place." Daniel says.

"He doesn't," Jill replies, "I tried your house first, but when you weren't there I thought I would come here. But he did send me to talk to you, although he did not explain to me why. "

"I think I know why," Daniel says, "I think Tom and his team know what I have been doing."

"Not necessarily," Jill says, as she approaches him slowly in what appears to be a consoling manner. She reaches out to him and touches his hand.

"But I do think he knows what *we* have been doing," Jill says, as she wraps her arms around him and she embraces Daniel with a deep kiss."

"I guess you *would* know about this place, wouldn't you?" Daniel says.

"Of course, I would," Jill replies, "some of my best memories have been made in this very room, bedroom if I may be perfectly honest."

Daniel turns and walks a few steps away and then turns back to Jill.

"So what are you going to tell Tom?" Daniel asks.

"I will tell him my *version* of the truth." Jill answers; "That you were not at your house, and then I went to meet a friend for a few hours at the St. Regis, ordered some food, and then had a screaming orgasm….the *drink*, of course," She finishes with a sultry wink.

"You are a sneaky little minx," Daniel says.

"I have been since college." Jill says, as seductively as she can, and as she moves in for another deep kiss, "Part of that is your fault for making me that way all those years ago."

Jill moves in and they kiss even more intensely than before, as Jill takes Daniel by the hand and leads him towards the bedroom. The lovers walk into the bedroom and shut the door behind them so we cannot see a thing.

No, not a thing.

Sorry, this just isn't that type of novel.

So, as the couple engages in the most passionate and fulfilling lovemaking that either of them can remember, and torrents of emotion come flooding back to them that remind them of their lost youth, let's back up just a little bit.

By now it is likely evident that this affair has been going on for some time, and it has. For the past year, Daniel and Jill have been involved. The catalyst being the point at which Jill learned of Tom's one night stand. Tom's latest affair was only the most recent of many incidents of womanizing that Jill had learned to live with.

This incident was her breaking point, and she sought comfort in Daniel's arms, the arms of her college sweetheart. She never expected the love to return, but it did.

From what was initially rationalized as being just a onetime fling, Daniel and Jill quickly both realized that they still had deep feelings for each other but had no idea how they could realistically deal with the complexity of those feelings and specifically the impact on their current marriages.

They made the decision to stay in their marriages until a better opportunity would appear for them to ultimately be together. Jill made the first move by filing for the legal separation; this was to be a slow process that would eventually result in divorce, and Jill's freedom.

Daniel had similar plans and was all set to take a similar course of action with Carrie, but had to be careful and not time it too closely with Jill's move or it might seem connected. He was to wait about six more months after Jill was divorced, and only then request the separation, then divorce after that and then he and Jill would be free to get married.

It seemed like a great plan.

But one visit to the doctor's office changed all of those plans.

Carrie had requested that Daniel take her to her checkup appointment which he thought was odd until he saw the ultrasound image. There it was right in front of him, the image of what would be his first child, a son. Carrie had waited to tell him because of so many unsuccessful attempts in the past.

It's difficult to explain exactly what changed inside Daniel at that moment, but he definitely knew that he could not possibly leave his pregnant wife and his unborn son. When he told Jill, she was disappointed but she understood. They would continue their affair, but have to wait a little longer to be together officially.

Daniel knew that leaving a wife and child would be bad, but deserting a pregnant wife would be borderline immoral and he simply could not do that. That would not be right.

Then, The Reaper attack on Daniel's home and Carrie's death really ended this grand plan. This incident not only derailed the plans but caused several chain reactions as well.

Perhaps if Daniel had viewed the event selfishly or opportunistically, Carrie's death would have been ideal for him to move forward with his life with Jill. Jill would complete the six-month separation, file for divorce and he would be free to begin dating her afterward.

But Daniel didn't respond to it that way.

The guilt that Daniel had harbored in his heart for taking his best friend's wife was bad enough, but when his wife Carrie and unborn child were killed this created some type of crushing, not-quite-psychotic break inside him.

He became Dark Vengeance on this quest, this mission to correct those mistakes in his professional life, most of which he has corrected already.

Back in the bedroom, it is now PG-rated so we can enter as the couple lies beneath the luxurious silk sheets, Daniel holding Jill in his arms. She feels more comfortable than she has for a while, this being only the second time they have been together since Carrie's death.

"I think this situation calls for a little bit of the bubbly," Daniel says, "Will you join me?"

Daniel walks from the bed over to an armoire, where the phone is located.

"Sure," Jill responds, "champagne sounds good. Don't forget to order my screaming orgasm so I will be telling Tom the truth later."

Daniel laughs, "Will do, but I am not sure if they serve those at a place like this. I am half embarrassed just to order it."

"Just order the damn drink will you!" Jill replies playfully, as she rolls back over in the bed seemingly content and happy.

Daniel prepares to dial and then looks back over to Jill.

"One other thing," Daniel continues, "let's both agree to not mention *Tom's* name while we are still essentially naked, it's just kind of creepy."

"Ouch," Jill winces, "yeah, that is a great point, sorry."

Daniel places the call and orders the champagne, but not the requested screaming orgasm. He walks back over to the bed to greet his lover.

Jill's expression moves from smiling and laughing to a serious gaze.

"I have to tell you something, Daniel," Jill says.

"Sure Jill, what is it?" Daniel asks.

"During our last counseling session, I had to tell Tom that I was seeing *someone* during the separation," Jill says.

Daniel's eyes show a look of shock, "you didn't say *me*, right?"

"No, no, I didn't give a name. I don't even think he would suspect you at all." Jill says.

"What are you planning to do about the final decision?" Daniel asks.

"We have two more meetings with the counselor and then I will make the decision. I would like to meet with you before I tell Tom." Jill says.

"Okay, but we might want to make it in the next few weeks."

Jill says nothing, but looks up as if to say "why?"

"Do this for me, though, Jill." Daniel continues, "Tell Tom that you met with me....obviously omitting certain 'details' of our meeting."

"Of course," Jill replies.

"Tell him that I would like to meet him in two days, at this building but only in the St. Regis lobby, no need to let him in on the secret of my apartment here. Hopefully, that stays between the two of us."

"No problem, Daniel, would be happy to."

"Thanks, Jill. Thanks for everything, I really do love you, you know." Daniel embraces Jill in a passionate hug.

"I love you too."

***

Now that the time for romance has ended, Daniel's thoughts return to the final few steps that he has left before he can end it all.

He made the promise to Alex Martin not to turn over the incriminating video that would doom Officers Martinez and Kinzer. He did make that promise but he never said anything about not paying them a visit in person. For such a visit, he used one of his other investigators to determine that Officer Martinez would not be alone for enough time, but Officer Kinzer would be vulnerable for a few hours.

Later that night, Daniel Aronson is in a conflicted mood as he waits outside of the apartment of Officer Roger Kinzer. Killing a police officer is a capital offense, and could ruin any chance that he has of getting out of this series of events. Such a cliché, but this could really be the actual point of no return.

He realizes that he promised Alex Martin that he would not turn over the video evidence, but he never said anything about not killing them.

Well, maybe it was implied, but he never actually did say it.

At around 1 AM, Officer Kinzer finally comes walking down the hallway towards the door of his apartment. Daniel hangs back out of sight until he sees Officer Kinzer start to put his key in the door and then Daniel approaches him.

"Officer Kinzer," Daniel says as he approaches Kinzer.

Kinzer looks up and doesn't say anything, apparently a slight bit intoxicated.

"Do I know you?" Officer Kinzer asks.

"No, but I know *you* and we need to talk." Daniel continues menacingly.

"Talk about what?"

"Charles Murphy, you murdering son of a bitch!"

Daniel hits Kinzer with a hard right cross, a true cold-cock shot to the face, and Kinzer falls over into the door, knocking open the slightly ajar door and falling through the front doorway of the apartment.

Daniel seizes the opportunity to drag the stunned Kinzer into the apartment and then shuts the door behind him.

Kinzer struggles to compose himself as Daniel removes his .500 Magnum beast of a weapon and prepares to fire at Kinzer.

"Wait…wait, you don't want to do this." Kinzer pleads.

"You're right, I absolutely don't want to, but you and your partner gave me no choice. You shouldn't have killed that kid." Daniel says.

"That was all Martinez, man." Kinzer continues to plead, "He hates blacks, he hates Jews, and he hates *everyone* really. I swear to you man he killed that kid, shot him twice right in the stomach."

"How do I know that you are telling the truth?" Daniel asks.

"You don't. But if you are looking to take down Martinez, I know how you can do it." Kinzer replies.

"How is that?" Daniel asks.

"Martinez is one of several in my precinct and an even wider group within the NYPD that don't play by the rules. And when I say that it really diminishes the full impact of what they are doing, some of it is really bad, just like what happened to the Murphy boy."

"If this is really true, then why didn't you speak out against your partner?" Daniel asks.

"That's a great question, man," Kinzer replies very sarcastically, "well maybe I just wanted to stay alive you know? Stupid me, right

"Why should I believe that you are willing to help me now?" Daniel asks.

"The gun is a little bit convincing for one thing. For another, I can't take his bullying anymore nor can I live with my conscience."

"Martinez bullies you?" Daniel asks.

"Yeah, like I said he hates almost everyone, and he especially hates gays," Kinzer replies.

At that moment, from an interior bedroom a thin, muscular white man walks into the living room, rubbing his eyes as he apparently just woke up.

"Honey, is everything okay out here?" The man asks.

"Buddy, yes, I am just having a conversation with someone from down the hall, and he was just leaving," Kinzer says.

"Okay, well come to bed soon, you know how I hate to sleep alone," Buddy says.

Daniel waves, and then nods to Officer Kinzer and walks towards the door to leave.

"Listen, if you want to take Martinez down I can help you." Kinzer says, "But you have to protect me, can you do that?"

"If you have serviceable information, then I can definitely protect you," Daniel says.

"I can give you more than information," Kinzer says, "I can tell you *exactly* how you can get him."

"You can?"

"Absolutely I can. Just one condition, though."

"What is that?" Daniel asks.

"I want to *be* there. I want to be there when you take down the racist, murdering, homophobic son of a bitch." Kinzer says with a smile.

19

CALL ME DEVICE-MAN

The following morning, Tom and Shane McWilliams are in the apartment of Will Harrison, the man whom Daniel had defended several months ago who featured the "Professor Light" devices. They feel that he is 'at risk' due to being such a recent case.

They walk around his apartment trying to command the attention of the easily distracted scientific genius. The apartment is a combination of beyond state of the art technical equipment, empty snack bags, and soda cans. Tom picks up an impressive, yet odd-looking electronic item from a table and starts to examine it while Shane speaks with Will Harrison.

Tom examines the item, which is nothing like he as ever seen before. It appears to be a wearable device about the size of a vest, but bulkier with several wires extending out from it.

"Please be careful with that." Harrison directs to Tom, "It is only a prototype, and I am still testing it."

"Plus," Harrison says under his breath, "It's also a little bit *unstable*."

"Back to our conversation, Mr. Harrison," Shane continues, "If you will just give us ten minutes of your attention, *undivided attention*, I think it would be in your best interest to hear what we have to say."

As they talk, Will Harrison continues to work on an electronic device in his hand that looks like a remote, never maintaining eye contact with either Tom or Shane.

"I cannot imagine how I could be of any interest to you," He says, "I was acquitted of all weapons charges, and have not done anything remotely criminal."

"We didn't say that you had," Shane says.

"Well, what then? Am I like a suspect or something?"

Tom walks over from where he had been standing to join in the conversation.

"No, you are not a suspect, quite the opposite actually," Tom says.

"How so? Please explain." Harrison asks.

"Your defense attorney," Shane says, "he has been apparently abducting some of his former clients."

"Abducting?" Harrison asks, with a slight smirk on his face.

"Well to be honest," Tom says, "he has killed at least two of them, and the other two are missing and presumed dead."

Now, Harrison looks at Tom and Shane directly with a very concerned look.

"Killed? Oh, my God." Harrison says.

"It might be a good idea to leave town for a few weeks," Shane says.

"Leaving town is not an option, I have too many commitments." Harrison says, "But I think I have some ways to protect myself, I will be ready for him if he comes by."

Harrison motions to all of the devices lying on the tables around him, implying that he could use said devices to defend himself.

"Remember," Tom says, "that if you see anything suspicious, see him around you or anything like that. Please call us."

Tom and Shane move towards the door, but Tom has one final question.

"By the way, what was that device that I was holding, it looked really interesting," Tom asks.

Harrison walks over to the table and picks up the device, and starts to describe it.

"This is a prototype of a directional charge wearable body unit," Harrison says.

"Say again?" Shane asks.

"Do you want the technical or the *non-technical* explanation?" Harrison asks.

Shane and Tom look at each other and then reply in unison, *"Non-Technical."*

"Yeah, that's what I thought. Okay, it is supposed to channel an energy charge forward, but in a controlled manner. The idea is to enable someone, say a police officer, or secret service agent to wear this and be able to repel someone at close range."

"I had a tentative contract with the secret service, but it is on hold pending further testing." Harrison continues.

"That sounds interesting. How has the testing gone so far?"

"Not as good as we expected," Harrison responds, "The charge is not directional enough and is too strong, so instead of stunning a person it would kill them."

"How is it triggered?" Tom asks.

"Ideally, it would be triggered via a wired mechanism somewhere on your body," Harrison says.

"Not wirelessly?" Shane asks.

"No, that would be *far* too dangerous" Harrison says, "Let me show you why."

Harrison places the device back down where it was laying originally, and moves back away from it about ten feet.

"Oh, you might want to back up a few feet, and you might want to cover your ears also."

Will Harrison clicks a button on the electronic device he has been holding this entire time and the directional charge fires, exploding outward with an energy shock wave three feet up and four feet wide.

Tom and Shane both jump back, shocked at what has just gone off in front of them.

Tom especially is surprised since he had been holding the item and had no clue of the danger.

"As you can see, it still has a few bugs," Harrison says.

"I...I was holding that thing," Tom says nervously, "Do you mean you could have set that off any time you wanted to?"

Harrison looks at Tom and then Harrison winks and smiles and says.

"Aren't you glad that you didn't arrest me?"

"I think I know why they call you the 'Gadget Guy," Tom says.

"Actually, I am not 'Gadget Guy' anymore, too *immature* sounding. Call me 'Device-Man'."

"Yes, sir," Tom says, as he exits the door and shuts it behind him, not knowing what to make of this so-called 'Device-Man'.

Shane looks to Tom as they walk down the hallway.

"What about *arresting* him?" Shane asks.

"Why would we do that? " Tom replies.

"There are enough questionable devices in there that we could arrest him on weapons charges, and keep him in custody for his own protection."

"Not a bad idea," Tom replies, "But not right now, right now we have bigger problems to deal with."

***

Back at Precinct 17, the four key players in the precinct, Tom Justice, Shane, Parra, and Barnes, all sit at the card table in the game room discussing The Reaper case, which they have now been permitted to work again.

"I was surprised that Mayor Lockhart let us back in, quite honestly," Tom says, "I thought that we would be permanently put on the 'ignore list' after Tarrytown."

"Same here, Tom," Shane adds, "Why did he suddenly have a change of heart?"

Barnes looks up and points over to Parra.

"You might want to thank my partner because he spoke to Lockhart directly," Barnes says.

Tom looks over at Parra and raises his hands as if to say "what the hell?"

"Parra?" Tom says, "You did this without consulting me?"

"Sorry, Tom, but I felt like the Mayor was personally mad at you, and if I approached him about it logically…." Parra says.

"..Then maybe it's not personal anymore and he actually would listen to you?" Tom finishes Parra's thought

"And there's more…." Parra says.

"And?" Tom asks.

"I actually met with your wife Jill to get some information that hopefully the Mayor would listen to."

Tom turns and looks to Shane, and responds to Parra, "You mean you got my wife involved in all of this?"

"Yes, Tom," Parra responds, "when all of us had dinner together Jill told my wife Cyndi that she was extremely close to Lockhart's wife, and I felt that I could use this approach once the Mayor finally cooled down."

Tom shakes his head, "It worked out for the better, but I still need to talk with you privately about these methods….this cannot continue, understand? I understand that you are ambitious, but this needed to be handled another damn way!"

Parra nods, "Sorry, sir."

"Now that we are back on the case, have we been able to make any sense of that 'Agente Oscuro' reference that Bill Tucker told us about before he was killed?" Shane asks.

"No luck, we really stopped looking at it, Shane," Tom answers.

"What the fuck is an 'Agente Oscuro'?" Barnes asks with his usual charm.

"We don't really know," Shane responds, "I have run the name and nothing comes back, not locally anyway."

"Perhaps we are being too literal," Parra adds, "I mean in an organization that has a 'Reaper' and a 'Mr. Impossible' it's not exactly a stretch to assume that this is an alias or nickname of some sort."

"Good point," Tom says.

"Actually, and I am ashamed I didn't see this sooner," Parra says, "'Agente Oscuro' could be Spanish for 'Dark Agent' or 'Agent Dark' depending on how you translate it."

"Dark Agent? What could that mean?" Shane asks.

"Or it could be a symbolic interpretation of that," Parra suggests.

"What about *initials*?" Barnes adds, "Some of these covert types love to hide the truth in their code names, sort of like an in-joke."

"D.A.?" Tom says, "No, I think District Attorney Garcia is clean, I have known and worked with him for years."

Shane and Parra nervously look at each other and then Shane adds,

"*Daniel....*" Shane says.

"*....Aronson?*" Parra finishes, as they both stare nervously over at Tom.

Tom looks up, pondering the possibility that this could be real.

"That's not really possible, *couldn't* be possible," Tom says.

"I don't know, Tom," Shane says.

"Don't know what?" Tom asks, his tone getting more combative.

"It would actually explain a lot," Shane says, "Such as why The Reaper did not kill Daniel or take the flash drive that he still hasn't turned over to us to this day."

"But then that means that Daniel had his own wife killed," Tom says, "And that all of these revenge killings were just what....a diversion?"

"It could be Tom," Shane says, "Think about it: if you didn't ever believe Daniel was capable of doing these killings, who knows what *else* he might be capable of?"

"But he did not need to have his own *wife* killed, that makes no sense," Tom adds.

"I agree unless he had a really good reason to want her out of the way," Shane says.

Tom's mind is overwhelmed by conflicting thoughts, as he tries to process everything he has been told, and then he thinks about Jill, he now is not sure Parra is the other man after all and then has one other sickening thought.

"Oh my God," Tom says to himself, as Tom thinks of one *other* motive Daniel might have had to kill his own wife.

***

That same evening, technically early morning the next day, Will Harrison is awakened by a sound in his living room. Heeding the warning that was given to him not twelve hours earlier, Harrison gets one of his defensive devices and walks into the living room slowly.

The lights are all off, and there is no apparent sight or sound of anyone in the room. Finally, he hears a slight motion in the living room and heads that way. Slowly, he turns on the main light in the living room and notices a figure sitting on his living room sofa. The unknown figure gets up slowly and walks in Harrison's direction.

Harrison is still holding a menacing looking electronic device but does not use it.

The figure is Daniel Aronson, who continues to approach Harrison, who appears to be completely paralyzed by fear.

"Will Harrison," Daniel says, "We need to talk."

***

At that exact time in an industrial looking area not far from LaGuardia airport in Queens, four large military style Hummer H4 vehicles approach an isolated industrial warehouse building and pull directly in front of the last building in the complex.

As the vehicles pull in, four men emerge from each vehicle and they start to speak amongst themselves.

A light rain falls on the cool early morning day, as the steel garage door type door opens in the warehouse unit, and Bippus and Mercado walk over to the vehicles to speak to the drivers, as Mr. Impossible and The Reaper stand in the doorway.

"What do we have here?" Mr. Impossible asks.

"Washington has sent us sixteen men, and these vehicles to help with transport to our target." The Reaper responds,

"For what purpose?" Mr. Impossible asks.

"We have been ordered to do an extraction," The Reaper responds, "two men, at the same location."

"Do we know who and when?" Impossible asks.

"Not a specific day, but I know it has to happen this week." The Reaper responds, "and not sure exactly who, but the chatter is that it might be the Mayor."

"I just don't think so, man" Impossible counters, "No way. I don't think we are even close to being ready for something like that."

"Will you just shut the fuck up, Impy!" The Reaper shouts, "This is not our call, this comes from the top."

"Yeah, the 'top'" Impossible replies sarcastically, "some douche named 'Agente Oscuro' that we have never even met. He's probably some fucking whack job."

The Reaper turns to Mr. Impossible and moves in towards him, slamming the diminutive man back on the floor with a powerful right cross. Mr. Impossible falls backward onto the floor, knocking over multiple boxes and spilling their contents.

The Reaper stands over Mr. Impossible menacingly.

"For the last time, Impy, know your fucking place!" He exclaims, "Just stay the fuck in here and let me, Bippus and Mercado handle the real work and get these guys checked in. I don't want to see your weasel face anymore tonight!"

Mr. Impossible continues to lie there on the floor, visibly upset. He is upset more out of confusion than anything else. This upset look quickly gives way to one of extreme rage and intensifying anger. Inside, Mr. Impossible is seething. Now, any doubts regarding his position in the organization have been made clear. It is painfully evident that he is disposable in this plan.

Impossible has been tiring of The Reaper's psychotic bullying and this might be the breaking point. He remembers all too well what The Reaper did to his own brother so many months before, and has no intention of being the next "ally" to be sacrificed to this madness.

He stands up and looks out into the parking area, noticing that all of the men were busy unloading the vehicles with a virtual arsenal of weaponry. He starts to get very concerned because he was not informed about any of this, whereas before he was consulted and involved in every step along the way.

He realizes that this is the third major decision that he has not been informed about.

Now that the warehouse was empty of all other individuals, he moves back into the rear of the building far away from the entrance where he can be neither seen nor heard.

Taking out his mobile phone, he makes a call.

"Yeah, it's me," Mr. Impossible says on the phone. "The date has been moved up. Right, now it's sometime this week."

"Same location that we talked about, although I think we are also being given a decoy location. You will need to watch both just to be safe."

"Listen, listen, if you are going to act you need to act now. Be in position once I give you the fucking date!"

Mr. Impossible disconnects the phone and then moves towards the front of the warehouse to again watch the arsenal being unloaded. The Reaper looks back at him with a dismissive gaze as Mr. Impossible holds his defiant stare back at him.

***

Later that same morning at approximately 10 AM, Private investigator Alex Martin walks with his briefcase into the hotel lobby of the St.

Regis Hotel. Daniel Aronson sits in the lobby waiting for him, and motions towards Alex for him to come on over.

"Were you able to make any sense of the files that I gave you?" Daniel asks.

"Needed some help," Alex responds, "But I got a lot of what I needed. To that point," Alex continues, looking around nervously, "it might be wise to take this conversation to somewhere a little less... public."

Daniel nods and then leads Alex to the hotel elevators as they head up to his residence upstairs on the 17th floor.

Once upstairs, Alex Martin sets down his briefcase and opens it, removing three items. He removes the original binder notebook, the flash drive and an additional black binder notebook that he has created.

"What do we have here?" Daniel asks.

"We have all of your original material, and then a new notebook full of the cross-referenced information, basically a translation of the coded information in the notebook."

"How comfortable are you with the translations?" Daniel asks.

"Well there is some guesswork involved, but based on some of the messages and threats that I have received I think we are on the right track," Martin says.

"Threats? Really?" Daniel asks, "That tells me something right there."

"We have obviously hit a nerve, which tells me we are doing something right," Daniel says.

"I want you to read this all for yourself, but to summarize the reach of this organization spans internationally, but we should probably focus on the local connections first."

"Can you summarize the local connections.?" Daniel asks.

"All the way to the top, Daniel. It includes several high-ranking officers in the NYPD."

"That makes some sense, based on how this case seems to never get anywhere, almost as if it is being sabotaged from the inside,"

Daniel says, "I had assumed that The Reaper tampered with the jury himself, but it had to be somebody *higher*, which is why he turned that flash drive over to me, it is now all starting to fall into place."

"There is one *other* name you might be interested to see," Martin says.

"Can you tell me who?" Daniel says.

Alex Martin does not look up, instead opening the black binder notebook and pulls out a piece of paper from inside. He hands the piece of paper over to Daniel.

"Maybe you should check for yourself," Alex says.

Daniel takes the page and begins to review it, his eyes widen and he looks back at Alex Martin.

"Are you sure about this?" Daniel asks.

"For him, I double checked," Martin responds, "The addresses match, the days of the meetings, and multiple deposits made to an account in the Caymans all tie back up to his name."

Alex Martin looks seriously at Daniel and continues.

"This is becoming too dangerous, there is no way that we can handle this all by ourselves, and we have no chance," Alex says.

"I have been recruiting help, but so far it is definitely not enough," Daniel says.

"So, what is the next move?" Martin asks.

"Now, I have to confront Tom and find out the truth," Daniel says.

"And if he admits it, what do you do if it **is** the truth?" Martin asks.

"Well, then I may just have to let them arrest me and then I can tell my side of the story."

"Let them *arrest* you?" Alex asks, "that's not much of a plan."

"I suppose not. Hopefully, though, I would have some degree of protection on the inside. Also, if that other piece of Intel is correct, I need to be at the precinct office in the next few days."

20

NEVER SURRENDER

As per Daniel's request a few days prior, Jill had notified Tom that Daniel wanted to meet with him privately. Tom agreed and as part of the deal, Tom promised to come alone and unarmed and speak with Daniel in the lobby of the St. Regis hotel.

At around 11 AM, Tom Justice enters the ornate lobby of the St. Regis and sees Daniel waiting for him. Tom walks over and the two greet each other and exchange pleasantries.

"Daniel, it is just fantastic weather outside, how about we do a walk and talk?" Tom asks.

Daniel looks around suspiciously for anyone else and then nods in agreement.

"How about the park? It's a great day for it." Tom asks.

Daniel isn't sure about this but then reasons that being out in the open might actually be safer than being in the closed confines of the hotel lobby and it is a fantastic day as Tom said.

They exit the hotel on to 55th street and then to 5th avenue for the short walk over to the park. As they arrive at Central Park, Tom takes them over to a fresh almond street vendor, and they each get some cinnamon almonds to consume during the walk and talk. It is a fantastic spring day, the sun is shining, there is a light breeze, the trees are green and the flowers are in full bloom.

To this point, Daniel and Tom have not said a single word, probably the most awkward and uncomfortable situation in their entire friendship. They continue walking in silence until they come upon a picnic bench over by the main body of water known as "The Lake". They take a seat across from each other and *finally* begin to talk.

"Any updates on The Reaper case?" Daniel asks.

"We actually have a new lead that I was just now following..." Tom says, "And it turns out that it might somehow be connected to four other cases."

"How so?" Daniel asks.

"We aren't sure yet," Tom says, "But there is one other thing that I need to talk with you about Daniel."

"What's that?"

"It's about five people, three of whom were found murdered and two others are missing, presumed dead."

"How does this relate to me?" Daniel asks, playing it cool.

"These were all cases of *yours*, Daniel, and not only that, these men were all those that you told me personally that you considered guilty."

"Just coincidence, Tom," Daniel replies, "You know that you don't have anything substantial or you would have arrested me already."

"I know, and maybe you are right." Tom admits, "We had an eyewitness who gave a description and the image is a virtual spot on match..."

"...But eyewitness testimony is easy to discredit." Daniel replies.

"Yes we know," Tom replies, "and in the cases of the two bodies we found, one was shot with his own gun, and one was shot with a gun we have not been able to identify, nor find."

"No murder weapon. What about fingerprints, DNA, or anything else significant?" Daniel asks.

"No, nothing that we can find," Tom replies, "in fact in each case there was enough inconsistent evidence to really complicate the investigation."

"In fact," Tom continues, "it is almost as if the killer knew enough to create *reasonable doubt*."

"That is very interesting," Daniel replies, "did you find anything concrete that could lead you to your killer?"

'No, nothing useful, that is, until I found this." Tom says, as he takes a small flash memory card and holds it in front of Daniel.

"What's that?" Daniel asks.

"This is the memory card from the video camera at Bruce Stephens' apartment." Tom begins, "I took it from his place and hid it until only I could take a look at it."

"Why does this concern me, Tom?" Daniel asks.

"Because you are on it, Daniel," Tom replies, "**you** are the killer."

Daniel does not respond.

Tom continues, "So I am watching the video and sure enough, there you are plain as day, walking in with gun drawn the same day that he was killed. I almost destroyed this, almost destroyed evidence because of our friendship. But I simply couldn't do it."

Daniel knows that he is backed into a corner. He sits back in a relaxed pose and takes in the view of the lake in front of him. He envies the happy freedom of the many people out rowing their boats on this gorgeous day.

He is even surprised to see a full Venetian style gondola rowing out on the lake in the middle of all of the other boats. He thinks that if events had occurred in a different sequence that maybe that could have been he and Carrie out on that lake together with their son.

Daniel then wonders if he should have just gone off with Jill for a happier life, wonders if maybe he should have ended it all several months before.

He then thinks that Tom made a critical mistake by not checking him for a weapon, since his ankle holster is set with a weapon that he could easily use to shoot Tom and escape right then.

But no, Daniel realizes that it is time to give this up.

Daniel looks around and notices Barnes and Parra at different points not far from where he and Tom are sitting. Parra was harder to spot, but Barnes was fairly easy to see with that four-donut-per-day gut of his.

Daniel turns back to face Tom and shakes his head.

"I guess you didn't understand what I meant by 'Come alone'," Daniel says.

"Sorry, old pal," Tom replies, "Not this time, I simply couldn't take the risk."

"Fine, I am tired of running anyway. Here is the deal:" Daniel says, "I will give you a full confession, tell you where to find the bodies, but I only want to talk to you. I don't want any of your other cronies in your office with us."

"Can you promise me that?" Daniel continues.

"I can agree to that," Tom says.

"Fine, then I formally surrender to you," Daniel says as he puts both of his hands on the table in a surrender pose.

Tom begins to speak into his microphone located under his shirt sleeve,

"He has surrendered willingly, please move in and help me secure the prisoner. No undue force!"

As Barnes and Parra move in and, as per the request, handcuff Daniel in a fairly calm manner with no unnecessary force, Daniel and Tom look at each other with a melancholic gaze, that of a lifetime of friendship now gone.

There is no question that if there even is still a relationship there that it will never be the same again.

Back at Precinct 17, it is a somber mood inside Tom Justice's office, but a very frantic and chaotic atmosphere out on the main precinct floor.

Tom Justice sits inside his office along with his prisoner and prime suspect in this Reaper case, Daniel Aronson. Not a single word has been spoken during this very awkward meeting, as each man waits for the other to initiate the conversation.

Breaking the silence, Shane McWilliams approaches the office, and then enters without knocking.

"Tom, they have found Ballenger's body," Shane says, "it was exactly where Aronson said that it would be."

"Good news, what about the others?" Tom asks.

"No sign of them yet," Shane replies, "we have checked the locations that Aronson provided, but have not found Gomez or Harrison yet."

"Okay, let me know as soon as you hear anything." Tom says.

"Tom, the Mayor has asked Parra and me to go debrief him at his office, are you okay with that?" Shane asks,

Tom hesitates a moment and then speaks,

"Yes, you can go ahead, but leave Parra behind," Tom says.

"Why is that?" Shane asks,

"I still need to visit with him to put him on written warning for going over my head," Tom replies, "And I especially didn't like the fact that he involved Jill in all of this."

"Okay, Tom, I understand," Shane replies, "But I will be sure to put in a good word for you with the Mayor."

"Oh, I am sure you will, man," Tom says, "And you will take *none* of the credit for yourself."

"Don't you think that it is a little premature to be debriefing the Mayor, you know this case is not quite closed, and you cannot be this excited about capturing *me*," Daniel says.

"Not sure about that Daniel," Tom replies, "It looks very strongly that we might have a key member of that organization right here in front of me...isn't that right, 'Agente Oscuro'?"

Daniel looks back at Tom with a puzzled look on his face, not knowing what in the hell Tom is talking about.

"What the hell is an 'Agente Oscuro'?" Daniel asks.

"Don't pretend you don't know, Daniel," Tom replies, "it all really ties together nicely."

"What ties together nicely? What on Earth are you talking about?" Daniel asks.

Tom stands up and starts to pace, his typical habit when addressing people in his office.

"Once I found out about the people you had killed, it took some time to process and truly believe that you could do something like that." Tom begins, "but once I stepped back and started to think objectively, think like a Cop and not your best friend it all became clear to me."

"Again," Daniel says, "if this is some sort of game, enough with it. If not, please tell me what you are talking about Tom!"

Tom slams his fist on the desk and shouts.

"Enough with this charade, Daniel!" Tom shouts, "We know it was *you*, know that you had your own wife killed, we know that you are behind everything!"

"Wait…you think that *I* am tied in with The Reaper??" Daniel exclaims, completely surprised that his friend could suspect him of something like this.

Daniel stares straight ahead, and cannot say another word. He is frozen, stunned that his best friend could truly believe that he was capable of such a thing.

Finally, Daniel speaks, but it's more of a faint whisper.

"Do me a favor real quick, open up your email and look for a file from an A. Martin." Daniel instructs. "It should be in your inbox by now."

"Whatever," Tom says dismissively and angrily, as he complies and opens his Outlook files and scans his email. He opens the email and looks at it."

"Okay, I have it open, now what exactly am I looking at?" Tom asks,

"This is the smoking gun, Tom," Daniel says, "This is the file that The Reaper gave me. After a great deal of waiting I had it decrypted and interpreted, and what you see here are the results. I have the original in a safe place."

"How does this help us?" Tom asks.

"Every single individual, every agency, connection, individual on the payroll they are all inside this file," Daniel says, "They are all in here."

"All in here?" Tom asks.

"To a certain point," Daniel responds, "I doubt that *every* person is listed in this file, because I doubt that The Reaper was privy to every last detail."

"What is this address in Queens listed in the email subject header?" Tom continues.

"I have confirmed that this is the last operating address for the organization. We most recently spotted a disturbing escalation in personnel." Daniel responds.

"Who is the 'We' that you keep referring to?" Tom asks, "Is this Alex Martin and his team? You know I don't trust half of those guys."

"But I *do*." Daniel responds, "And through those connections, he was able to use a drone to do some aerial reconnaissance. You should look at the pictures in there. According to the photos that were taken just this week, there are between 2-4 military vehicles and somewhere between 10-15 men."

"Does that include The Reaper's normal crew?" Tom asks.

"No, that's 10-15 men in addition to the normal team," Daniel responds.

Tom begins to review the additional files in the email attachment and is visibly concerned with what he is viewing.

"This may be helpful," Tom adds, "but how would I know that you are not just sending us into a trap? We already had that with Tarrytown."

"I wouldn't expect you to go in their blindly, I was going to have Martin turn over the drone to your precinct so that you could use it and then coordinate with other agencies. But we have to work this *together* like I was suggesting all along."

"Well, we aren't ready for anything like this, not quite yet," Tom replies, "But what else do you have that we can use?"

"There is more, I think you really should look at page 15 in this document, under NYPD: Precinct 17."

Tom scrolls through the document to reach the noted page and then looks back to Daniel, then back to the document.

"This can't be right," Tom says, "It says under NYPD Precinct 17 Payroll: Tom Justice and Shane McWilliams."

"Yes," Daniel says as he nods, "that is exactly what it says, would you care to explain?"

Tom continues looking at the file, his mind trying to process exactly what is going on here.

"Tom, I had Martin follow up on all of the details in there, it doesn't just list your name it also has a bank account in the Cayman Islands which is registered to an LLC on which only you and Jill are shareholders. Can you explain this?"

"I have no such account, and furthermore no LLC, no business of any kind." Tom insists.

"I didn't think so, and I also know one thing that others might not know about you," Daniel says.

"You actually feel *guilty* about being rich, therefore, money would not be a motive for you to break the law, much less commit murder." Daniel continues. "This is an obvious frame by someone unaware of your true financial net worth."

"A frame? So wait, let me get this straight, you intended for us to arrest you and bring you here to let me know that I was a suspect?" Tom asks.

"Wouldn't a phone call have served the same damn purpose?"

"That's only one part of it, Tom. I also know all about the rumored extraction plan and I knew exactly where and when I had to be when the planned attack was going to take place."

"Be where?" Tom asks.

Daniel cranes his neck over to look at the clock on the wall.

"Right *here*," Daniel responds.

Tom looks over at Daniel with an even more perplexed look.

"Daniel, what in god's name are you talking about?" Tom says, and tries to keep speaking but is cut off mid-sentence.

The sentence is never finished because at that very moment the main precinct floor is shocked with two large explosions.

The glass door and glass walls of Tom Justice's office shatter, and the concussive force of the blast knocks both Tom and Daniel to the ground.

Papers, equipment, bodies all fly in a chaotic display of carnage. Time seems to stand still as people lie on the floor, the few survivors remaining cry out for help. The bodies of four dead officers lie directly outside Tom Justice's office and five more bodies lie motionless and presumably dead out on the main floor.

Three officers come rushing into the main precinct floor in an attempt to rescue any survivors. Tom gets up from underneath his desk to try to make sense of what is happening.

He looks out on to the main precinct floor and sees Officer LeCorgne calling for help as four other officers tend to a young female officer who is alive despite having had her leg severed at the knee.

As Tom watches Officer LeCorgne on the phone, he sees bullets cut LeCorgne down where he stands. Similarly, the two officers trying to help and the wounded officer are hit and instantly killed by a barrage of gunfire. Five men in full SWAT gear, armor from head to toe and helmets that include facemasks enter the main precinct floor, shooting anything that moves.

The apparent leader of the group motions for them to move back towards Tom's office. They move with a purpose, this is no random attack as their actions clearly indicate that they know where they are going.

As the leader stands back, the other four masked gunmen take their assault rifles and slowly walk towards the office. At this point, everyone in the office appears to be dead, except for Parra and Barnes, who lie under their desks, about halfway between Tom's office and the entrance to the precinct.

The masked gunmen move row by row checking for any survivors and they are only one row away from Parra and Barnes desks. Tom sees that Parra has his gun drawn, and looks ready to engage. Tom desperately tries to get his attention, waving his arms like an umpire's safe sign, his way to try to tell Parra to not engage.

Parra shakes his head, and with a look of resignation, he moves out and fires at the armed gunmen, hitting two of them but failing to do any real damage against the body armor. Parra tries to avoid the men, but they cut him down with a synchronized barrage of gunfire, ripping him to shreds.

Seeing his partner's fate, Barnes decides to at least try a formal surrender, still unsure if he will receive any kind of mercy at this point.

Barnes stands up, holding his hands in the air and says, "I give up. I surrender."

One of the gunmen prepares to fire at him when the apparent leader shouts.

"Hold your fire!" The leader shouts, "We need this one alive."

The leader moves in, and at this point removes his helmet and mask and reveals that it is, in fact, The Reaper himself. The other men remove their masks and helmets and reveal themselves to be Bippus, Mercado and two of the military reinforcements sent from Washington, only known by their codenames "Mr. Brown" and "Mr. Pink".

Bippus and Mercado move over and secure Barnes, making sure that he has no weapons, and put a set of tuff-tie hand restraints on him, placing his hands behind his back. They secure the large man and hold him in front of them as they move forward towards Tom's office.

"Bippus and Mercado, bring the big man with me towards the office." The Reaper orders as he moves ahead of Bippus and Mercado towards Tom Justice's office.

"I know that you want a piece of us," The Reaper yells towards Tom's office, "but you are heavily outgunned. We also have your boy here so any sudden moves and fat boy here takes one in the head."

Daniel looks over to Tom and shrugs his shoulders, "I don't think we have much of a choice, do you?"

Tom looks extremely angry, but that angry look yields to common sense.

"We have our orders to take both of you alive, so no need to worry." Reaper barks.

"As if I trust that man," Daniel says.

"But what other choice do we have?" Tom asks.

Tom stands up and puts his hands in a surrender position. Daniel stands up too, although he cannot raise his hands as his are cuffed to the chair.

The Reaper moves into the office and motions for Bippus and Mercado to bring Barnes into the office with them.

Bippus brings Barnes in and The Reaper orders, "Just set him over on the floor over there."

Mercado walks over behind Tom Justice and puts the tuff-tie restraints on him and then brings him around to The Reaper.

The so-called Mr. Brown comes into the office carrying a leather bag. He takes the bag and removes a syringe from it. Mercado unrolls Tom Justice's sleeve, and Mr. Brown injects something into Tom's arm.

He then moves over to Daniel and injects him with the same solution, using the second syringe. As quickly as he started, Mr. Brown then moves out when The Reaper motions for him to do so.

"You and Mr. Pink guard the front and radio Impy that we need to get the Beta team in position, the Alpha team can move out now. Go!"

The Reaper walks over to Daniel in a taunting position, "Counselor, how nice to see you again."

"I would love to say the same, but not under these conditions," Daniel replies, "considering that you have just poisoned us."

"Oh *that* no, nothing of the sort." The Reaper continues, "That is just to help you sleep, so we can get you out of here. No, you two have a guardian angel, somebody wants you two alive for some fucking reason."

Bippus walks over to The Reaper and says.

"Boss, but we only have the two stretchers," Bippus says.

"What do we do with the big man over there?"

"Oh damn, you are right," Reaper replies, "I wasn't thinking this through."

The Reaper turns to Barnes and speaks to him in sort of a mock-apologetic tone,

"Sorry, big man, change in plans!"

The Reaper casually and coldly aims his rifle at Barnes fires but misses him, apparently intentionally.

"I was just kidding, big man. As I told him before, we need you alive," The Reaper says, now turning to Bippus, "For now, just give him the sedative and throw him into the back, no stretcher needed. Cover him with that tarp and put him in the back."

Bippus picks Barnes up off the floor and leads him out into the main precinct floor area. Mercado comes over and injects Barnes with the sedative and the two men walk him out.

At that time, the sedative has taken full effect and both Daniel and Tom go unconscious.

In front of the precinct house, the four military vehicles that were parked there drive away and these vehicles are supposed to return to Washington to leave no trace of their connection to this attack. This is the so-called "Alpha Team", and as they drive away, two emergency vehicle ambulances drive up with their lights flashing and sirens blaring.

By now, The Reaper and his men have dropped their weapons, removed their body armor and black SWAT uniforms and have replaced those with the uniforms of paramedic personnel.

So now at this point, all that a casual observer would see is two men being brought out on stretchers and loaded into two separate ambulances.

This perfectly choreographed scene enables them to drive down 55th street and back to their location in Queens at breakneck speed.

21

BLURRED LINES

Hours later, Daniel Aronson finally regains consciousness having been sedated and then taken on that trip from Manhattan to the Queens Warehouse building.

Daniel looks around, trying to find confirmation and determine exactly where they might be but is almost positive it is the warehouse building that Alex Martin had identified and of which he took the photos with the drone.

Daniel is fully bound, his chest tied with rope, to a steel chair which is bolted to the ground. His arms are bound behind his back and his legs are bound at the ankle. He is not gagged because the site is so remote none need worry about him screaming.

He looks around that sees that Tom Justice is right next to him similarly bound, and is still unconscious. The room is approximately 1200 square feet, with no windows, a room that resembles an interrogation room, albeit significantly larger. Daniel scans it for any apparent weaknesses, but after some basic thoughts of escape possibilities, Daniel quickly comes to the conclusion that any escape attempt ideas would be futile.

With Tom still unconscious, Daniel tries to get his attention. As he calls out to Tom, he looks over in the front corner of the room where a body lies face down, still and motionless within a pool of blood. As he looks closer at the body he recognizes that it is Shane

McWilliams, whom The Reaper's team intercepted before he could make it to the Mayor's office.

Shane's body lies in the corner of the room next to Barnes' body which they also brought back from the police precinct building. Daniel just shakes his head at this unnecessary carnage.

"Tom, Tom!" Daniel yells at Tom, which startles him and causes him to stir, albeit slowly.

"Uggh." Tom says, slowly regaining consciousness, "What the hell happened, are we dead?"

"No," Daniel responds, "But I have a sinking suspicion that our time here is definitely limited."

"What is going on here?" Tom exclaims.

"I don't know," Daniel responds, "They took us captive for some reason. I thought we were as good as dead."

"I don't understand why they didn't just kill us at the precinct," Tom adds.

"Nothing in this case is that easy, Tom" Daniel replies, "It is like some warped psychodrama or something."

Tom nods in agreement and then looks down to see Shane on the floor.

"Oh God, they got Shane too!" Tom exclaims, "Where does it stop"

Tom struggles a moment to see if he can somehow break free, but, of course, the restraints are far too strong for this.

Then Tom looks over to Daniel with a look of resignation on this face.

"Can you, at least, tell me one thing?" Tom asks, "Why did you kill those men? What was your motivation?"

"Guilt, mostly," Daniel responds as he shakes his head.

"Guilt?" Tom asks, "Not revenge?"

"Not really revenge in a true sense," Daniel says, "if you look at the people that I killed, they had not done any harm to me *directly*."

"That is true," Tom says.

"But the guilt that had built up slowly as I was defending these sick, warped men year after year just broke me down. And the final straw was when Carrie was killed, essentially because of me." Daniel says, "You even warned me not to take The Reaper case, and I arrogantly, almost defiantly, took the case that was so important to you and let's face it, I screwed you over."

Tom nods, and then adds, "If that is your form of an apology, I accept and appreciate it."

"If we are going to die at least we don't die as enemies," Daniel adds.

"Man, that sounded really cheesy," Tom says jokingly as Daniel cracks a smile and laughs lightly in agreement.

"But, I do realize that I have gone too far," Daniel says, "I have become almost as bad, if not worse, than these people that I killed."

"That's what happens with rage," Tom replies, "no matter how you try to justify what you did, all that you were really doing was executing vengeance and it *consumed* you."

Daniel nods.

Slowly, the door to the warehouse room opens, and slowly one by one, The Reaper, Bippus, and Mr. Impossible walk inside, shutting the door behind them.

"Ah, our gracious hosts finally arrive," Tom says, sarcastically. "Can we just get this over with, you have destroyed my entire precinct, killed some of my best friends, so what do I have to go back to now??"

The Reaper walks over to Tom and gets right in his face.

"Trust me, if I had *my* way, I would have put a bullet in your brain back at the precinct," The Reaper says.

"He can't make that call because *he* is not in charge," Daniel says defiantly.

Tom doesn't understand that comment and nervously looks over to Daniel.

"Daniel, come on, please don't tell me it really *is* you, after all of this," Tom says.

"No, but I did receive a clue as to who it might be," Daniel says, "I received a call telling me that I was wanted alive, but it was still a major, major gamble. The word was that it was somebody at the precinct on the inside."

Tom looks over at Daniel with an angry and confused look.

"Anonymous call? Someone at the precinct that is behind all of this? Are you nuts?" Tom exclaims, becoming more and more agitated, "Everyone at the precinct was killed; we saw everything, it was right in front of us."

Daniel shakes his head, "Think about it for a minute, did we actually see *everyone* get killed?"

Tom thinks, and then remembers that The Reaper said that he needed Barnes alive. He saw his body on the floor and simply assumed that Barnes was dead.

Suddenly a muffled voice calls out from an unknown source across the room, a voice that sounds hauntingly familiar.

"He *is* right you know." The voice calls out.

At that moment, Shane McWilliams stands up slowly from his supposed death pose, and shakes himself off, as he says in an eerily cryptic and menacing voice:

"See, I told you they should have made me Captain."

Tom cannot say anything. His eyes, however, say everything.

Daniel just nods, as if he half-expected this all along.

It all falls perfectly into place now. Daniel thinks, "Who else would have had insight into the entire investigation? Who else would have known that Daniel was going to turn the files over to Tom?"

"Son of a bitch," Daniel says softly, under his breath.

Shane walks over to Tom and Daniel in a position of perceived dominance and power.

"This fake blood is some nasty, nasty stuff," Shane says, wiping his body off and clearing the fake blood off of his face. "A little theatrical maybe, but I thought it was a nice touch."

"That was clever putting your name with Tom's on the file so I would suspect Tom first." Daniel says, acting like he is not completely surprised at the turn of events, unlike Tom who is visibly shell-shocked by this betrayal.

"That was the entire point, Aronson," Shane replies. "The entire point of all of this was to put both of you against each other, except that I had hoped the two of you would *kill* each other. That would have saved us all a great deal of work." Shane finishes, motioning to the other members of his team.

Daniel responds, "But I knew it wasn't Tom because I had that LLC checked, the one through which he was supposedly getting payoffs, and there was no link at all to Tom directly, which is when I knew that was a frame. I knew it was someone else in the precinct..." Daniel responds.

"But you didn't know *who*." Shane finishes.

"No, I knew an attack was coming," Daniel says, "but I just thought they were coming to capture Tom, I had no idea that the entire precinct would be killed."

"That investigator of yours does good work," Shane replies.

"You're right, that was a last minute plan change." Shane continues, "It was supposed to be just an extraction, but this turned out to be better, this will help me more in the long run."

"How will this help you, Shane?" Tom asks, "The precinct was destroyed, how does that *help* you, man!!!?"

"He plans to make himself the hero, and get the Medal of Honor," Daniel says.

"There's your winner. It's called the 'martyr effect', Tom," Shane says, "I will be the lone survivor in a horrific attack on the precinct, and then...."

"They will promote you to Captain," Tom says.

"Just for starters," Shane says, "After that, I will be the sympathetic choice for future promotions and no telling how far that I could go."

Tom shakes his head at Shane, and adds:

"You are making too many assumptions, Shane. You are no *hero* in this case; you are just the lone survivor. That actually makes you look suspicious, why do you automatically assume that you will benefit from all of this?" Tom asks.

"Very simple, Tom," Shane replies, "I will benefit because I was the hero who followed the masked gunmen and killed all five of them by myself."

"But you didn't," Daniel says,

"Didn't I?" Shane asks, "Take a look behind you."

Shane nods his head towards Bippus as if it were some kind of a signal.

Bippus walks over to a wooden pallet located in the back of the room that is covered with a large tarp. Bippus pulls the tarp from the pallet and reveals the dead bodies of five of the men, dressed all in SWAT attire with their assault rifles. In a classic criminal multiple betrayal, he had these hired guns killed by The Reaper and his men shortly after the precinct attack.

"Looks like I am a hero after all," Shane says.

"I really thought it was funny how you missed the entire 'Agente Oscuro' clue." Shane continues, "So you translate the words and then take the initials from it and conclude it is secretly your best friend??"

"What a stretch! That's just so ridiculously stupid." Shane continues, "Of course, I kind of helped lead that entire line of thought, but you went with it."

"Dark Agent?" Tom says, finally clicking to the meaning, "*FBI* Agent, you used to be with the Bureau."

"Exactly, I put the clue right in front of your face and you still missed it," Shane replies, "Who else do you think would know FBI procedures and protocols and where they like to stay so that their hotel could be bombed?"

"You had your former colleagues and friends killed?" Tom asks.

"They were getting too close," Shane replies coolly.

"Enough of the personal bullshit, Shane," Daniel says, "I get why you did this to get a promotion, and how Tom stands in your way, but why did you ever have to involve *me* in all of this, I hardly even know you."

Shane walks over to Daniel and stands over him.

"That is a great question," Shane says, as he punches Daniel with a right cross across the face,

"*I just don't like you!*" Shane says, with a sinister grin.

"Once I saw your arrogance, that sham of a trial that you had, and then I saw how close you and Justice were, I knew what I had to do," Shane says, "Once I realized how close you two really were, that's when I had this idea."

"This is ridiculous Shane," Tom interjects, "Why not just kill us at the precinct, we were complete sitting ducks!"

Daniel shakes his head.

"He doesn't just want to kill us, Tom," Daniel interjects, "He wants to kill….."

"….Your *reputations*." Shane adds. "You are exactly right, counselor. As I said earlier, once I saw how close you two were, it sort of made sense to set up a scenario in which the two of you were working together all along."

"You two will be found wearing the same armor as the others with enough evidence to connect you to the entire plot. Then the aftermath will be tremendous, all of the cases that you were involved with would have to be reinvestigated, it will be legal chaos which is just what my organization wants."

"Then I will be left to handle everything, all while directing a criminal organization at the same time. Probably safe to assume I won't be arresting any members of my own organization, right?"

"Seems like you have thought of everything," Daniel says.

"Of course. Think about it, a police captain and defense attorney, lifelong best friends. It will not be difficult to make this connection." Shane continues, "I have even found a way to make it look like you helped provide Daniel information to get the acquittal in this case and several others."

Shane walks back over to Tom.

"I bet you were wondering how Jill found out about that one night stand in Texas….that would be from me." Shane says, "I just loved hearing all of your pathetic whining about Jill and the separation, I laughed inside every time you would confide in me, you pathetic little wuss."

"So what about Daniel and his little crusade, was that part of your plan also?" Tom asks.

"I wish I could claim that, but no," Shane replies, "That was just a bonus. We thought by killing his wife and giving him the file incriminating *you* that he would come after you right away."

But I had no idea he would take so long to decrypt it and then start killing his fucking former clients along the way. This plan had to keep changing and evolving based on his actions. This was supposed to have been finished months ago."

Shane laughs in a dismissive tone, sort of a "man that was crazy" kind of laugh. "I had no idea that Daniel would turn into some 'dark avenger' and go on a killing spree"

"He did not make it that easy for us," Shane says, "Oh, and if you've ever wondered why he killed your wife and not you, well those orders came from even above my pay grade. You have no idea how far and high up this goes."

Shane walks back over to Daniel and stands right in front of him, hovering over him like a belligerent interrogator over a political prisoner.

At that moment, as Shane continues his tirade, Tom looks over at Daniel and notices something strange about Daniel's shirt. He noticed it initially back at the precinct but was so preoccupied that he never asked about it. He notices that Daniel's shirt appears bulky in the front, but Tom doesn't know exactly why.

"I was kind of entertained by your killing spree, Aronson, but there was one thing that I never really understood," Shane says, "Why did you have to kill Will Harrison, that Gadget Guy, he never killed anybody. Talk about a harmless little fuck."

Daniel turns towards Tom and mumbles something under his breath that Shane cannot hear.

"What was that?" Shane replies, starting to get increasingly frustrated and angry, "Speak up you little bastard, why did you kill Will Harrison?"

Daniel turns back to face Shane but continues not to speak.

"Answer me!" Shane shouts as he strikes Daniel twice with a right cross, causing Daniel's lip to start to bleed. Shane stands over Daniel in a domineering position, his eyes full of hate and fury.

Looking back at Shane, blood flowing from his lips, eyes tightening their focus, brows furrowed, and a resolved and angry look on his face, Daniel finally responds.

"I didn't kill him. Actually, he works for *me* now."

Suddenly, Daniel turns to the left and presses his chin down on his collar bone, where there is a small and unseen button located underneath his shirt, the device that Tom Justice had noticed earlier.

The button is pressed, and immediately a large concussive energy blast explodes up and outward from Daniel's chest striking Shane full force in the head and chest, the explosive charge knocking Shane backward across the room and killing him instantly.

Daniel is wearing the directional explosive device that Tom had seen earlier at Will Harrison's apartment.

The force of the blast is so strong that it also strikes The Reaper and tears into his right leg knocking him down to the floor. At the same time, Daniel's chair is blown backward by the force of the blast and he falls back on the floor, and it is not immediately obvious if he survived the impact or not. At a minimum he is unconscious.

As the blast hits The Reaper, his gun slides across the floor in the area near Mr. Impossible. Impossible picks up the gun and rushes over to Tom Justice, placing the weapon up to his temple and prepares to fire. Daniel continues to lie unconscious, still bound on the floor in front of them.

"What are you waiting for, Impy!" The Reaper shouts "Shoot him!"

Mr. Impossible looks down at Tom, readies to fire, as Tom closes his eyes in anticipation of oblivion.

Then, Mr. Impossible removes the weapon from Tom's head and aims it instead at his Boss, The Reaper.

"Not this time, *bitch*," Impossible says with a menacing grin. "Your bullying days are over, motherfucker."

"Impy, what the fuck are you doing?" The Reaper yells, "Bippus, shoot this back- stabbing little worm!"

Bippus takes aim on Mr. Impossible, and Impossible turns back to him in a stand-off, but neither man fires. The two men, former allies, stare each other down. Two men who don't particularly want to shoot each other, but will if they absolutely have to.

Impossible looks around like he is waiting for something and then calls out in his professional voice, dripping with sarcasm, as if someone is listening in the other room.

"***NOW*** *would be nice*!!!!" Impossible shouts.

At that moment, the room door flies open and Gabe Gomez rushes in holding a large shotgun in his hands. He sees Bippus and takes aim. Bippus is startled but fires once, without aim, and misses Gomez completely.

After Bippus fires, Mercado moves back into the room and takes aim at Bippus which distracts him. As Bippus loses focus, Gomez moves forward and fires a shotgun blast that places a foot-wide hole in Bippus' chest, the impact knocking him back across the room to the pile of victims that Shane had created earlier.

Impossible ducks out of the way and then moves towards the front door, and then calls out through the door to others who are not yet visible.

"All secure!" Impossible yells, not obviously apparent to whom, as he continues to hold his aim on The Reaper, who is sitting on the floor with his hands up.

At that moment, Will Harrison walks in, clearly having waited until the violence had ended to emerge.

"Is it over?" Harrison asks, "Did it work?"

Gabe Gomez puts down his shotgun and walks over to tend to Daniel, who still appears unconscious, and might even be dead.

"Aronson!" Gomez says, lifting Daniel up off of the ground, "Speak to me!"

Daniel starts to move around a little, but is still not fully coherent.

"Will, get over here and let's get him untied!" Gomez says, as Harrison goes over and they untie Daniel and bring him to his feet.

Nobody has untied Tom yet, and he is still trying to process what is going on here. Daniel, slowly regaining his composure, walks over towards Tom. He takes off his badly-burned shirt and removes the explosive device from his chest, and a thick white pad underneath it.

"I am really glad that you added the extra padding," Daniel says, "without it, I think I am a dead man."

Will Harrison, a.k.a. Device-Man, nods in agreement. "Yes, that is highly likely."

"Is that the same damn thing I saw at your house?" Tom asks.

Harrison nods.

"I thought you said that thing was just a *prototype*," Tom says to Harrison.

"I may have lied to you a little," Harrison replies, "Although it does still have a few bugs to work out, obviously."

Mr. Impossible looks over to Daniel, as he continues to hold his gun on The Reaper. The Reaper sits silently, pondering his next move. Mr. Impossible looks back over to Daniel for direction.

"Can I shoot this motherfucker now, please?" Impossible asks.

Daniel walks over and looks straight at The Reaper.

"You know if I were all about *revenge*, this would be my moment right here, my therapeutic triumph, and I would shoot you in the head," Daniel says to The Reaper.

"*I'll do it.*" Mr. Impossible says with his menacing smile, indicating that he really means it.

"No, no." Daniel says, motioning to Impossible to stand down, "I have realized that this never was about revenge for me, but rather setting things right. Killing him won't bring my wife back to me, and it also will help to have a witness to confirm what Shane did."

Daniel then turns to The Reaper and again speaks to him directly.

"If we spare you, can we count on you to cooperate, and testify to what happened here today?"

The Reaper hesitates for a moment and then weakly nods in agreement with a look that doesn't particularly evoke confidence.

"Gomez, Mercado, let's put him in this chair, just get some cuffs and we will bind him that way." Daniel orders.

Gomez moves over, and Impossible motions for The Reaper to be seated in the chair as Gomez binds him and puts his hands in the cuffs and then secures those cuffs to the chair.

Tom has been fairly quiet up to this point but now has to comment on the chain of events that have transpired up to this point.

"I do not have a clue what is happening here, you are working *with* this guy now? He is one of them." Tom says, indignantly as he motions to Mr. Impossible and Mercado, "And so is that other one behind him."

"I *was* one of them." Mr. Impossible replies, "I am a douchebag, a criminal, I know, but even I have my *limits*. Mercado felt the same way once I explained everything to him."

"Plus I realized that their plan was to kill Mercado and me, too. Ain't that right boss?" Impossible continues.

Mr. Impossible looks over to The Reaper who smiles and nods as if to say "well yeah".

"Mercado and I realized that we were both expendable, and decided that we would rather not end up as two more bodies on the pile back there," Mr. Impossible says.

Daniel walks over to Tom, who is still bound to his chair, as nobody makes any attempt to untie him.

"Impossible called me after the Carrie incident," Daniel says, "he apologized for his part in it, and swore that he did not know it would happen. I didn't believe him right away, but later he backed it up by providing me some useful information."

"I didn't know about that, I swear." Mr. Impossible adds, "I just thought we were supposed to kill *you*."

"Oh, I probably shouldn't have said that," Mr. Impossible adds sheepishly, "Sorry."

"After Tarrytown, he called me again and said that he wanted out, but he knew he couldn't trust the cops because there was a minimum of one dirty cop, and he just didn't know who it was. He actually thought it was you, Tom," Daniel says.

"You never know who you can trust." Impossible adds.

"How can you trust *him* now?" Tom asks.

"Hey," Impossible continues, "Who the fuck do you think told him about the attack on the police station?"

"That would be *me*. Mr. 'anonymous phone call' right here." Impossible says.

"He did, Tom, that's why I had to get you to take me back to the precinct," Daniel says,

"A whole lot of good that did, Daniel," Tom says, "my entire precinct was destroyed and everyone was killed."

"I know," Daniel replies, "we didn't know about the full extent of the plan, I think Shane just added that part at the end."

"Seriously, man." Mr. Impossible adds, "They were just supposed to take the captain and then frame both of you for all of the crimes, that's all."

"Daniel, you really think that you can trust this man, he was a willing partner all along." Tom continues,

Mr. Impossible walks over to Tom to make his case.

"I understand your point, but I am not joining with him to be some choir boy." Impossible says, "I still get to do what I do but for a different side."

"Is this right, Daniel?" Tom asks.

"To a point, yes," Daniel responds, "Both he and Gabe provide access to criminal organizations that I need. I spared Gabe because he promised me that he would help in my cause and I promised to help him get back at the men that were really responsible for those girls' deaths."

Gabe Gomez walks over to Tom and makes his point as Mr. Impossible walks away.

"When you are in a gang," Gomez says, "you follow orders or you die. I couldn't say anything before or else I would have been as dead as those girls. It was the leader, Frederico Loria, who raped and killed the girls; I was just a soldier that was ordered to take the fall."

"Mr. Aronson promised me that if I helped him, we would deal with Loria in a different way altogether." Gomez continues.

"Do you really think we can put gang leaders on trial?" Daniel asks.

"You can if you want to *die*," Gomez adds. "You know how many potential witnesses I have silenced just myself, much less the entire gang?"

"So, Daniel, this little vengeance spree, it was just an act?" Tom asks, "I really don't get it."

"Not at all." Daniel replies, "I killed three men, and I would do it again. Morality is a tricky thing, Tom. For now, I have more work to do, and once it is finished, I will confess my part in all of this and pay for my crimes. The men who deserved to die, are dead. Those who had different circumstances are still alive."

"One other thing that I don't understand, why hasn't anyone *untied* me yet?" Tom asks.

Daniel walks over to him, and says, "We can't. You need to be here and be found by the Feds, who have already been called. Then you will be anointed the hero once they find you and learn the true story, which cannot involve us at all I am afraid."

"But you cannot be conscious when they find you." Daniel continues, as he looks over to Harrison and motions for Harrison to walk behind Tom.

"Why can't I be cons….." Tom tries to ask, as Harrison walks behind and charges Tom with a handheld, Taser-like device, shocking Tom and rendering him unconscious.

As Tom sits there now unconscious, the others continue to discuss next steps.

"Now, Harrison have you destroyed all of the security tape footage? Daniel asks.

"Yes, it will be as if we were never here, and all of the planted evidence will make Justice and McWilliams look like the heroes, just as you requested."

"All we have to do now is get the hell out of here," Harrison concludes, "We probably have no more than fifteen minutes."

"First, let me untie Tom and make it look like he was knocked unconscious in the struggle," Daniel says.

Gomez, Harrison, and Daniel move towards the front door as they plan to exit leaving behind Tom Justice and The Reaper.

Mr. Impossible is in no hurry to leave the room, and hesitates.

"Guys, are we sure we want to leave this guy behind?" Impossible asks.

"You are making some bold assumptions that he will testify as you expect him to." Impossible continues, "If anything, he is more likely to tell what we don't want people to know."

Daniel walks back towards Mr. Impossible, as Gomez and Harrison continue to leave the room since they don't feel that this concerns them.

"No more bodies at this time," Daniel says, "Like I said, this isn't about *revenge* anymore."

"Revenge my thick, lily-white dick!" Mr. Impossible exclaims as he starts to get more irritated, "You cannot *trust* this piece of shit! He killed his own brother, then he and that corrupt cop were going to kill me, plus he killed your *wife* for Christ's sake!"

Daniel remains calm as a counter to Mr. Impossible's rage.

"I know, but that is the past, we have to give him the benefit of the doubt that he will cooperate. We discussed it before and that was our agreement that was our plan."

Daniel turns back to look at The Reaper.

"If he doesn't cooperate and he betrays us, then he is *all yours*," Daniel says.

Mr. Impossible hangs his head as if to concede defeat. He will comply, he thinks, but he still strongly, vehemently, disagrees with this move.

Daniel walks out of the room, and Impossible puts his weapon down to his side and begins to slowly walk outside of the room.

As he walks in that direction he looks back at The Reaper who stares at him defiantly.

Then, The Reaper winks and makes a kissing face to Impossible. Impossible knows what that means, it means that The Reaper intends to betray them just as Mr. Impossible suspected all along.

"*Change in plans, bitch,*" Impossible says to himself.

Mr. Impossible turns, raises his weapon and aims at The Reaper, firing and hitting him twice in the chest. Then the final kill shot right in the head, forcing The Reaper over backward.

"No way in hell you would have supported our story." Mr. Impossible says.

Daniel comes rushing back into the room to see what has happened and yells at Mr. Impossible.

"What did you do?? I said this was not about *revenge* anymore," Daniel exclaims.

Mr. Impossible looks back to Daniel with a sharply focused look but then cracks a little smile.

"Maybe for *you* it wasn't," Mr. Impossible replies,

"But for **me**, yeah, it was a fucking little bit about revenge."

22

EXPECT THE UNEXPECTED

Four weeks later, after everything has been sorted out and a significant amount of evidence presented to Mayor Lockhart and the Police Commissioner, Tom Justice, and Shane McWilliams are considered to be heroes.

Yes, both Tom and Daniel struggled with the ethical dilemma of protecting Shane's legacy. They were protecting the reputation of a ruthless, betraying killer but they realized that it had to be done this way. They realized that if it became public knowledge that a police lieutenant was a part of a large criminal organization, that many of the cases that Shane worked on could warrant a new trial.

This legal chaos was the result that the organization was after in the first place, of course, they wanted to have Tom Justice as their fall guy, or "patsy" with Daniel being his co-conspirator.

The official story had to be that Tom and Shane were captured by the organization and that Tom and Shane fought back together, and that ultimately Tom was able to defeat the entire group, except for Mr. Impossible and Mercado who both escaped.

Tom initially thought this story was too far-fetched, but then realized that this story is far more believable than the way it *actually* happened.

Any real forensic investigation would quickly discredit this story, considering the variety of weapons used and shooting angles, etc. This doesn't matter, it is quickly handled and the case is wrapped up with no additional investigation. The FBI quickly took over the crime scene and it was decided that all evidence would be structured in such a way as to support the official story. This is not something that the FBI is unaccustomed to doing.

So, as far as the general public knows, Daniel Aronson, Gabe Gomez, and Will Harrison were never at the warehouse and had nothing to do with this event. The 'inside man' Mr. Impossible is still considered to be wanted and has been moved up on the FBI's Top 10 most wanted list to number 3.

This is all by design, as they expect to allow Mr. Impossible to operate from within the organization and then relay information back to them.

***

The gathering occurs inside One Police Plaza, Downtown Manhattan. This very plain, borderline ugly brown building is the headquarters for the NYPD, and today is the site of a very special ceremony.

Normally ceremonies take place outside the building, but it is raining today so they have moved things inside. In this large auditorium, Mayor Lockhart stands at the podium, flanked by the Police Commissioner as Tom Justice sits down to his immediate right. To the left of the Mayor sits Director Maxwell of the FBI.

The Mayor addresses the packed auditorium which is filled with Police officers all wearing their formal blues.

"Ladies and Gentlemen," Mayor Lockhart begins, "It is my extreme honor and pleasure to be here for this joint New York Police Department and Federal Bureau of Investigation award ceremony for Captain Tom Justice."

The auditorium erupts in thunderous applause, as Tom Justice nods to display his appreciation.

"Normally we do these award ceremonies once per year, as you know, but in this instance, we felt a special out-of-cycle award was warranted." The Mayor continues, "In conjunction with the Federal government, we agreed that we would jointly present two awards for Captain Tom Justice. To present the first award, let me present FBI Director Edward Maxwell."

Edward Maxwell stands up and walks over to the podium to speak. Maxwell, a sharp dressed 50-ish African American with glasses, begins to speak.

"On behalf of the Bureau, I would like to give my sincere and heartfelt thanks to Tom Justice," Maxwell says, "for his unrivaled bravery taking on a criminal organization and bringing them to justice. No pun intended."

The audience laughs mildly.

"For his bravery, in bringing down the organization that was responsible for the deaths of 10 Federal agents, and several officers of the NYPD, we wish to present the FBI Medal for Meritorious Achievement to Captain Tom Justice."

The audience stands and erupts in applause, as Tom walks over to the main podium, shakes Director Maxwell's hand and accepts his award. He then walks back to his seat and sits back down.

Mayor Lockhart walks back to the podium to continue speaking and shakes Director Maxwell's hand.

"Thank you, Director." Mayor Lockhart says.

"And now, for the second award of the day, and the most prestigious award that any officer within the New York Police Department can ever receive, it is my honor to present the Medal of Honor to Captain Tom Justice."

Again the auditorium erupts in applause and there is about a five-minute standing ovation as Tom walks over to receive his award. The Mayor and Police Commissioner shake his hand and pat him on the back with big sincere smiles. Tom smiles back truly appreciating the grand moment.

He looks into the front row and sees Jill standing there waving and yelling in appreciation. As he stands there he looks back to the rear of the auditorium and sees Daniel Aronson leaving the room.

Tom locks eyes with Daniel as Daniel nods at him and Tom nods back. Daniel continues on and leaves the room. Daniel should be a fugitive, but Precinct 17 was the source of the investigation into his crimes and it has been completely destroyed. Tom had decided to destroy the flash memory card upon which the video evidence was located. Still, Daniel realizes that his life will be far from normal going forward.

Tom will continue the investigation into Daniel's crimes, but was going to discuss it in greater detail with District Attorney Garcia to see if there were other options other than a full prosecution.

***

About an hour after the ceremony, Tom walks with Jill down the street with an umbrella to protect them from the light drizzle that falls.

"I must say that you look rather dashing in your formal blues," Jill says.

"Thanks, Jill," Tom replies, "And I must say that you look stunning, but I must ask, why the black?"

"Simple answer to that one, you *love me* in this outfit," Jill replies. "Because I look so good in it," Jill finishes with a wink.

"No argument here," Tom answers.

"So, did you enjoy the ceremony? You certainly deserved it." Jill adds.

"Yeah, but I felt funny up there, kind of like I didn't deserve it or something," Tom replies.

"That's silly, *of course* you deserved it. I am sure that if Shane were here he would say how happy he is for you."

"Maybe," Tom says, "at least the Shane that I thought I knew."

Jill looks at Tom with a puzzled look on her face.

"What did you mean by that?"

"Oh, nothing.....I guess I am still bothered by his death."

"I am too," Jill replies, "and Juan, and Barnes. This was a real tragedy."

"There is some good out of it," Tom says, "When they rebuild the office they are going to add a new wing and it will be the New York command center for joint ventures with the FBI."

"That is great," Jill says, "But how long until they rebuild?"

"About nine months or so," Tom responds, "I am really looking forward to it. This might be a turning point for the city."

"Did you see Daniel?" Tom asks, "He was in the back of the room, but had to leave early."

"No I didn't see him, but he said he would call us later today," Jill replies, "I told him we had that appointment with Dr. Elsbury tomorrow."

"The 'big decision'," Tom says playfully.

Jill doesn't laugh, but looks straight ahead, instead wanting to change the subject.

"Which reminds me," Jill says, "I think a certain someone owes me a *massage* tonight."

"Only if I get to pick, well, you know…" Tom says suggestively.

Jill punches him in the arm, "Tom!!"

***

A few hours later that afternoon, Tom and Daniel are on the phone speaking.

"I have to say that you looked awfully sharp up there in your formal blues," Daniel says.

Tom laughs at the pseudo-compliment. "That's just what Jill said, only I think she actually *meant* it."

"Yeah, I guess I really know how to rock the uniform don't I?" Tom replies.

"I had a long conversation with District Attorney Garcia," Tom says, "He actually likes your idea."

"So what does that mean?" Daniel asks.

"For now, it only means that I am not to prosecute you in any way." Tom replies,

"As far as we are concerned, you and Mr. Impossible are no longer suspects in any cases. We are keeping Impossible on the Most Wanted List, however."

"You told him that Impossible assisted our cause, right?"

"Yes, but it is going to be difficult to sell the fact that he has been completely rehabilitated, but we are willing to try for now." Tom continues.

"That's definitely a start, Tom." Daniel replies, "I don't fully trust him either, but if we keep an eye on him, I think he can help us to get the information that we need in a way that you or I simply cannot."

"So, he is back in with the organization?" Tom asks.

"Yes, in deep cover," Daniel responds, "As soon as he provides us some operational Intel, we will be poised to move."

"Where are you going to base from?" Tom asks, "You shouldn't probably stay in Manhattan."

"No, I agree," Daniel responds, "With Gomez and Harrison in the city, I am looking somewhere in either Westchester or maybe Greenwich, close but not too close."

"I guess we shouldn't meet for a while, right?" Tom asks.

"I think it would be best, don't you?"

"I agree," Tom replies, "Okay, I probably should get going, let's touch base once Impossible provides you some more Intel."

"Okay, well congratulations for the awards, they were well deserved. I will talk to you later." Daniel says, disconnecting the phone.

Tom walks from his office into the main living room, where Jill is sitting on the sofa reading a book on her tablet.

"Is everything okay with Daniel?" Jill asks.

"Yeah, he is doing great. He apologized for not being able to stay longer." Tom says.

Tom walks over, sits down on the sofa next to Jill, and puts her arm around her.

"I'm glad everything turned out okay," Tom says, "Sometimes bad things happen for a reason I guess."

"Sometimes," Jill responds, getting comfortable, nuzzling up to her husband on the sofa.

"Like you and your *boyfriend* for example," Tom says.

Jill's eyes widen, and she moves slowly away from being nuzzled against him to being seated in an upright position and stares at him in a nervous, frozen manner.

"I am really sorry about Juan, I am sure that this loss has hurt you greatly," Tom says. "He was a great man, and a great detective, and I can say with all sincerity that he will be missed."

Jill has a surprised look on her face; because she had no idea that Tom suspected Juan Parra was her boyfriend. She wants to correct him but quickly realizes that it is to her benefit if Tom believes that it was Parra, regardless of whether it is true or not.

"It's okay, Jill," Tom says in a consoling manner, "I wasn't okay with you dating Parra at first, but after my initial anger faded, I realized that maybe this was the shock we both needed to light a fire back in our relationship."

"It just hurts that you did this with someone close to me." Tom continues, "We probably should keep it a secret from his wife Cyndi also. No point in her knowing the truth at this point, it would only tarnish the memory of her husband."

Jill can't speak, merely nodding, still feeling very vulnerable.

"We can survive this, Jill," Tom says, "What is most important is that we let the past be the past and move forward."

"Right, the past is the past," Jill says as she starts to sob lightly.

"Its okay, Jill," Tom says, "Like I said, we can move past this. I love you too much to let this get in the way of our happiness."

Jill nods but continues to sob.

"Mayor Lockhart wants to meet me and a few of the other key officers at Connolly's to discuss initial plans for rebuilding," Tom says, "Will you be okay by yourself for a couple of hours?"

"Sure, let me walk with you downstairs, I could use some air myself," Jill says.

Jill and Tom exit their townhome and begin walking in the direction of Connolly's pub. About five blocks down, Jill decides to stop at Starbucks for a latte. Tom proceeds onward to Connolly's and Jill sits down to enjoy her warm beverage. She takes her mobile phone from her purse and dials Daniel on the phone.

***

Daniel doesn't answer because he is wrapping up a lunch conversation with an old friend Richard Murphy.

"So you are telling me that the two officers that killed my brother have been dealt with?" Richard asks.

"It turns out that it was only one of them, the other was just as much a victim as Charlie," Daniel replies.

"So, the one officer is going to jail for my brother's murder?" Richard asks.

"Well not exactly, I am afraid." Daniel says, "But we got him for something else."

"I don't understand," Richard says, with a puzzled and concerned look on his face.

"There wasn't enough evidence to convict for your brother's murder," Daniel says. "I saw the evidence, but we could not use it in court."

Richard starts to become agitated.

"Wait, you mean this man is going to skate and get off with nothing??"

"No, just no charges on your brother's murder. As part of a deal I made, his partner provided enough video evidence on a series of rapes that will put Officer Martinez away for a long time, and he is of course off the force and will forfeit all benefits and his pension."

"Oh, I understand. What about his partner, shouldn't he pay for his role in all of this?" Richard says.

"Actually, we have come to a sort of *understanding* of sorts. He will be working for me now providing me information from the inside on other dirty cops." Daniel says, "This way, hopefully, there won't be any more victims like Charlie in the near future."

"Okay, Mr. Aronson, thank you for that update, I have to admit I was kind of hoping you would tell me that you killed them or something, but I guess this is better for everybody."

Daniel chuckles, "Yeah, me a killer, I don't see that happening."

Richard smiles, as he walks away. "You're the best, Mr. Aronson, thanks again."

Daniel looks back sternly. "Richard, as I keep telling you.....call me Daniel."

Richard just smiles and exits the restaurant.

Daniel takes a minute to reflect on this and has a feeling of joy for a moment thinking that at least some justice has come from this. But then that joy shifts to melancholy as he realizes that none of this will ever bring back Carrie, his unborn son, or Richard's brother Charlie.

***

Daniel checks his phone and notices a missed call from Jill, so Daniel calls Jill back and they begin speaking.

"Hey, Jill," Daniel says, "Sorry about that, I was just finishing up a meeting. What's going on?"

"I just wanted to touch base with you, Daniel," Jill says.

"Nice to hear your voice, Jill," Daniel replies.

"I was thinking about Carrie today," Jill says, "Yeah, I am having a latte at what was 'our' Starbucks, she loved this place. God, I miss her."

"That she did," Daniel replies, "Three-latte-a-day habit," Daniel says laughing. "Of course, I miss her, too."

"I still miss her every day," Jill says, "and I can only imagine how you feel. Both of us lost best friends on that day."

"I lost more than you even know," Daniel says.

There is a slight pause, and then Jill resumes the conversation, not the best transition, but this is what Jill has been waiting to say.

"On a slightly different topic, I have made my decision Daniel," Jill says.

"Decision about what, Jill?" Daniel asks.

"Tom and I are supposed to meet with our marriage counselor for our final separation decision tomorrow," Jill replies.

"And?" Daniel asks.

"And I have decided that I want to...." Jill starts but stops with a nervous pause.

"You want to...what, Jill?" Daniel prods.

Jill regains her nerve and proceeds very stoically, although she is nervous inside. "I have decided that I want to divorce Tom and marry you, or, at least, *date* you. Not sure what our future might be, but I want to give it another chance." Jill says, with a look of hope in her eyes, not sure how Daniel will take the news.

She tries to contain her excitement and nerves as she anxiously awaits his response.

There is a noticeable pause and no answer on the other end of the line. Finally, after a pause that seems like an eternity to Jill, Daniel responds.

"I cannot do that, Jill," Daniel responds.

"You...you can't?" Jill responds weakly, feeling a tear starting to well up in her eye.

"I just cannot betray Tom like that, and right now I don't think I would be any good to anyone in a relationship," Daniel says.

Jill stares straight ahead, speechless, doing everything that she could to hide how hurt, how emotionally devastated that she is. Even though he cannot see her face, she does what she can to conceal the hurt in her voice.

Daniel continues, "I will truly always love you, this was a great experience and I think we both felt twenty years old again. But we are *not* twenty years old anymore, and sometimes we have to recognize that the past is the past."

A tear streams from Jill's eye as she truly was not expecting this response and now must try to shift the topic and hide the pain in her voice.

"Okay….so, well what will you do?" Jill asks, not being very clear, not able to hide her disappointment very well.

"I don't really know. I think finally I have finished most of my cases and I really should get away for a while and process things." Daniel continues, "Carrie's death has affected me more than I let on."

Jill wants to plead with him and beg him to stay and start a new life with her, but she plays the part well and continues the small talk.

"I understand. I think that is a good idea….I mean going out of town….Where will you go?" Jill asks.

"Somewhere in Spain, I think," Daniel responds, "Then maybe the Greek Islands for a week or so. I just need to try to clear my head of all that has happened."

"Well keep me posted, Daniel," Jill replies still trying as hard as she can to mask her pain, "I will miss you."

"I will miss you too, Jill. *Goodbye.*" Daniel says.

The word 'Goodbye' echoes to Jill, and sounds almost permanent, not merely a friendly ending to a conversation. It sounds more like an ending. It sounds like the ending of a friendship, the ending of a relationship.

The full impact of this hits her like a brick wall.

Before she can even disconnect the phone, another teardrop falls, followed by several others. She does what she can to compose herself, since she is out in public, but she cannot.

Jill disconnects the phone, and proceeds to drink half of her coffee and then walks back to her townhouse. As she walks back inside the door of her home, the full impact of the possibilities starts to overwhelm her. She sits down on the sofa, but cannot stop crying as she drops her coffee cup onto the floor, spilling the remaining coffee all over the rug.

She realizes that she should have told Daniel the truth, told him why she ultimately chose him over Tom, but she just couldn't. She froze, being truly surprised at this response, something that she hadn't emotionally prepared herself for.

Jill doesn't know when it changed, but she is not in love with Tom anymore, the cumulative effects of his cheating and the fact that he has put his job ahead of her time and time again. She wanted to reconnect with Daniel for this very reason.

Jill gets up and walks over to the powder room and shuts the door behind her. After procrastinating as much as is humanly possible, she realizes that she must go on and find out the truth one way or another.

"The past is the past, the past is the past" Jill keeps mumbling to herself.

She walks over to the sink, upon which she had placed a small white device that clearly has an indicated plus sign on its display.

She holds it up, knowing the results before she even looks at it.

Jill Justice is pregnant.

For a moment, Jill thinks that this will be a great way to move forward with this relationship, rescue the strained marriage, and build a family which they have not been able to have yet, and hopefully a greater happiness would follow.

Jill collapses to the floor of the powder room and cries uncontrollably. What should be a happy occasion is now something that could change her life forever.

She should tell Tom right away, and, of course, Tom should be ecstatic at the good news.

She knows he would be happy if he heard that news.

He *would* be happy, except that the baby is not *his*.

"How can I raise a child," Jill thinks, "if his father is no longer around?"

THE END

Made in the USA
Middletown, DE
17 January 2019